THE **CLARK GABLE**
AND **CAROLE LOMBARD**
MURDER CASE

*Also by George Baxt
in Large Print:*

The William Powell and Myrna Loy
  Murder Case
The Tallulah Bankhead Murder Case

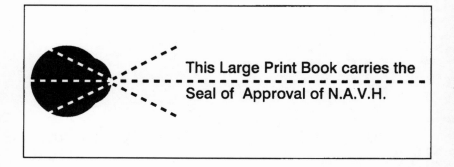

THE **CLARK GABLE** AND **CAROLE LOMBARD** MURDER CASE

GEORGE BAXT

Thorndike Press • Thorndike, Maine

Published in 1998 by arrangement with
St. Martin's Press, Inc.

Thorndike Large Print ® Cloak & Dagger Series.

The tree indicium is a trademark of Thorndike Press.

The text of this Large Print edition is unabridged.
Other aspects of the book may vary from the original edition.

Set in 16 pt. Plantin by Juanita Macdonald.

Printed in the United States on permanent paper.

Library of Congress Cataloging in Publication Data

Baxt, George.
    The Clark Gable and Carole Lombard murder case /
George Baxt.
        p.   cm.
    ISBN 0-7862-1543-7 (lg. print : hc : alk. paper)
    1. Large type books.   2. Gable, Clark, 1901–1960 —
Fiction.   3. Lombard, Carole, 1908–1942 — Fiction.
4. Actors — United States — Fiction.   I. Title.
[PS3552.A8478C57   1997]
813′.54—dc21   98-26426

*For
Kelley Ragland
for services above and
beyond the call of duty*

ONE

On December 14, 1939, David O. Selznick's epic production of *Gone With the Wind* was scheduled for its world premiere in Atlanta, Georgia. Atlanta was where the author of the book, Margaret Mitchell, lived with her unimpressive husband. While writing the book in long hand at her kitchen table, she never dreamed she was creating a behemoth that would take the world by storm and solidify her place in literary history. She had called it *Tomorrow Is Another Day*. Her publisher retitled it, and when Hollywood maverick David O. Selznick bought the film rights for a bargain at $50,000 he was soon under siege by every star in Hollywood who saw herself and only herself as the book's heroine, Scarlett O'Hara. Selznick capitalized on this by starting a worldwide hunt for the right actress to play Scarlett. For the film's hero, Rhett Butler, Selznick and the reading public agreed that screen heartthrob Clark Gable was the only choice. The one person who disagreed was Clark Gable. He was soon convinced to change his mind. But until this happened, major stars came knocking at

Selznick's door, Errol Flynn, Ronald Colman, Robert Taylor, and Ray Milland among them.

One warm afternoon Selznick stared across his desk at William Claude Fields. Fields had been badgering him for a meeting for several weeks and Selznick finally succumbed. He was now wishing he'd had time to commit suicide. "Bill," said Selznick, his voice shaking, "I don't see you as Rhett Butler."

"That's because you're nearsighted," said Fields, taking a swig of gin from one of several flasks he always carried. He stood up and twirled his ever present cane while strutting around the office in what he was positive was a display of male sexuality that would cause Selznick to change his mind. He boomed, "Carlotta sees me as Rhett Butler!" Carlotta Monterey was his live-in lover, an actress of dubious talent but a loyal and faithful paramour. Fields was lighting a cigar and after a fit of coughing said, "If she didn't see me as Rhett Butler, I threatened to paste her one in her kisser. A very nice kisser, I might add." He flicked ash on the rug while Selznick groaned inwardly. Fields was one of his favorite people despite his alcoholism. They were together at Paramount Pictures some five or six years earlier when Selznick was a fledgling producer. It was Selznick who four years ago convinced Louis B. Mayer at MGM to hire Fields for *David Copperfield*, replacing Charles Laughton, whose temperamental outbursts were unnerving the company. Fields as Micawber was a triumph, setting both critics and audiences on their ears.

Much as he liked and respected Fields, Selznick was growing impatient and Fields recognized this. "David, I will give you a few days to think this over. I'm sitting on an offer from England's Old Vic to play *Julius Caesar* for them. I told them I'd consider it if Julius doesn't die. I know, I know" — he waved a hand at Selznick — "the poor sap traditionally gets himself assassinated, but if he had listened to the old witch who warned him to beware the Ides of March, he'd have taken a chariot back to his villa and run up a game of croquet. Croquet," he mused, scratching his head. "Haven't played in years. How long's it been since you've played croquet?"

"Bill." Selznick spoke the name with exaggerated patience. Fields recognized exaggerated patience when it was laid out before him.

"I know, I know," said Fields, raising a hand like a cop halting imaginary traffic. "I have overstayed my welcome." He looked at his wristwatch. "Ye gods, I'm late for an appointment with Greta Garbo. She wants me to consider doing Ibsen's *A Doll's House* with her. But no woman leaves me and slams the door for good measure. And who wants to see *A Doll's House* with anybody in it? Ibsen's finished, we both know that."

Selznick was escorting Fields to the door that led to his waiting room. "It was nice to see you, Bill. We should get together more often."

"We will, we will," the comedian assured him, "when I sign my contract to play Rhett Butler. Of course I get top billing, keep that in mind, David."

In the waiting room, Hazel Dickson, Hollywood's most avaricious purveyor of gossip, dropped the trade paper she'd been reading along with her chin on seeing Fields exiting from Selznick's office. On recognizing Hazel, Fields tipped his straw hat and said warmly, "Why, my precious little kumquat, how are you, Hazel?"

Hazel got straight to the point. Maybe here was a piece of gossip she could sell at a fancy price to one of her many columnist clients. "What are you doing here, Bill?"

He drew himself up and proudly and said, "Hazel, here before you stands Rhett Butler."

"Where?" asked Hazel, looking past Fields and seeing no one but Selznick's overworked receptionist and several people waiting patiently for an audience with Selznick.

"Are you blind, my passionate petunia? Right here. Me. I. *Moi.* Rhett Butler! Can you see anyone else in the part?"

Hazel's look of astonishment changed to one of horror and then, in an instant, to one of sympathy. "Why, Bill, I had no idea David was given to such original thinking."

"I gave him the original thinking," boomed Fields. "I presented myself today as Rhett Butler." The receptionist crossed herself. "Had David sneered or scoffed or favored me with an old-fashioned raspberry" — he raised his cane high over his head — "I'd have crushed his skull like it was a ripe casaba melon." He brought the cane down on an imaginary melon, Hazel stepping backward as she felt the breeze stirred up by the downward motion. The ferocious look on Fields' face softened as he asked Hazel in a tone both courtly and concerned, "Did I frighten you, my priceless cream puff?"

Hazel patted his cheek gently, considerate of the many veins that populated his cheeks and nose. "Bill, darling, you're a priceless old fraud."

"Ah yes!" agreed Fields munificently,

11

"and I command a very high salary. Tell me, my pussy willow, is it necessary you see Selznick or can I kidnap you to the nearest bar for some alcoholic libation?"

Kidnap. Hazel asked, "Bill, don't you have a bodyguard?" Hollywood had been besieged in the past several weeks by an outbreak of kidnappings and, as a result, bodyguards were at a premium.

Fields raised the cane again. "I will pulverize any kidnapper who dares threaten me. I shall mash them into pulp, do you hear me, *pulp!*" He turned to the receptionist, who had slammed a phone down, and bellowed "Pulp!" The receptionist yelped and Fields immediately assuaged her. "Fear not, my precious concubine. I wouldn't harm a hair of your beautifully coiffured head." He stared at the homely woman and repressed a shudder. Then he said to Hazel, "Who chooses Selznick over Fields would choose dishonor before death! I shall go forth and commit a good deed."

"Oh good," said Hazel affably. "No good deed goes unpublished."

"Well said! Well said!" Fields was headed out of the reception room. "Remember me to your mother."

"My mother's dead."

Fields continued on his way, his bulbous

nose leading him to his car, which he would guide to one of his favorite watering holes, Romanoff's.

Finally ushered into the presence of the presence, Hazel settled into the chair previously occupied by W. C. Fields and rummaged in her oversize handbag for a pad and pencil. She asked Selznick, "Doesn't W.C. know that *Gone With the Wind* is completed? I mean this nonsense of his playing Rhett Butler. Poor bastard."

"Hazel," said a solemn David O. Selznick, "treat W. C. Fields with respect. The man's a genius. He's one of my heroes. Had it occurred to me, I'd have had a part written into the picture for him."

"Robert E. Lee?" asked Hazel with a cocked eye.

"Why not? They say he fought the war half crocked. How are you, Hazel? Worried about being kidnapped?"

She asked archly, "Who would have the good taste to kidnap me? If they did, Herb Villon wouldn't pay the ransom." Herb Villon was Hazel's long-suffering and patient lover of almost a decade, and a respected detective with the LAPD. "Among others, and a lot of others, Dietrich is scared out of her wits. Not for herself but for her kid, Maria."

"They better not touch Marlene," growled Selznick. "I'm optioning *The Paradise Case* and there's a terrific part for her, if Garbo turns it down."

"Attaboy, David. First things first. 'Don't kidnap my star, I've got a great part for her.' "

"Hazel, why do I put up with you? When you're sarcastic, you send a shiver up my spine. You sound just like Irene discussing a menu with our cook." Irene was Mrs. Selznick, the younger of Louis B. Mayer's two daughters. Mayer loved his daughters, who loathed each other.

"I hear Clark doesn't want to go to Atlanta."

"Clark is a pain in the ass. He's been a pain in that vicinity since the picture went into production. He made me fire George Cukor as director and replace him with Victor Fleming, a *man's* director." He selected a cigar from the elegant humidor on his desk. As he spoke, he rolled the cigar knowledgeably between his fingers, then sniffed it and held it to an ear, listening for God knows what, thought Hazel. Finally he laid it to rest in his mouth after clipping off one end and lighting it. He inhaled and then exhaled a magnificent smoke ring, which flew past Hazel's cheek while she waved her hand to clear the air. "Then Clark goes into a snit when he learns Vivian Leigh and Olivia de Havilland are being coached on the sly by Cukor." He settled back in his chair. "What they do in private is none of my business and their performances in the picture are superb. Everybody in the picture is superb. The picture is superb. A fitting epitaph for me."

"You planning to go someplace, David?"

Now his eyes narrowed. "What are you after, Hazel?" She must know something he didn't know. Hazel Dickson always knew something everybody else didn't know. She had an uncanny nose for news, the way a pig knew exactly where to snuffle under earth for truffles.

Hazel crossed one shapely leg over the other, ignoring the beginning of a run in the stocking on her left leg. "Have any of the cast received a kidnap threat?"

"Not that I know of."

"How about Carole?"

"Not that she knows of. Anyway, Louis B. has assigned them two bodyguards. Two athletes, young bucks under contract to Metro."

"If they're gorgeous hunks, Clark will slit their throats." She sighed. "That clod. It's okay for him to bang or try to bang every starlet on the lot, but if Carole's antenna rises when she sees an attractive man, he goes to pieces. Poor Carole, little did she know she was biting off more than she could chew when she finally roped him."

"Clark's deeply in love with Carole."

"I'm sure you're right. But there's deeply and there's *deeply*. Like Herb Villon is deeply in love with me from the picture *The Bride of Frankenstein*." She thought of the detective and then shook her head from side to side to clear it.

"What's Herb's take on the kidnappings?"

"No stars."

"What do you mean no stars?"

Hazel was lighting a cigarette. "No real stars have been kidnapped. Just small fry. And as Herb says, you can't cash in on small fry."

"What about Lydia Austin? She's been missing about a week now."

"She's no star," said Hazel flatly, condemning the young actress to a very minor position in the firmament.

"Nice breasts," said Selznick with a faraway look in his eyes.

Hazel flicked cigarette ash in the tray she found on a small table near her chair. "If you're into breasts . . ." She knew what Selznick was into — everything but his wife. "Why should anyone want to kidnap Lydia

Austin? Her sole claim to fame is being one of Carole's four protégées she's grooming for stardom. Four protégées! Now if ever there was a publicity ploy."

"It isn't. You know Carole. Her heart is always in the right place. She'll always give a kid a leg up. She's genuinely interested in these girls. Christ, she certainly auditioned enough of them before choosing these four. She made me screen-test all four of them."

"Oh yes? Can I see the tests?"

"If Carole says so, you can see them." He examined the ash at the tip of his cigar. "The girls aren't at all bad. I'd have used them for the ball scene in *Wind*, but it was already in the can. Carole's got Russell Birdwell doing their publicity." Birdwell was an ace Hollywood publicist, an eccentric given to wild ideas such as sitting on an ostrich egg all day to see if he could hatch it (he didn't).

Hazel thought for a moment and then said, "I'll bet he arranged Lydia's kidnapping!"

"Carole's already asked him. He denies it vehemently. Damn — do you suppose Dietrich is in danger?"

"Whoever snatches her deserves the consequences. She'll be on her hands and knees scrubbing the floors, then she'll do their laundry and after that she'll bake some German pastries and cook them a lush sauerbraten for dinner."

Selznick said sadly, "If that's the case, they'll never let her go." Then he said, "Are you canvassing every producer in town to see who they've got under contract who's a likely candidate for kidnapping?"

"A few have told me who they'd like to see kidnapped."

Selznick's face brightened. "Names, Hazel, names."

Lombard and Gable lived in a handsome, rugged ranch in the San Fernando Valley near Encino. They had purchased it from the director Raoul Walsh with Carole's money, Clark having been taken to the cleaners in his divorce settlement with his ex-wife, Ria. In her own right Ria was a very wealthy woman, a formidable woman in Hollywood society of whom Carole said, "She has lots of society friends but very little class." At the same time Hazel was interviewing Selznick, Clark was illustrating how to clean and oil a hunting rifle for their raptly attentive young bodyguards. Roy Harvey and Sammy Rowan were college athletes discovered by an MGM talent scout who immediately hustled them out to the studio where they were tested and placed under contract. Not for their acting talents, which were minuscule but for their physical attributes, which were most impressive. Carole commented on first meeting them that they'd make marvelous bookends. Clark liked his captive audience; their naiveté was refreshing and he liked the way they called him "sir" and Carole "ma'am." There wasn't much of that kind of respect in motion pictures. Clark tossed the rifle to Roy Harvey, who had shaggy blond hair and was all of twenty. "Try this one for size, Roy." The youngster stared at the gun in his hands. "What's the matter, Roy? Never used a rifle before?"

"When I was a kid, I had a BB gun." He added shyly, "I was a lousy shot."

"Just raise it to your shoulder and take aim. Don't be afraid of it, it's not loaded."

"Yes, sir." Roy raised the gun until he could look through the barrel sight. He chuckled. "If it was loaded, I'd catch you between the eyes."

On the landing above them, Carole screamed. She had emerged from the bedroom she shared with Gable carrying a script, wearing blue jeans and one of Clark's plaid shirts.

"It's okay, honey. It's not loaded."

"That's what Russ Columbo's pal Lansing Brown said before he shot and killed poor

19

Russ." She said sharply, "Young man, put that gun down." Roy Harvey handed the rifle back to Gable, who stared at Lombard with the familiar look of exasperation that made his dimples stand out. Women adored his dimples almost as much as Gable did. Carole had thought of Russ Columbo often since his so-called accidental murder in 1934 from a gunshot from one of Lansing Brown's antique pistols.

Hazel Dickson had her own theory about Columbo's death, as did most of the movie industry. "Those two were closer than peas in a pod. When Russ told Lansing he was planning to marry Carole, Lansing popped him." Herb Villon didn't disagree, but the Hollywood powers wanted the matter hushed, especially Carl Laemmle at Universal Pictures, where Columbo was being groomed for stardom. So the matter was hushed, and a loyal Carole abetted Columbo's siblings in feeding their ailing mother the fiction that Columbo was away on a world tour, even arranging for letters and postcards to be mailed to her regularly. She especially treasured the ones from Italy, where she had been born.

The bodyguards quietly admired Carole as she descended the staircase. "Having a nice time, boys?" They smiled their appreciation.

"I'll have the cook prepare some snacks. You must be famished. I didn't think those thick steaks you ate for lunch would be enough." Then she yelped "Pappy!," her nickname for her husband.

"What, Mommy?"

"This script is so beautiful. It's really touching. It's a perfect vehicle for me and Jimmy Stewart." She murmured, *Made for Each Other*."

"Soppy title," said Gable.

"It is not," said Lombard defensively as she crossed the room and pushed open the kitchen door and asked sweetly for some sandwiches. She then sat on a couch next to the two bodyguards, facing Gable, who was buffing the rifle's barrel with a piece of chamois. "It's a perfectly beautiful love story. Selznick has such good taste. He really has an exquisite story sense."

"You mean Kay Brown has such exquisite story sense." Kay Brown headed Selznick's story department and had found and acquired *Gone With the Wind*.

"I wish he was a detective," said Carole.

"Who?" asked Gable. "Selznick?"

"He'd be a marvelous detective," said Carole, warming up to the idea. "I'll bet he'd track down this gang in no time."

"What gang?" asked Gable.

"The gang of kidnappers," said Carole.

"How do you know it's a gang?"

"Don't kidnappers work in gangs?"

"It took one man to kidnap the Lindbergh baby."

"Clark, stop aggravating me!" She said to the athletes, "Why don't you boys go to the kitchen? Agnes will turn out the sandwiches faster. Clark, you want a sandwich?"

"Not right now."

"I don't have an appetite either. Thinking of poor Lydia. The girls up at the house are so upset." She watched the bodyguards as they went to the kitchen. "Especially Mala Anook, the Eskimo."

"Eskimo!" snorted Gable. "If she's an Eskimo, then I'm a Lithuanian."

"You're a Lithuanian, because she's really an Eskimo. She has a picture of herself harpooning a narwhal. That's a kind of walrus or something. I'll bet she's in the kitchen up at the house chewing on a piece of blubber and fighting back her tears. She adores Lydia. She was teaching her the art of blubber chewing."

"That's an art? The very thought of gnawing away at a hunk of whale fat nauseates me."

"On the subject of nauseate, how's Miss Crawford behaving on the set?"

"Now don't be cruel to Joan."

"She's determined to steal you away from me."

"No she's not!"

"Did she tell you that?"

"No, damn it!"

"So how do you know?" On her face was a sly smile.

"Listen, baby. I love you and only you. I gave up a hell of a lot for the privilege of putting a wedding ring on your finger."

She sat up and said with mock haughtiness, "I'm worth every nickel. Oh put that damn gun down and pay attention to me!"

"I heard you!" he insisted. "You're worth every nickel."

She smiled, crossed to him, and kissed his cheek. "I'm going to call David and tell him I just adore the script." She went to a desk, sat and dialed. After a few moments, she spoke sweetly into the mouthpiece. "Hello?" She said grandly (the way Janet Gaynor in *A Star Is Born* announced proudly into a radio microphone that she was Mrs. Norman Maine, Maine being the once famous star dead by a drowning suicide), "This is Mrs. Clark Gable."

Gable asked, "Are you sure you don't have to give which number wife you are?"

She ignored him. Into the phone she said,

"David? How are you, darling?" Gable wondered briefly if they had ever had an affair. "David, I absolutely adore the script. What do you mean, which script? *Made for Each Other.* You still want me to do it, don't you?" At his end, he assured her he most certainly did, Lombard being box-office insurance. Hazel Dickson paused in the application of fresh makeup to her face to try and figure out who he was talking to. Selznick assuaged her curiosity by mouthing Lombard's name, while Carole was telling Selznick to phone his brother Myron, her agent, and set a deal. Hazel shouted, "Remind her I'm doing an interview with the two of them at Chasen's in a couple of hours." Selznick did so and Carole asked him to assure Hazel she hadn't forgotten. She said to Gable, her hand over the mouthpiece, "Hazel Dickson at Chasen's in a couple of hours."

"For crying out loud, didn't we just give her an interview?"

Carole said, "You can never give Hazel enough interviews." She returned to Selznick. "David, I'm really frantic. It's Lydia Austin. Isn't there any word on her?" Selznick had nothing new to tell her. "This is awful! She's supposed to start shooting *Darkness in Hollywood* for Oscar Levitt next week and we all know Oscar. He works on such tight budgets that he can't afford a delay and he'll replace her. He mustn't replace her! She's my most talented girl!" She sounded like a madam determined to set up one of her girls with a choosy client. Selznick knew Carole was a mother hen furiously determined to protect one of her chicks and admired her for her loyalty and tenacity. From his own experience he knew there was a lot of tenacity in Hollywood but very little loyalty.

"David? Do you hear that crackling noise?"

"What crackling noise?"

"That's the sound of my heart about to break." Gable shot her a look and thought her display of intermingled pathos and sorrow was admirable, considering she'd had no rehearsal.

"Now, Carole," chided Selznick, "I'm sure Herb Villon is giving Lydia's return every possible consideration."

"Lydia who?" asked a suspicious Hazel Dickson.

"Austin," said Selznick and then reminded her of the kidnapped actress.

Hazel muttered under her breath, "Probably dead somewhere at the bottom of a quarry." After over a decade in the business of gossip, Hazel had had her fill of ingénues who get into trouble.

Carole listened as Selznick told her, "Herb's a crackerjack. He'll bring back Lydia safe and sound." To Carole Herb Villon now sounded like a prototype of the big-game hunter Frank "Bring 'Em Back Alive" Buck. Carole had a momentary vision of Lydia Austin tied to a bamboo pole while native bearers transported her to the safety of a studio set.

The bodyguards were back in the living room, having wolfed down the sandwiches in record time. Clark referred to them as human vacuum cleaners.

Carole was finished talking to Selznick for the time being. Matters of the director and who would design her clothes could wait until Myron Selznick squeezed every last dollar out of his brother for Carole's services. She looked forlorn and Roy Harvey, the athlete with the shaggy blond hair, asked sympathetically, "Mrs. Gable, is there something we could do?"

"Not much unless you're bloodhounds. But thanks anyway." She stood at a sideboard on which she had long ago placed framed photographs of her four protégées. She had her hands crossed across her chest and Clark presumed when she spoke there'd be a sob in her voice. She spoke, but blissfully a sob was absent. She commanded the athletes, "Look at my darlings." They looked. Both young men were interested in laying all four of the girls but tactfully kept silent. She held up a portrait. "This is Lydia. She's the girl who's missing. Isn't she gorgeous?" Sammy Rowan was about to say he certainly wouldn't kick her out of his bed but bit his lower lip instead. "And here's Nana Lewis. She has a smaller role in the movie, but if Lydia isn't found in time to start shooting, Oscar Levitt says he'll give Nana the part."

Gable spoke up. "If Nana knew this, maybe she arranged for Lydia to be kidnapped."

Carole raged, "Clark, you don't mean that!" Clark, not Pappy. She was really angry.

Gable persisted. "Makes sense, doesn't it, boys?"

Carole glowered at the young men, who wisely elected to voice no opinion. They didn't care who played the lead in the Levitt movie.

Carole took a moment to simmer down and picked up the next photograph. "This girl is Nell Corday. Look at those smoldering looks. She claims she's descended from Charlotte Corday." The boys didn't dare ask who Charlotte Corday was. Carole rescued them. "Charlotte Corday. She assassinated Marat." The boys were stumped again. "Marat was a politician at the time of the French Revolution," said Carole in response to the blank looks on their faces. "But I'm wondering about that because Nell doesn't speak any French. And here's Mala Anouk. Believe it or not, she's an Eskimo. We don't get many Eskimos in Hollywood, do we, Pappy?"

"No, there's no great demand for them. And an igloo wouldn't last long in this climate." Carole clasped her hands together dramatically, and crossed and stood in front of Gable. "They've got to find Lydia, they've just got to. So talented, so sweet, so . . ."

"Don't say 'so innocent,' honey, Lydia's been around."

Lombard's hands were on her hips. "How do *you* know?"

Gable got to his feet and chucked his wife under the chin. "Honey, there are very few virgins in Hollywood."

"Yeah! Not since you got here!" Gable flashed a wink at the athletes. They were so young. So naive. Built like brick ovens, but would they be of much use if an attempt was made to kidnap Carole?

He hoped he would never have to find out.

Carole snapped her fingers. "I know I'm right!"

"Now what?" asked Gable.

Carole ignored him. "I know I'm right." She was at the phone dialing.

Clark asked with suspicion, "Now who you calling?"

"Oscar Levitt."

"What do you want with Oscar?" Oscar Levitt was one of Clark's hunting companions. Carole waved him to be quiet. Into the phone she said, "I'd like to speak to Mr. Levitt." She said grandly, "This is Mrs. Clark Gable."

"I know," said the receptionist in Levitt's office.

"You always know," said Carole. "You're so clever." Carole waited, and then Oscar Levitt said, "Hello sweetie."

"Oscar," Carole spoke his name with a tear in her voice, "is there any news?"

"About what?"

"Lydia!"

"Not a word. Not a damned word."

Her voice deepened. "Oscar, I want the truth."

"You sound angry. Why are you angry?"

"I'm not angry. I'm merely speaking through clenched teeth." She took a breath.

"Oscar, level with me. We're old friends. I want you to level with me."

"About what?"

"About Lydia's kidnapping. Is it a publicity stunt? Did you arrange it?"

"Christ, no!"

"You wouldn't lie to me, Oscar? We've been friends for years!"

"Two years," Gable said to the athletes. "I introduced them."

The boys slyly exchanged looks. Who the hell was Oscar Levitt?

"I'm not lying!" He was staring at a framed photograph of Lydia Austin on his desk. It was in color and Lydia's best feature, her flaming red hair, reminded Oscar Levitt of a forest fire blazing out of control. Her lips were also a flaming red and were an invitation to a night in paradise. She wore a low-cut blouse which displayed the sort of cleavage that drove men either to drink or to take the pledge.

"Oh God!" he heard Carole wail, "maybe she's dead!"

Oscar swallowed. "God forbid," he said softly.

"Sure God forbid," said Carole sullenly, "you're just worried about the starting date of the picture."

Gable glanced at his wristwatch. It was

time to leave for their date with Hazel Dickson. He waved his hand at Carole while pointing to the wristwatch. "We'll be late for Hazel's interview."

Carole was listening to Oscar Levitt telling her he had spoken to Jim Mallory that morning. Jim was Herb Villon's partner with a unique penchant for envisioning himself in erotic situations with just about all of the cinema's leading ladies.

"Did you learn anything?" asked Carole impatiently.

Oscar said, "Nothing new. There's been no ransom note."

"Nothing? Not even one of those cockamamie demands with words cut out of newspapers? God," she said to the ceiling, "if kidnappers are smart enough to kidnap you'd think they could write a ransom note. Oscar, if anything turns up let me know right away." She hung up.

Oscar stared at Lydia's photo on his desk. Poor kid, he thought, poor kid.

Carole paced the room, reminding the young athletes of a panther on the prowl. Gable reminded his wife they were due at Chasen's in about an hour, but his wife was busy lighting a cigarette. "Oscar sounded shattered. His voice broke twice." She exhaled smoke and shrieked, "What the hell are the police doing?" Gable was placing the rifle in the gun cabinet with tender loving care. "Why aren't they out with bloodhounds yapping and baying? They should be beating the underbrush, sloshing through swamps —"

Gable cut into her monologue. "We don't have any swamps."

"No swamps?"

"No swamps, no alligators, nothing."

She spoke with her hands on her hips. "Florida's got it all over us. They've got swamps, alligators, and juicier oranges." Then, "Shouldn't we be headed for Chasen's?" She had glanced at her wristwatch. "Damn it, if we're late she'll start drinking doubles and she'll be pissed out of her skull by the time we get there." She clapped her hands as she hastily ascended the staircase. "Boys! Front and center! On to Chasen's!" She was taking the steps two at a time. "Clark! Come on! We'll be late!" Gable sat in a chair. At the head of the stairs, Carole turned and shouted, "This is no time to sit! You've got to change!"

"Into what?"

Carole snapped, "Your best ball gown."

"Don't be snippy. And don't you take an hour deciding on what to wear. What you've got on is perfectly fine. Casual chic."

"Oh really?" she squeaked. "Boys! How do I look to you?"

Good enough to eat, Roy wanted to tell her but instead said, "You look real great, ma'am." Sammy agreed with him.

Carole said sweetly, "You boys have such exquisite taste. Such lovely manners, I just might adopt you both."

Roy crossed his fingers in hope. Sammy's grin was crooked and boyish. Clark's look was his usual one of dimpled exasperation. Carole was in the bedroom selecting a handbag and then a jacket. Both were incredibly expensive. She looked in a mirror and approved of what she saw. She knew Gable did too and that was all that mattered. She hurried downstairs where he was getting into the leather hunting jacket that he selected from the hall closet where he stored a variety of jackets. Gable watched Carole as she poked her head into the kitchen. "We're off to be interviewed. We should be back in three or four hours." Then she warned the staff, which consisted of Agnes, the cook-housekeeper, a middle-aged woman who adored the Gables, her husband Albert who tripled as handyman, chauffeur, and butler when they needed any buttling which was rarely, and Ada, maid of all work who mostly saw to Carole's needs, "Beware of strangers. All the things in the gun closet are loaded. There's more ammunition in the drawers. And Albert, don't forget to feed the horses. You know they tend to get peckish. Bye!"

Sammy held the front door open for them as Clark and Carole, followed by Roy, hurried out of the house to one of the family's several cars. Clark led the way to a black Cadillac, which Carole insisted was for gangsters and not for movie stars, but it was Clark's favorite vehicle. He didn't look favorably on Carole slipping behind the wheel but knew better than to argue with her. She was a marvelous driver and the only time she'd been in a serious accident was back in 1926 and she wasn't driving at the time. Her left cheek was cruelly disfigured. Just when Carole's film career was beginning, she thought it was over. But a young plastic surgeon came to her rescue, and within a few months after the delicate surgery, all that remained was a slight scar, which careful lighting disguised. Carole studied up on lighting and was soon an expert, sharing her knowledge with the cameramen assigned to her films. Now she felt like singing, but the thought of the danger Lydia Austin was in discouraged her. She pulled out of the driveway and caught a glimpse of Roy and Sammy through the rearview mirror. So young, so fresh, so innocent, and so adorable.

She remembered her mother telling her, "You were born mature. You weren't young like the other girls in your crowd. I remember when Monte Blue interviewed you for the part of his little sister in *A Perfect Crime*. He said, 'So this is the scrappy little kid Allan Dwan discovered. She's not scrappy, she's a perfect little lady.' "

Allan Dwan was a respected director, who while visiting friends noticed the twelve-year-old in the next yard badgering all the kids, and thinking, There's the kid I need for Monte's picture. Eventually, Monte Blue agreed with Dwan and Jane Alice Peters became Carol Lombard, the *e* added later, presumably on the advice of a fortune teller. But that wasn't how it happened. Carol with an *e* mistakenly appeared on a movie poster and the actress liked her name spelled that way and decided not to change it.

Carole heard Clark say, "Honey, you're strangling the steering wheel."

"Hmm? What about the steering wheel? It's a perfectly lovely steering wheel." She said over her shoulder, "Boys! Don't you think this is a lovely steering wheel?"

Roy looked at Sammy who said, "Oh yes, ma'am!"

Carole smiled while stealing a look at the

man she loved seated next to her. He was staring straight ahead now, probably seated in a duck blind preparing to knock off a slew of them. She reminded herself of the horoscope she had Carroll Righter prepare on Clark before marrying him. Righter was known as the Astrologer to the Stars, a jovial poof who was making a fortune preparing charts for anyone in Hollywood who could afford him.

Righter told her as they sat in the drawing room of his elegant Beverly Hills home, "Clark is an Aquarian with a moody Cancer moon. Saturn created some friction with his highly sensitive moon, perhaps the cause of trouble for Gable with both his mother and the women in his life."

Mother. Most of the women in his life, it seemed to Carole, were mother substitutes. His first wife, Josephine Dillon, was easily ten years older than him. She taught him all he ever learned about acting. Then he dumped her for the formidable Ria, who was fifteen years older. But she had money and class and connections and did Clark ever deny being an opportunist? Most of his significant affairs when he began in the theater were with older, influential women. Carole was humming "Melancholy Baby" as these women paraded before her eyes, every one of them a superb actress. Jane Cowl, Marjorie Rambeau, and Alice Brady topped the list. Clark wondered why she was chuckling to herself but knew better than to ask. She was chuckling because after Clark's star rose at MGM, Louis B. Mayer signed Rambeau and Brady to contracts and promptly assigned them roles in Gable's pictures. And Pappy apparently didn't bat an eyelash and besides, he was now having it off with Miss Crawford, who demanded — and got — a lot of attention, even from her husband of the moment, Douglas Fairbanks, Jr.

Roy and Sammy were wondering what had brought on Gable's sudden coughing fit. They hadn't heard Carole's softly spoken question, "Pappy, were Rambeau and Brady good in bed?"

TWO

"What time is it?" Hazel Dickson asked Maude Chasen, Dave Chasen's wife.

Maude said patiently, "I just told you."

"Tell me again, I have a short attention span." Without looking at her wristwatch, Maude told her it was a few minutes past three.

Hazel said, "You didn't look at your wristwatch. You pulled that number out of thin air."

"A few minutes ago I told you it was three o'clock. So now it's a few minutes past."

Hazel looked at her wristwatch. "You're right. It's a few minutes past three."

Maude saw into the restaurant foyer where Carole and Clark had just arrived, Carole assigning Roy and Sammy to the bar and cautioning them not to talk to strange men because any man in Hollywood not working at three in the afternoon is either up or down to no good. Sammy promised her they could look after themselves, while Roy sauntered to a bar stool and ordered a couple of beers. Casually, Sammy joined him while hearing Carole's high-pitched "Hazel! It's been so long! And look how you look!" Sammy wondered aloud how anyone could tell how anybody looked because like all Hollywood restaurants, the room was dimly lit. "Have you been waiting long?" asked Carole after blowing a kiss to Mrs. Chasen, who blew one back.

"Oh no, I just got here myself," Hazel lied. "Clark, you're looking handsomer than ever. And Carole, I *adore* your jacket."

"So does Pappy," said Carole. She smiled at a waiter who was hovering nearby and asked him, "Do you come here often?"

The waiter was an old Chasen hand and leaned down. "It's me, Miss Lombard, Wendell."

"Wendell!" shrieked Carole. "I didn't recognize you! Beaten up your wife lately?" Clark and Hazel sank lower on their chairs while Maude Chasen made a discreet retreat. Wendell was unfazed.

"Let me see now," said Wendell, "last time was about a month ago. She's been behaving herself since then." It seemed to Hazel that the waiter was unhappy about his wife's good behavior. Possibly he missed the exercise.

Clark interjected, "I want a scotch on the rocks. Hazel?"

"A very dry gin martini and leave out the

olive." She said to Carole and Clark, "They take up too much space. So Carole, you're going to do *Made for Each Other* for David." She reminded Carole, "I was in the office when you called. That Jimmy Stewart is coming up real fast. You're lucky to get him."

Carole stiffened. *"He's* lucky to get *me.* "

"Of course, darling," said Hazel. "Any actor's lucky to get you." She said to Clark, "How's the hunting?"

Clark said affably while smiling at Carole, "I haven't done much lately now that I'm an old married man."

"You've been an old married man twice before," Hazel reminded him but refrained from adding "to two old married women." "Do those two stunning specimens at the bar belong to you two?"

"Our bodyguards," said Carole.

"And who's *their* bodyguards?" asked Hazel.

Clark said, "They can look after themselves. They're young athletes, fresh out of UCLA. Louis B.'s got them under contract."

"Has Crawford or Shearer seen them?"

Carole said, "We wouldn't know. We don't have a hotline to either one of the ladies. Wendell, you've forgotten about me."

40

"Oh no I haven't. I've been waiting for you to make up your mind."

"I don't have to make it up. It's not rumpled. I'll have tea with lemon."

Clark asked with concern, "Aren't you feeling well?"

"I feel just dandy. But when I'm driving, I prefer not to drink." She smiled at Hazel, whose capacity for gin was a Hollywood legend. "Hazel, how's Herb?"

Hazel said with a sigh, "Up to his ears in these kidnappings. He practically has no time for me at all. I park my car at his precinct just for an excuse to poke my head in his office and ask, 'Remember me? I'm Pollyanna the Glad Girl.' "

"Oh Hazel, you're so cute," said Carole. "What's new with the kidnappings?"

"If you mean Lydia Austin, Herb doesn't have any leads. It's like she's vanished into gin air." She paused. "I mean thin air." Then Hazel said, "How're you enjoying the ranch?"

"Great!" said Clark, lighting a cigarette.

"I just adore it," said Carole. "All that fresh air all day and all night long. It's so healthy and invigorating." Hazel was taking notes in a small pad.

"What about coyotes?" asked Hazel.

"I'm sure they also find it healthy and invigorating."

"I hear you've got horses."

"Four," said Clark.

"And you keep them in the barn?"

Carole said, "There's too much furniture in the library." Hazel flashed her a look, which Carole ignored because she was busy stealing Clark's cigarette. He lit another one for himself. Carole then said eagerly, "I'll bet Herb's got a theory about these kidnappings but he's keeping it under wraps. Am I right?"

Hazel shrugged. "Ask Herb. Say, Carole, wasn't Lydia Austin mixed up with Mike Lynton?"

Carole was not about to speak without choosing her words carefully. Mike Lynton was Hollywood's most notorious gangster. His gambling casino in Marina del Rey was everybody's home away from home. He held gambling markers on everybody in Hollywood except Shirley Temple. Carole was not about to admit that she had done some sparring with the handsome racketeer. George Raft, who had gangland connections, had introduced them five years ago while he and Carole were co-starring in *Bolero*. As Carole explained her brief but heated romance with Lynton, "I'm such a sucker for a pretty face." And Lynton's was indeed a pretty face, exceptionally handsome for a thug —

chiseled featured and surprisingly enough no scars, which with other gangsters went with the territory.

Carole spoke through a practiced smile. "Do you mean, was she Mike's girl?"

"Of course I do," was the fearless Hazel's brisk reply.

"I don't know for sure," said Carole. The hell you don't, thought Hazel. Clark recognized the change of tone in Carole's voice. It was a warning to back down and change the subject. Carole was still that scrappy kid who had enchanted Allan Dwan fifteen years ago or more.

"Lately I gather she's been Groucho's girl."

"You're doing a lot of gathering, Hazel."

"That's my job and right now, Lydia is news." Bad news, Clark was beginning to think, and he wondered if either of the ladies knew about his brief fling with the ubiquitous Miss Austin. The waiter had returned with their orders and recognized the tension at the table. He served them quickly and vanished.

Carole created a laugh, albeit a feeble one. "I just can't envision Lydia and Groucho as an item. It's too surreal."

"No more surreal than Lydia and W. C. Fields," said Hazel as she lifted the martini to her lips.

Carole howled with laughter and when she simmered down said, "I'll bet it's Bill himself who's spreading that rumor. Poor old Bill, I think he's getting senile."

"You may be right," said Hazel. "He was in Selznick's office prior to my appointment, and demanding he be tested for Rhett Butler."

"My God," said Clark, "doesn't he know the picture's in the can?"

"Oh pooh," said Carole, with a disdainful wave of a hand. "Don't you recognize a Fields put-on when you hear it?"

"I didn't hear it. David told me after Fields left and David was very upset."

Carole said to Clark, "The world's gone mad!" She craned her neck toward the bar. "The boys seem okay." Then she clucked her tongue. "Poor Lydia. I know she's been playing around. All the kids play around. It goes with the territory. The only ones who don't play around are afflicted with paralysis."

Hazel couldn't resist. "Did you play around?"

Clark thought he heard a phantom bugle announcing a declaration of war. Carole leaned forward with an elbow on the table. "Hazel, there's playing around and there's playing around, if you catch my drift." Hazel was scribbling on the pad. A saucy Lombard quote was always good for at least ten bucks. "There are those who bed-hop and those who bed-wet and those who make a lot of noise about sex to cover up the fact they rarely indulge. I've had two serious involvements in my life, Pappy here and Bill Powell."

"What about Russ Columbo?" asked Hazel. If Clark guffawed Carole was prepared to kick him under the table.

"At the time," said Carole with her special brand of hauteur, "I was seeing the world through Russ-colored glasses."

"Oh brother," exhaled Clark to no one in particular. Actually he was grateful Carole hadn't drenched Hazel in a downpour of vulgarity. Carole Lombard had a notorious reputation for letting loose with curse and swear words that would give a longshoreman a stroke. But Carole had put the lid on the vulgarities out of deference and respect to the two bodyguards. As far as she could see they were two innocents and she had a deep respect for innocence, an emotion she had never experienced. Before and more so after the car accident, she built a reputation as Hollywood's wild girl. During the flapper era other flappers flapped with envy. When she signed with Paramount in 1930, she was up against the imports from Broadway and England who were hired because they could "talk." And talking pictures badly needed good diction and style. When Carole checked into the studio, she had among her credits a short series of knockabout comedies for Mack Sennett and some undistinguished roles in B features.

Now at Paramount she was being served an opportunity to make it in the big time. But other newcomers offered strong competition. There was Miriam Hopkins, a terrific comedienne with a volatile temper. There was Sylvia Sidney, who made crying a high art and also snared studio head B. P. Schulberg for a boyfriend. There were Wynne Gibson and Virginia Bruce and the most formidable and gifted actress of them all, Ruth Chatterton, who in turn was up against the two clotheshorses Kay Francis and Lilyan Tashman. Amazingly enough, all the ladies were terribly friendly. They were even friendly with Paramount's two major stars, the instant hits Claudette Colbert and Marlene Dietrich. And it was rumored they were more than just friends, frequently appearing in public in matching tuxedos. As Carole commented to her mother, "Oh what the hell. What does it matter if girls will be boys." Carole's mother, Bessie, said it was

46

fine by her as she believed in live and let live and she hoped they went often to confession. Carole's brothers, Stuart and Fred, were thoroughly disillusioned as both had a crush on Dietrich, little knowing that Dietrich also had a crush on Dietrich.

"That's a long pause, Mrs. Gable. Are you trying to move the conversation away from the late Mr. Columbo?"

"No, I'm only trying to squeeze some lemon in my tea. Poor Russ, I hope he's resting in peace." Which was more than she was getting at the moment. "He could have had a brilliant career in films. Universal was looking for a story to co-star us." She smiled at Gable. "Your silence is deafening, Pappy. Hazel is supposed to be interviewing both of us."

"Oh, I'll soon be getting around to him," Hazel assured Carole. "Were you friendly with Jean Harlow?"

Carole responded, "Hazel, is what you're really after is do I know of Bill Powell ever having an affair with her, you'd do better to ask Pappy. He was on the Metro lot with both of them. You know he co-starred with Jean in lots of pictures. Pappy, did you ever screw Harlow?"

Gable said with a phony smile, "I'm the one who didn't."

"Now there you go spreading nasty gossip," scolded Carole.

"What the hell are you talking about?"

"You're inferring Jean was fair game for every man at the studio!"

"Okay, if it bothers you, I'll rephrase the sentence. She wasn't interested in me and the feeling was mutual. Every man she married or was involved with was a replacement for her father. Even that slimy stepfather of hers, Mario Bello."

"God damn it!" bellowed Carole. "Let's talk about the dark cloud hanging over our heads!"

Hazel stared at the ceiling with curiosity. "What dark cloud?"

"The kidnappings!"

"All I know is what I read in the papers," pleaded Hazel.

"Ha ha ha. You've got a direct line to the cops," Carole said. "You can't tell me Herb Villon isn't blabbing to you about what he knows!"

"Blabbing is hardly a verb I'd use for Herb Villon. There's a man who doesn't gossip, doesn't discuss his work, keeps a tight lid on everything, and when he orders food, he whispers."

"What a catch," commented Carole wryly.

"And he doesn't refer to them as kidnappings. He calls them disappearances."

"Very strange character, your Mr. Villon."

Hazel leaned toward Carole while Carole took a sip of her now very lukewarm tea. "Carole, there's something seriously missing from these cases."

"Yeah?"

"No ransom notes."

"If there are no ransom notes, maybe they weren't kidnapped. Maybe they just upped and disappeared. A lot of husbands and wives who are fed up with their marriages do."

Clark said, "That's an interesting point, baby."

"There's another interesting point," said Hazel. "As far as I know, Lydia Austin is the only woman who's vanished."

"Lydia's the only woman reported missing?" Carole said with heated indignation. "Why, that's discrimination! Don't you agree, Pappy?"

"Whatever it is, it's still a crime. There's another point you ladies seem to have missed."

"Go on," egged Carole.

"Most of the men were Japanese."

Hazel was scratching her chin. "That's a pretty good observation, Mr. Gable. I'm sure

Herb's aware of it. Let me see . . ." Hazel did a hasty calculation. "Seven Japanese as opposed to three white men. Most of them influential in business circles."

"Well, they're usually loaded financially," reasoned Carole, "which makes them the most favorable victims. Sayyyy, a lot of us in Hollywood have impressive savings accounts."

"I don't," said Clark glumly. Hazel was busy scribbling. Carole was staring into her tea cup.

"Can anybody here read tea leaves?"

In Herb Villon's office at the precinct, Detective Jim Mallory had flung open the two windows at Herb Villon's pleading. Cigar smoke polluted the room and the perpetrator was pacing back and forth in his familiar half crouch. Off screen Groucho Marx wore real glasses for his nearsightedness as opposed to the painted black ones he sported in films. He was singing one of the songs associated with him since he introduced it in *A Day at the Races*, and it seemed most appropriate to the current situation afflicting the film colony. " *'Oh Lydia, oh Lydia, oh, have you seen Lydia . . .'* " Jim Mallory chimed in and Herb Villon exploded. "Oh, shut up the two of you!"

"Why don't you get another off-key cop in here and the four of us will make it a barbershop quartet. Of course, it'll be a close shave." Groucho stopped and stared at Herb. "Forgive me for that one. On the other hand, forgive Chico because he thought it up. While I" — he feigned moroseness — "stand here in sorrow. If you had a bed, I'd lie in a bed of pain. We'll have to make good with a vale of tears." He leaned across the desk and Villon shrank back. "I want you to know I'm very sweet on Lydia Austin. I don't want to marry her, I just want to be sweet on her. As I recall, lots of men have been sweet on Lydia. Men gather around her like moths around a flame. I wonder if Mike Lynton's our man. He's perfect casting for a culprit. Culprit! How's that for a fancy word? And they say I have no class. I have lots of class but no pupils. I suppose I could call Central Casting and tell them to send over a couple of dozen pupils. But no, I'd have to feed them." He sprawled across Herb's desk and affected a seductive pose. "Can I interest you in Mike Lynton? Or a double dozen of a dozen damask napkins? Didn't you know Mike was one of Miss Austin's boyfriends?"

Herb knew but chose not to answer. He didn't have to. There was no chance to get a word in edgewise. Groucho babbled on like an undammable brook. Jim Mallory was enjoying himself immensely. One of the perks of being Herb Villon's partner was the variety of drop-in trade. There'd been a lot of Groucho Marx since Lydia's disappearance. Also Lydia's three housemates, quite a delectable lot, especially the Eskimo even if her lips were always greasy.

Jim heard Groucho persisting. "Well, what about Mike Lynton? It would be so sweet of you to put him away where he can't keep calling in my markers. That's my darling Lydia, little Miss Marker."

"That was Shirley Temple!" crowed Jim Mallory.

"What was Shirley Temple?" asked Groucho.

"Little Miss Marker! One of her first starring roles!"

Groucho said to Herb Villon, "Don't you realize this young and handsome flatfoot is being wasted around here?" He zeroed in on Mallory. "Have you no ambition? Don't you wish to make something of yourself? If I bought you some wool and some knitting needles, *then* would you try to make something of yourself? Of course not!" He hopped off the desk. "Lydia couldn't knit. She couldn't crochet. She couldn't even tat lace.

But she knew how to collect jewelry. Mike Lynton showered her with jewelry. Pearls, diamonds, emeralds, lapis lazuli imported from the Far East, zircons imported from Woolworth's . . ."

Jim Mallory was awestruck. "You're kidding us."

Groucho went dramatic. "No I'm not. I'm not in a kidding mood. There's a *zaftig* beauty missing and the older I get, the harder it is for me to snare for myself a *zaftig* beauty. Lydia loved to parade around in her beautiful jewels. Sometimes she wore a dress. She's always trying to get me to give her jewelry. I bought her boxes of Crackerjack. There's usually a prize at the bottom." He raised himself to his full height and raged, "Ungrateful wench!" He paused and then said, "Did I ever tell you the one about the plumber and his ungrateful wrench? It wouldn't screw. Oh no no! Forgive me! That was beneath me!" He was solemn again. "I bought Lydia dinner. When we went to a movie I bought her popcorn. She's crazy about popcorn. I wish she was as crazy about me as she is about popcorn. I suggested she wear strings of popcorn but she wouldn't hear of it, they'd stain her dress. Oh, how I wish she was standing before me, stains and all."

Herb Villon had tuned out on Groucho from the moment he mentioned Mike Lynton. Take his gambling house in Santa Monica. It was never raided despite its being illegal. But the word had come from above, and words from above had to be taken seriously and obeyed, so Mike Lynton's casino was never raided. Herb and just about everybody else in the know assumed the chief of police was on the take. Los Angeles was notorious for its crooked police force. Only stupid L.A. cops didn't own a house and a car. The only person in L.A. who collected better than the cops was its queen gossip columnist, Louella Parsons. Lydia Austin had collected from Mike Lynton, or so she claimed. Did she have anything serious on him or was he genuinely generous? And if so, how could she cast aside Lynton's generosity for Groucho Marx?

Herb heard Groucho saying, "Maybe I've got Mike Lynton all wrong. I'll bet there are lots of people who would like to get Mike Lynton all wrong. Why would he kidnap Lydia? He's got lots of girlfriends." His voice brightened. "Maybe he can spare me one! I'll pay her cab fare if she doesn't have a car. Maybe she's thinking I'll buy her a car. Ha! Fat chance she's got of getting a car out of me. The scheming gold digger. I want no part of her! Keep her, Mike, she's yours!"

Herb Villon was staring at a page in his notebook. On it he had listed the missing abductees. The Japanese outnumbered the others two to one. Only one name among them was familiar to him. A businessman named Takameshuga. Ito Takameshuga, an investor. He had an interest in the Futamara in down L.A. on the fringe of Chinatown. It was beautifully constructed, offered superb cuisine, had a splendid staff, and served a very select clientele. The staff was polite and discreet, which made it a perfect venue for forbidden trysts. Herb had been there himself on several occasions when he hungered to vary his Hazel diet of sex and gossip. He had seen Gable there prior to his marriage to Lombard with a well-known MGM featured player. He'd recognized the face but couldn't attach a name to it. It didn't matter. He liked Gable. He would never betray him to Hazel, who was always badgering him for some of the dirt he was often privy to.

Herb read the names for the umpty-umpth time. He was looking for a possible connection. Maybe they all knew each other or were associates in one of the many so-called secret organizations Orientals created. The Chinese had mostly tongs, but they were family affairs. The Japanese had the Yakuza, but they were a lethal group of killers. Maybe the Yakuza was behind the disappearances. Herb leaned back in his chair and stared at the ceiling where two flies, oblivious of his prying eyes, enjoyed some indiscreet fornication. Herb transferred his curiosity to his limited circle of Japanese acquaintances. There was Takameshuga, but he was, so to speak, out of town. There was the movie star Sessue Hayakawa, but when Herb last heard, he was filming in France, talkies having put paid to his once thriving Hollywood career. There was a pretty actress, Toshia Mori, but she had disappeared from the Hollywood scene several years ago.

While Groucho's stream of consciousness inundated the room, much to his own egoistic satisfaction, he was unaware that Herb and Jim had tuned him out. Jim had sensed Herb might be on to something and quietly joined him at the desk. Herb said to him, "Somewhere there's a link between these jokers. And there could possibly be a link to the three Caucasians, Nathan Taft, Elmer Rabb, Oscar Nolan. What do we know about them?"

"Not too much," admitted Jim. "They're war veterans for one, and all three were highly decorated. I contacted Washington like you told me to but the FBI wasn't much help." He added sardonically, "They're still straightening out their files. The guy I spoke to offered me some stuff on John Dillinger and Baby Face Nelson, and I explained with great patience that those two weren't missing, they were just dead."

"God damn it, so where does Lydia Austin fit in?"

"In my boudoir!" exclaimed Groucho, "which she sprays with 'Essence of Eve' every time she pays me a visit. 'Essence of Eve.' I can smell it now. Or is that a hamburger and onions wafting from across the hall? I'll be right back." He scurried out of Herb's office and Herb and Jim exhaled a collective sigh of relief. Herb said, "I love the guy but he's best in small doses."

Jim said after deep thought, "Why does Lydia Austin have to fit in at all?"

Herb stared at him. "That's a good thought. You might be right." He scribbled a note to himself. Groucho came rushing back into the room. "There's no hamburger and onions in the office across the hall. Only a crap game." He began stalking back and forth. "They wouldn't let me play. Just like the gang on my block when I was a kid on the Lower East Side of New York. They wouldn't let me play with them. What a blow to my psyche. I still bear the scar. Want to look at my scar?" He was pulling out his shirttail.

"For crying out loud, Groucho!" yelled Herb.

"Oh come on," urged Groucho coyly, "just a little peek. Please? Pretty please?"

Herb folded his hands on the desk and rested his head on them. Jim asked, "Can I get you something, Herb?"

Herb moaned, "Out of here."

In the front seat of the black Cadillac, Clark sat next to Carole. In the back seat, Hazel sat between Roy and Sammy and thrilled at the touch of their muscular thighs. She wondered if athletes were ever traded or sold to civilians. Carole was saying to Clark, "Seven Japanese missing, three local whites, and Lydia. Clark, Lydia doesn't belong there."

"I think you're right."

"I'm positive I'm right. It's just a coincidence she's disappeared at the same time the others did. As a matter of fact, I think her kidnapper took advantage of the other disappearances to make it look as though she was part of the chain."

Said Clark, "We'll ask Herb when we get to the precinct. How's your landing gear?"

"Oh shut up. I'm driving very carefully. I know you're a nervous Nelly when I'm behind the wheel." Over her shoulder she asked Hazel, "Do I turn off left or right?"

"You turn right, but we've got a way to go." She was looking through the rearview mirror. "I wish we didn't."

Clark didn't like the darkness in her voice, "Why?"

"I think we're being tailed." Roy and Sammy turned their heads with difficulty to look out the back window. Carole and Clark studied the rearview mirror.

"It's a delivery van," said Carole. "Slightly beat up."

Hazel said grimly, "That's the kind they use in gangster pictures." Then she said, "What do we do if they pull up alongside us?"

"Scream," said Carole. She patted Clark's knee. "I'm not making a pass, I just want your attention."

Clark grunted.

Carole said, "I prefer we use the eye blink system. One if you understand what I'm saying, and two if you're frightened shitless."

"I understand what you're saying and we Gables know no fear. What's on your mind?"

She spoke with confidence. "I know you've got your gun."

"No you don't."

Her voice went up a few octaves. "You

59

don't have your gun? Then what do you have?" she raged, "a peashooter?"

Clark asked the boys in the back seat, "You guys got guns?"

"Not me," said Sammy, "I'm afraid of them."

"Oh swell," said Carole. "A bodyguard without a gun! Roy! Don't you have a gun?"

"No, ma'am. I don't have a license." He reassured her, "I've got my fists. I'm an intercollegiate boxing champion."

Carole said blandly, "I just had my nails done. I can do a mean job of scratching."

Hazel told them, "The van's passing us."

They saw two old ladies in the front seat. The one who was driving bore down on her horn to get Carole to give them room to pass.

"Daredevils," Carole muttered.

Hazel said, "I think they're adorable. One looks like my mother shortly after she died."

"Which one?" asked Carole.

"The one driving, of course."

"Oh look!" squealed Carole. "They recognize us." She shouted out the window. "Yes, it's us! Mr. and Mrs. Gable! Clark and Carole! This is your lucky day!"

One old lady asked the other, "Why's the stupid bitch yelling at us?"

"Pay them no mind, Daphne. Just pass. If you have to, knock off a fender."

"Whatever you say, Tootsie." She bore down on the gas and left the Cadillac in a cloud of dust.

Said Carole, "I guess they didn't want autographs."

Hazel yelled, "Turn right at the Orange Julius stand. Did you hear me?"

"They heard you in Pasadena. Damn damn damn! I can't get Lydia out of my mind. Maybe Herb'll have some news. Maybe she escaped her captors and was found wandering on a lonely road, dazed, babbling . . . oh God . . . probably raped!"

Said Hazel, "Some girls have all the luck."

THREE

In Villon's office, Groucho was voicing his own wacky version of Lydia's escape. "I can see her now making her dash for freedom in her anklestrap shoes, dodging a hail of bullets." He was looking into an imaginary distance, his right hand raised dramatically. "There she goes, zigzagging her way to safety like a football player running for a touchdown. Or like Chico when he's being pursued by a horde of creditors. But good old Lydia. She's always fast on her feet. I should know," he added with the famous Groucho leer, "I've chased her often enough."

At the front desk, Hazel breezed past the sergeant in charge with a cheerful "How are you, Hymie?" while Carole told Sammy and Roy to sit on a bench or read the Wanted posters pinned to the bulletin board. Clark grabbed Carole's hand and pulled her in the direction Hazel had taken, leading them to Villon's office. Carole said to Clark, "Hazel acts as though she owns the place! Shouldn't we have been announced? This place looks familiar," she said as she pattered behind Clark, shaking her hand free. "I think this is the place where I was fingerprinted and mugged after I socked a cop outside of the Mocambo. That was years ago. I was such a crazy kid."

Gable believed her. He sometimes thought she was such a crazy adult, like the time she gave an all-white-clothes party and arrived in an ambulance on a stretcher and made the front page of just about every newspaper in the United States. But he loved her dearly. She had gone out of her way to adapt to his style of living. She learned to hunt and shoot and to favor her wardrobe with jeans and dungarees. She gave steak and potato dinners for his pals while managing to turn a blind eye to his indiscretions. She taught herself to accept the fact that Gable's eyes were bigger than his stomach where women were concerned. She was long used to the fact that though a good performer in the sack, he was not terribly well endowed. As she put it to her mother, "There's less to Pappy than meets the eye."

Hazel entered Villon's office. At the sight of her, the detective groaned inwardly but then cheered up on seeing the Gables. They were two of his favorite actors. They greeted each other warmly and Jim Mallory's face went red when Carole kissed his cheek and said, "I'm sure we know each other. Do we?"

Mallory admitted they hadn't met before and Carole said with a laugh, "Well, now we know each other!" Groucho had scurried across the room and held Hazel in a passionate embrace. "My favorite yenta!" He showered her with kisses while Hazel screeched. "Don't resist me! Don't even try! I'm one in a million. I'll call my broker and maybe find out I've got two million. With any luck he'll give me a clean bill of wealth." Hazel pulled free while Groucho said to Villon, "When are you going to make her an honest woman? You've had a longer engagement than Hearst and Marion Davies. Marry the harlot or I'll sell her into slavery. She ought to bring a pretty penny." He eyed Hazel dubiously. "On the other hand she might bring a homely penny."

"Groucho!" remonstrated Hazel.

"She's got to bring something, if only a bag of tollhouse cookies she baked with her own gin-stained hands." His gaze dropped to her hands. "Ah yes. She does have hands. That's a good manicure, Hazel." He rounded on Jim Mallory. "Why are these people here? Are they under suspicion? Are they under the weather?" Swiftly he grabbed Carole. "Come with me to the Casbah. They're having a spring sale. Every kind of *shmatte* your heart desires."

"Let go!" cried Carole as she pushed him away. She yelled at Clark, "I'm being man-handled and you stand there with that silly smirk on your face."

Groucho said, "It's his face. He can have anything he wants on it, including some egg. I wish it was my face. And if it was, I probably wouldn't know what to do with it."

"How are you, Groucho?" asked Gable, knowing Marx's off-the-wall sense of humor camouflaged a very sensitive and very loving soul.

"It's about time you asked," Groucho said. "You have the audacity to steal the gorgeous Lombard from under my phony eyeglasses and you dare to inquire as to my health?" He said to Hazel with a new variation of a leer, "It's my health and you keep your hands off it." He said to Gable, "I have a warm spot for Carole. In fact, I have two warm spots for Carole but I'll never tell you where they are." He said sotto voce to Carole, "Would you care to come to my hacienda in Brentwood for a private viewing of my warm spots?"

Carole stood with her arms folded while Gable and Hazel sat in the chairs Jim Mallory offered them. "Knock it off, Groucho. There's fun and there's fun and much as I adore you you sometimes go too far. I know you're upset about Lydia and for crying out loud so am I. She could be lying dead somewhere. Oh God, I hope not." Villon was at her side with an arm around her shoulder. "It's been over a week now, Herb."

"Carole, we're doing our damnedest to break this case. It's a hell of a puzzler. Sit down? You want some coffee?"

"Black, no cream or sugar."

Jim Mallory crossed to a hot plate on which there rested a pot of hot coffee and poured a cup for Carole. Hazel said, "The same for me. Clark?" He shook his head no.

Carole rummaged in her handbag and found a cigarette. Groucho bent over and held a lighter to it. "Thanks, darling," she said. She exhaled, the smoke pouring from her nostrils making her look like an evil dragon on an Oriental tapestry.

Villon asked Carole, "How well do you know Mike Lynton?"

"Knew," corrected Carole, "past tense." Then she asked, "You got him on your list of suspects?"

"He's a likely candidate. As good as anybody else. And Lydia Austin was his girl for a while." Groucho had poured himself a cup of coffee. He pulled up a chair to Jim Mallory's desk and sat and sipped.

"Kidnapping's not Mike's style," said Carole. "He may be a gangster, but he's got class. Of course when he felt it was necessary he was not beyond ordering somebody's legs broken." Hazel grimaced.

Clark spoke. "Mike has hunted with Oscar Levitt, the other boys and myself a few times. We've had long talks around the campfire. I know he was sweet on Carole briefly."

"Back in the Ice Age," said Carole. "He caught me on the rebound from Bill Powell when we were divorcing. He was good company. He's not your everyday run-of-the-mill mobster. He comes from a good family in Baltimore. I know because he spoke of them with affection, and he frequently spoke of them. And it's rare for someone in the mob to discuss his relations." She stared at the glowing tip of her cigarette and told Villon, "I called Mike when Lydia was reported missing. It was natural to think he might know something. But he was still recovering from losing her to this nudnik over here." She indicated Groucho.

Groucho said, "I called him too. So help me Hannah. That's how desperate I was. He was very nice. He understood how I felt. But he had nothing to tell me."

Herb said, "Jim and I were there when you called. We were in Mike's office in the casino. It was late last Friday, and there was little action."

Mike Lynton had spoken into an intercom. "Hold all my calls. That means everybody." Then he gave his attention to the two detectives sitting across from him. "You guys like a drink?" Both refused. "Mind if I have one?" He went to the bar and poured himself a Drambuie. He held the glass up to the light from a window and was satisfied with the texture of the liqueur. "It's a Drambuie. Superior stock. You sure you won't join me?" But he had no takers. He sat behind his desk and said, "A superior drink considering its lowly origins. It originated in a fire in an Edinburgh distillery. There were iron vats of scotch all over the place and the distillers, being Scotch, despaired at the prospect of a big financial loss. So when the fire was finally out, there they were with iron vats of burnt scotch. Some guy decided to taste it. Not bad, he thought, and got his partners to try some. They all agreed there was something tasty about it. So they decided to try bottling it as a liqueur. It was a sensation. They called it 'Drambuie' because, like today, anything French-sounding commands respect and a good price. I have yet to dine in Paris without suffering a severe case of indigestion.

Their meats and fish are so inferior, which is why they created fancy sauces to camouflage the bad qualities." He smiled. "But I still like to visit Paris." He said sadly, "Of course, it'll be a long time before I'll be able to return to Europe. This war is going to be a very long war. But that's not why you're here."

"No it isn't," said Herb. "Mike, when did you last see Lydia Austin?"

"That's what Groucho just asked me. And the answer's still the same. A couple of months ago. Imagine losing a broad to Groucho Marx?"

"I know a guy who lost his to Jimmy Durante," countered Herb.

Mike chuckled. "What do these comics have that we seem to lack?" He said without an underlined ego, "I've got looks, money, and more connections than I need. And Lydia trades me in for Groucho." He shrugged. "Whatever it is he's got, Groucho should package it and market it. More power to him." He sipped the liqueur. "What about these other johns who've gone up in smoke? The Japs? The three other guys? I've been thinking about it but I can't come up with a connection between them and Lydia."

"I'm beginning to think there isn't one," said Villon.

"You mean Lydia might be a copycat kidnapping?"

"I'm sure it's no publicity stunt. Oscar Levitt swore on his wife's grave he didn't engineer a stunt."

"Oscar's wife is alive."

"I guess it was wishful thinking on Oscar's part."

Mike Lynton put his drink aside and began toying with a square box that contained small pellets and a series of holes in which you were supposed to drop the pellets. He wasn't very good at it.

Villon asked, "Was Lydia in hock to you?"

Lynton said, "Is she dead?"

"What makes you think that?"

"You asked *was* Lydia in hock to me, not *is* Lydia in hock to me. 'Is' says she's alive. 'Was' says she isn't."

"Sorry. As far as we can tell, we assume she's alive."

"I hope so. She's a good kid. And Oscar's offering her a big chance. I've read the script. It's a dog. He's been trying to get me to invest in it. But it's not for me." He tossed the box aside and became interested in the liqueur again. Villon had been studying him closely as he always did when on an interrogation. He'd met Lynton before on several occasions, mostly social. Mostly when Hazel was covering a Hollywood party and if he was free, Herb went along for the food and drink, which was usually top drawer at Hollywood parties. The Basil Rathbones gave the most lavish ones, Ouida being a superb hostess. They knew everyone worth knowing but Herb never felt out of place. Despite the fact that he looked like one, Rathbone was not a snob. In fact he was quite democratic, and slept with both men and women. Back in 1934 on an American tour with Katharine Cornell's company, he seduced a young actor named Tyrone Power, and now he was filming with Power in *The Mark of Zorro*. On the set, both behaved admirably although there were times during their sword fights that Rathbone thought Power was out to draw blood, despite the fact that their swords were tipped for safety's sake.

It was at a party of Ann Harding's that Herb and Lynton started discussing hunting and Herb learned Lynton was a hunting partner of both Clark and Levitt. He thought he detected a note of distaste when Lynton discussed Levitt but then, though Levitt was normally a decent enough fellow, he could be a nuisance when raising money for his independent productions.

Lynton asked Herb, "You ever go hunting?"

"What do you think I'm doing now?"

"I hope Lydia's okay. I sure hope she's okay. There's been no ransom note?"

"None."

"That's not good. Snatches are instigated for money. Who would pay for Lydia's release? She has no money. She has some good jewelry I gave her but in the big time what she's got is penny ante. Her family's dirt poor. They couldn't help."

"There's you. There's Groucho."

"And there's a small hotel," said Mallory.

Mike Lynton asked, "What about her housemates? Weren't they any help at all?"

Jim Mallory's eyes took on a romantic glaze as in his mind he flashed back to the three beauties who shared a house with Lydia Austin. These were Carole's discoveries, three of the four girls she thought could make it in pictures. And when Jim and Herb questioned them that sunny morning last week, they were impressed not only with their beauty but with their intelligence.

Mala Anouk had elected to serve tea to the detectives, a special jasmine tea sent by her mother. Herb was surprised that Eskimos drank tea or even were aware of its existence. But Mala assured him tea was as important a staple in the far north as coffee and cocoa. Preparing the tea, Mala performed a ritual which Herb seemed to remember he'd seen performed a couple of years earlier when he was in San Francisco at a detectives' convention. It was in a Japanese restaurant where geisha girls did the honors. Herb wasn't too sure about geisha girls in San Francisco but the girls, geisha or ersatz, put on a dazzling performance.

Mala's performance that morning was equally dazzling, almost as dazzling as the girl herself. Herb could tell they were in for a long morning as each girl seemed determined to answer his questions at inordinate length. In response to when they had last seen Lydia, each girl indulged in a long-winded explanation. They're actresses, Herb reminded himself. They're always long-winded when they hold center stage. But first Herb told Mala he had seen a similar tea ritual before but hers was more impressive.

"Oh thank you," said Mala with a sweet politeness. "This was taught to me by my aunt Suki, who studied at a university in Tokyo. It is very rare for an Eskimo girl to attend university. I visited her there three years ago, the year before I won the beauty contest." She said with pride, "I was chosen as Miss Arctic Circle of 1937, which is how I come to be in Hollywood. My prize was five hundred dollars in cash and a trip to

Hollywood and a six-month contract with Monogram Pictures. So here I am. Would you gentlemen care for some blubber? I've got lots in the refrigerator."

"Does she ever," commented Nana Lewis, the girl who was in line to inherit Lydia's lead in *Darkness in Hollywood*.

"Five hundred dollars," echoed Herb Villon.

"Oh yes," said Mala cheerfully. "I counted it very carefully. Would you like biscuits with the tea? I have a box of Hydrox cookies." Both detectives refused. Mala served the tea in dainty porcelain cups. She wore lounging pajamas that clung to her beautiful body provocatively. Nana Lewis sat in an easy chair, one leg crossed over the other, clutching a rubber ball in each hand with which she exercised. Nell Corday was poised in the center of the room holding a tennis racquet with which she returned a series of phantom serves. "I'm playing at Greta Garbo's this afternoon, doubles with Charlie Chaplin and Paulette Goddard."

"An all-star game," said Herb, having decided that as far as a career was concerned, Miss Corday was seriously on the make. Garbo, Chaplin, and Goddard were quite a coup for anybody in Hollywood, let alone a young actress.

"Charlie promised me if he needs an actress for a young gamine in his next picture, he would test me."

Knowing Chaplin's reputation and his taste for pubescent young ladies, Herb suspected that Nell had already been tested, with no film in the camera.

Mala urged Nell, "Do your impersonation of Charlie!"

Herb had a feeling getting any help from these young women as to what they knew about the missing Lydia might be a long-drawn-out process, and Herb was always pressed for time. He was about to suggest they could do without the impersonation but like most actresses on the make, Nell was walking jerkily around the room and twirling an imaginary cane. Jim Mallory was caught off guard by the performance and thought she might be having an epileptic fit. Mala clapped her hands enthusiastically, looking like a child being given a birthday gift. Nana Lewis was stifling a yawn, undoubtedly having suffered the routine a number of times earlier. She had the dubious distinction of having worked the previous week in a Three Stooges comedy, an ordeal as she was not partial to their knockabout antics.

"More tea?" asked Mala, standing over Herb and Jim, her right hand raised and giving Mallory the uncomfortable feeling she was about to hurl an imaginary harpoon. The men refused. Jim recognized Herb's impatience. Herb asked Mala to sit down, and from his tone of voice Mala knew he meant business, serious business.

"Ladies," Herb began, "I'm sure you understand kidnapping is a very serious business."

Nana Lewis said, "We certainly don't think it's a parlor game."

Herb countered, "That depends on the kind of parlor games you like to play."

"I don't like parlor games period," Nana said. "Why don't I begin? I last saw Lydia in this room last Saturday night. She said she had a date but didn't say with whom . . . or is it who?" Nobody answered her. "I thought it might be with Groucho Marx. In case you didn't know, he's her latest conquest."

Herb said, "I gather she piles up a lot of conquests."

"She is not promiscuous!" cried Mala, coming to Lydia's defense.

"Of course not," said Nana Lewis dryly, "she is one of those who live by that old bromide 'Variety is the spice of life.' "

Herb said, "You stand to inherit her part in Oscar Levitt's movie."

She leaned forward. "I can assure you, Mr. Villon, I didn't arrange her disappearance."

"I'm not inferring you might have."

"If I don't do that movie, there are plenty of other opportunities for me."

"I'm sure there are. For the three of you."

Mala said wistfully, "Oh how I long to play *Lady Precious Stream,* but no one plans to film it." She didn't seem to mind being ignored. Herb found himself wondering how she survived. Although Eskimo she could certainly play Orientals, but there weren't too many of those roles available. Even the formidable Anna May Wong, who was a friend of his and Hazel's was having difficulty getting parts, though while at the height of her career she had been wise enough to invest in a Chinatown apartment house that now gave her a comfortable income.

Probably Carole provided all the girls with an allowance. Herb hoped her bank account was at least as large as her heart.

"Miss Corday?"

She cocked her head coyly. "Yes?"

"Have you anything to tell me about Lydia?"

"She dyes her hair."

"I'm looking for answers as to her disappearance. Are Nathan Taft, Elmer Rabb, or Oscar Nolan familiar to you?"

"Nathan Taft is." Herb wanted to cry 'Bingo' but restrained himself.

"You knew him well?"

"Not well at all. I just knew him. At least I think it's the Nathan Taft I knew."

Nana Lewis said impatiently, "You recognized his picture in the newspapers."

"Now just hold on there! The guy in that picture was wearing a uniform and his hat hid part of his face."

Herb said, "Nathan Taft was a veteran. I prefer to assume you met him."

"I did meet him. I met him at a party for Pola Negri. She was back from making pictures in Germany."

"She worked for the Nazis?" asked Jim Mallory.

"Listen," said Nell Corday sternly, "when you've been on the skids the way Pola was for a couple of years, you grab any offer when it finally comes your way. I know Pola. We go to the same beauty parlor. You see, before she came to America back in the early twenties, she'd been a big star in Germany. The Europeans don't have the kind of short memories we have in this country. In Germany Pola will always be a big star. She'd still be there but one of Hitler's stooges was getting too friendly, so she lammed to France and from there came back here. She made good money in Germany and it was the stake she needed to try for a comeback here. Phillips Holmes was over there too, but a fat lot of good it did him. So he joined the Canadian Air Force."

"Wasn't ours good enough?" asked Nana Lewis.

"Oh belt up," said Nell. She said to Herb, "Pola had met Nathan Taft in Germany. I think he was in the export and import business. He did a lot of business in Germany." Jim Mallory was diligently taking notes. "And don't ask me what he exported and imported. I'm sure he told me but that sort of thing just evaporates when I hear it, it just doesn't interest me. And is this interesting you, Mr. Villon?"

"I'm mesmerized. Go on."

"He asked if he could call me and I said by all means if you've got a telephone. I'm big at checking things out so I checked him out with Pola. She didn't know him too well either. He seemed to be a friend of some minister or another. The Nazis are very big with ministers. Pola said what difference did it make anyway. He shleps back and forth on business trips so he's got to have money. Pola only deals with the well heeled. Her Dun and Bradstreet is very heavily thumbed. So Mr. Taft invites me to dinner."

"Oooh, that magnificent car he was driving when he picked you up," oohed Mala Anouk.

"A Hispano-Suiza," said Nell matter-of-factly, as though it was her due to be squired about in one of the fanciest and most expensive of European makes. Herb didn't think they made them anymore but decided not to say it was probably an overhaul bought at a bargain price, like Miss Negri. "We had dinner at Romanoff's."

"Did Prince Mike fall all over him?" asked Herb. Mike Romanoff, who owned the famous Hollywood eatery, insisted he was a Russian Romanoff and was Hollywood's most famous inside joke. But he was popular with many stars, Humphrey Bogart being his biggest champion.

"Romanoff greeted him in a friendly way, but there were no hugs or backslapping the way there usually are."

"You've been to Romanoff's before."

"I've been to lots of places before. And after."

Herb smiled. Miss Corday was one smart cookie. Whether or not she was descended from the infamous Charlotte Corday, she'd inherited from someone quite a nimble brain. "Did Taft do or say anything memorable?"

"Yes, he ordered champagne and didn't make a pass at me." She smiled. "And I don't care for either champagne or a pass. Anything else?"

"Did Lydia Austin know Nathan Taft?"

"Not that I know of. She might have met him at Mike Lynton's place. Nathan said he went there a few times a week. He took me after dinner. Mike bought us drinks, told us to make ourselves at home."

"If he did," said Herb, "then Taft must have looked as though he could afford to drop a bundle."

"He dropped some. But not a bundle. We played blackjack. The table was hot for the dealer, but not for us. Nathan didn't lose too much, even though he played flamboyantly. That, of course, was an act for me."

"Lydia wasn't around that night?"

"Lydia was at Groucho's. Or so she said."

"You don't care too much for Lydia."

"She's okay. We're not bosom buddies, but then, I haven't got the bosom for buddies."

Jim inhaled as he thought, you've got the bosom for this buddy. Herb stared at Jim as though he'd been reading his mind. Jim blushed.

Herb turned his attention to Nana Lewis. "Were you and Lydia friendly rivals?"

"In this town all of us ladies have rivals, friendly and unfriendly. Carole told me she has enemies she's never been properly introduced to. Lydia's a nice girl and once you find her, she'll go on being a nice girl. She's from the Midwest, cornfed and all that press agent crap. And I suppose you'll hold it against me if I tell you I don't think she's much of an actress. But the camera loves her and that's what really counts in this business. Oscar let us see the tests he made of us before deciding on Lydia for the lead. Lydia comes right out of the screen and knocks you for a wallop. The way that Rita Hayworth does over at Columbia. Can't act for buttons but you can't take your eyes off her."

Herb was amazed at her generosity toward other actresses and told her so. She shrugged while smiling and then said, "There's room for all of us. I don't give a damn if I make it to the top or not. My family sent me to finishing school and it almost finished me. Most of the girls there were spoken for by Juniors and Threes and Fours, meaning So and So, Junior, or So and So the Second, the Third, the Fourth and so on ad infinitum. They're the ones I envied. I was successful in drama class but they were the belles of the balls, to which I say balls and go on with my life. Would you believe Lydia was jealous of me? I get small parts over at Columbia. They like me there. Harry Cohn likes me."

Jim wondered if she had ever been invited into Cohn's legendary "secret room," the one presumably hidden behind a wall of his office at Columbia. Mallory had heard many starlets were given their initiation in that room. Cohn had a well-deserved reputation for brutality but no actress had ever filed a complaint against him. All the studio chiefs had their peccadillos (or as Carole called it, "peckerdillos").

Nana put paid to his curiosity. "I've made it without Cohn inviting me to a private party." She had lit a cigarette. "Mr. Villon, you know as well as we all do that lots of girls over the years have disappeared out of this town." She said firmly, "I won't."

"I asked Oscar Levitt if this might be a cooked-up publicity stunt. He denies it. What do you think?"

"If it is, Lydia would have told us. She told us everything. Right, girls?"

Mala Anouk spoke up. "I read her tea leaves the day before she disappeared."

"Was it a good read?" asked Herb.

"I will tell you the truth. I saw danger."

"Baloney!" snapped Nell Corday.

Mala said in a furious flow of words, "You

83

scoff at everything I say! I read danger in the leaves and I told that to Lydia. And she believed me!"

"Did Lydia have any idea what the danger might be?" asked Herb.

"She was afraid Oscar Levitt would change his mind. Give the part to Nana."

Nell Corday said, "That's every actress's fear. I don't know any actor worth his salt who doesn't suffer from fears of insecurity."

Herb said flat out, "I get the feeling you're one of the few who doesn't."

"Now look, when Carole brought us together I filed it under 'Too Good to Be True.' But I was wrong. Carole's the genuine article. She brought us to inspect this house. It was a hell of a lot better than where we were each living."

Nana Lewis said, "Lydia had a beautiful place on Beverly Drive. Don't ask me how she could afford it. Ask her."

"I'd like to. I'd really like to." He asked Mala Anouk, "Why do I get the feeling you know some of the missing Japanese?"

"You're very clever. There is the ectoplasm floating over your head." Jim Mallory didn't notice a thing over Herb's head except the ceiling.

Herb seemed to know what she was alluding to. "Is it good ectoplasm or evil?"

"Oh, not evil at all. It is good ectoplasm." She explained to the others, "We all have ectoplasm. It comes from the spirit world. My grandmother was a respected soothsayer. Hers was a very popular igloo. Actually, I am too modest. It is the most popular igloo in the settlement, the only one with a Sears Roebuck calendar."

Herb said, "I can't tell if your grandmother is alive or dead."

"Neither can we." Mala giggled. "Sometimes she goes into a trance. When she does my father says, 'There goes Grandma.' She sometimes talks when she is in this trance, but the voice is not her own."

Mallory suggested, "Maybe there's a ventriloquist in the igloo."

"Oh, you hush up," admonished Mala, sounding as though she came from south of the Arctic Circle. "Grandma is terrific. She told us Roosevelt would be elected for a second term and we hadn't even heard of Roosevelt. Ha ha ha. I wish she was here and she could maybe tell us where Lydia is." She turned to Herb. "I knew Ito Takameshuga. He's the only one I knew. I met him at a party in Malibu. I was hired to do the tea ritual by a lady who heard about me from my hairdresser. Takameshuga was very polite and respectful. But he was also very nervous."

"You mean he fidgeted a lot?" asked Herb.

"Oh no, nothing that simple. He had what I guess you would call a twitch." She jerked her shoulders as though demonstrating the Brazilian samba. "You see what I mean?"

"Very provocative," said Herb.

"Very mysterious. He looked upon everyone with suspicion. Except me. He said I was as cute as a cherry blossom. I thanked him even though I have never seen a cherry blossom."

"You saw him again after the party?"

"Several times. He was always very proper. We ate a lot at Nate and Al's Jewish delicatessen. He said they'd never heard of pastrami in Japan. I told him blubber was better."

"What did you learn about Takameshuga?"

She was quiet. She was thinking very hard. Finally she seemed to think of something worth telling Villon. "He missed Japan. He wanted very much to go back. His family is there. His wife and his sons. Two sons." She thought again. "Yes, two sons. He thought he soon would be going home. He burned a lot of incense to convince the gods to send him home. Though he had two grown sons — yes, they were grown — he did not seem terribly old."

"You do not have to be terribly old to have two grown sons," said Villon.

"Oh no? You should see my father. I have three brothers and my father is all shrunken, and his skin is shriveled. I send him jars of cold cream."

Herb studied her. She came across as a misplaced innocent, brought from her element into a world that would very probably ruin her, destroy the innocence.

Mala asked, "Why do you stare at me like that?"

"I'm sorry." He spoke with honesty. "I was thinking, you don't belong here."

"In this house?"

"In this city."

Mala was amazed. "But I do belong here. There is so much opportunity for me. Look around. Look at this house. Believe me, it's no igloo. Oh, how I love Carole Lombard. How I thank her. She is in my prayers every night."

Nell Corday spoke up. "Mala is terribly generous. I don't think she thinks ill of anyone."

Mala had a sweet smile on her face and Herb expected a halo to appear over her head but none materialized.

"I guess this does it," said Herb to Jim. "Thanks, girls. If you think of anything that might be useful to us, here's my card. Give me a ring at the precinct."

Nell Corday took the card and looked at it. "Why, Mr. Villon, are you possibly descended from the French poet François Villon?"

"I don't think so," said Herb, adding that he did admire his poetry.

"Ah yes! His poetry!" said Nell. And she quoted with passion, " 'If I were king, the stars would be your pearls upon a string . . .' "

"Oh, how sweet," said Mala Anouk.

Nell told them, "I'm directly descended from Charlotte Corday. You know, the woman who stabbed Marat to death in his bathtub."

Herb said, "I'm very cautious in my bathtub."

"Jim!"

"What? What?" He had fallen asleep. His eyes opened and he saw Herb bending over him and beyond Herb, Mike Lynton at the bar replenishing his Drambuie. "Sorry. I'm so sorry. It's so warm in here." Lynton left the bar to open a window.

As he did so, Lynton said, "Nana Lewis is the smartest one of the four of them. Maybe she won't become a big star, but once she makes it, she'll last a lot longer than the others playing supporting roles."

"You don't remember Nathan Taft at all?"

"I remember Nana being here with some guy, but if that was Taft, he's just a blur to me."

"That's a hell of an epitaph," said Herb.

Mike Lynton said, "You know how many people come to this place in a night? You think I can remember all of them? Taft doesn't strike a bell. And as for this Taka-whatever the hell his name is, we don't get much Oriental trade here at all."

"That's surprising. They're big gamblers," said Herb. "Maybe you should advertise in the Oriental papers."

Mike laughed. "I'm doing just fine without them. How's Gable and Lombard? I don't see them anymore. I miss them. They're lovely people."

Carole's face was aglow. "Did Mike really say that? Did he really? Did you hear that, Pappy? Mike Lynton said we're lovely people." She glared at Hazel, who was taking notes. "Damn it, Hazel, do you have to write down everything?"

"My memory's not all that good," explained Hazel. "So I try to write down everything and in the morning I sift through my notes looking for the nuggets. Like Nana

Lewis met Nathan Taft and Mala Anouk knew that Japanese."

"Takameshuga," Herb Villon said.

"You don't have to tell me. I've got it written down at home."

Carole was pacing the small office. She asked Groucho, "Did you see Lydia the night she disappeared?"

"If I had I'd have told Herb. In fact I will tell Herb, she stood me up. I was expecting her at my house for a quiet evening of dinner and then a game of gin. Then I chase Lydia around the room. She called to say she'd be late. She apologized and frankly, I was suspicious she was having a drink with another guy. Actually, I was grateful she'd be late as I'd had a tough day rehearsing some scenes with Margaret Dumont. You know we test some of our routines in vaudeville houses and Margaret's getting a little old, she's having memory problems."

Carole said, "Don't you dare drop her for somebody else!"

"Drop her? I can't even lift her!"

Carole said, "Don't be mean, Groucho. She's as important to you as your brothers. Even more important. Her timing is better than theirs."

"You keep your mitts off my brothers' timing. The only person in this business who can time a laugh better than my brothers can is Bill Fields. In fact he never seems to know he's timing a laugh. It's all instinctive with him. I'm thinking of killing him. Except there's no point in bothering. He's half shot from too many shots. He's been begging us to do another version of *Robin Hood* with me as Robin and Bill as Friar Tuck. Can you see Margaret as Maid Marian? Of course you can't. Who can? She can play Marian if Marian was triplets." He grabbed Carole's hand and kissed it, moving up to her wrist and then to her elbow, of which he commented, "This is one of my favorite joints." Carole pushed him away because the look on Clark's face was one of complete displeasure. Imagine anybody being jealous of Groucho. But on the other hand, he had stolen Lydia away from Mike Lynton. And what about Mike Lynton? She asked Herb Villon, "What about Mike Lynton?"

"I told you we had a session with him."

"I know. But something's missing. He doesn't strike me as the kind of guy who lets anything slip through his fingers, let alone Lydia Austin. Groucho, didn't he even threaten you?"

"The only Marx he can threaten is Chico who's into him for a fistful of markers. Chico places bets on numbers that have yet to be invented. And then there's Karl Marx."

Carole squeaked, "You're not related to Karl Marx!"

"Of course I'm not. Don't we boys have enough trouble? Has anyone checked to see if Lynton has a record? Maybe one by Bing Crosby? The Andrews Sisters? Kate Smith? Now I positively could never pick up Kate Smith."

Herb Villon said, while wishing Groucho would find some excuse for a quick exit, "We know he has the mayor and the D.A. in his pocket, but he doesn't seem to lean on them too often. Clark, did you know him in New York back in the twenties?"

"Oh sure. We all knew Mike, all the Broadway gang I hung out with. We used to play cards a lot, shoot craps . . ." When you weren't in bed with the ladies, thought Carole. "Take a flutter on the ponies. Mike Lynton was barely in his twenties when I met him. He was well heeled, a slick dresser, always a different girl on his arm. His people were upper class but they didn't approve of him. I think his father was a corporation lawyer. I met his family once, at the opening night of Sophie Treadwell's play *Machinal*. I co-starred with Zita Johann."

Carole asked sweetly, "How did she rate in bed?"

"I don't think she did much rating in bed, she just slept. Ask her husband. He's John Housman. He's out here with the boy wonder, Orson Welles." And he added, glaring at Carole, "and I don't know how he rates in bed either."

"He wants me to do Theodore Dreiser's *Sister Carrie* with him. I don't think it'll ever get done. Too raunchy. Did you know the character of Sister Carrie is based on Louise Dresser?" asked Carole.

Hazel's eyes widened. "*Our* Louise Dresser? Who's done pictures with Will Rogers, to name a few?"

Carole was pleased she could on occasion one-up Hazel. "Dreiser's brother was a writer of popular songs like 'My Gal Sal.' He was Paul Dresser. Louise was his girlfriend, to be polite about it, and she took his last name. I suppose he gave her permission." Hazel was swiftly taking notes and wondering what other obscure show biz tidbits Carole harbored.

Clark asked with an edge to his voice, "Why don't we get back to Mike Lynton?" Carole caught the look he flashed her. She had somehow displeased him but Clark's displeasures had a tendency to disappear when she withheld her favors.

"Everybody! We're going back to Mike

Lynton," Carole announced. "Now where did we leave him? Oh yes. Opening night of *Machinal*." She said to Gable, "Am I right in assuming he was there with his mother and father?" She was rewarded with another ferocious look from her husband. "Who else was in the party, Pappy?" She'd be damned if she'd call him "darling" with all those threatening looks he was giving her.

"Mike's kid sister."

"Hallelujah; He has a sister!" cried Carole.

"Had a sister," said Clark. "Her name was Loretta."

" 'Had'? 'Was'?" Carole held Clark in her gaze. "It sounds like she's dead."

"She's dead," said Clark. "She committed suicide in October of '29, at about the time the stock market crashed. And when she killed herself, Mike crashed. He cared a lot about Loretta and she did for him."

"If you've got something sick to tell us," said Carole, "I don't want to hear it."

FOUR

"It was Loretta who was sick," said Clark. "She had a slight touch of nymphomania. The family booked her with an alienist but he couldn't help her. Mike thought she didn't want any help. She wanted to screw to hell and gone. She had an occasional steady, but they soon bored her. I won't say any more because it's a very unpleasant story. Her death was very unpleasant. She drank lye and it didn't kill her instantly."

"Christ," whispered Carole and wondered how Hazel could continue taking notes so matter-of-factly. "I don't want to hear any more."

"Matter of fact, she looked like Lydia Austin," said Clark.

Groucho folded his hands in his lap and stared at them.

"I went to the funeral," said Clark. "It was a big, fancy affair in St. Patrick's Cathedral on Fifth Avenue. Everybody was there from Mayor Jimmy Walker to Jack Dempsey and Walter Winchell." Carole assumed Loretta had been to bed with all of them and then hated herself for what she was thinking.

Groucho said huskily, "That must be her picture on the sideboard in Mike's office."

"That's Loretta," said Clark.

"And I always thought it was Lydia. And if Lydia and Loretta were look-alikes, I'm harboring a very sick thought. Anybody interested in sailing into the harbor?"

Hazel said animatedly, "I hope you're not thinking *he* kidnapped Lydia because she looked like Loretta."

"I've heard of crazier motives," said Groucho.

"Well, you can scrub this one," said Carole. "Mike Lynton's no kidnapper! Or murderer! Or anything else like that. He's a nice, sweet gangster, and that's that, so there." She turned to Herb Villon. "You've got some smart instincts, Herb, what's your guess?"

"My guess is that a guy who owns a gambling casino wouldn't go in for anything so risky as kidnapping. Especially Mike Lynton, who I'm sure doesn't need the money and would most certainly not take the risk."

"You see!" cried Carole triumphantly.

Clark asked with a soupçon of suspicion, "Why all this championing of Mike Lynton?"

"Because you've been trying to put him in the hot seat and I know how it feels to get your behind singed in that situation," said Carole.

Groucho said staunchly, "Anyone who singes your behind will have to answer to me!"

Carole resumed, "It's not pleasant in any situation but in this town it's just plain awful. When Lansing Brown shot Russ —"

"— by accident," interjected Hazel.

"Bullshit." Carole spat the word. "He killed Russ because Russ wanted to marry me and Lansing wasn't about to give up Russ. The studio, with the help of the cops, if you'll forgive me, Herb . . ."

"Forgiven."

". . . cooked up the story of the boys examining an antique gun they didn't know was loaded. Lansing knew every gun in his collection. He was worse about them than any girl with a collection of dolls. But for a while there, the buzz was that I was in the house with them and I blew my top when I realized the boys were lovers. Realized! Ha! You had to be deaf, dumb, and blond not to know what was going on." She sighed. "I thought it was rather sweet. Russ was too young to die. Why just think of it! He might have been sitting here with us!"

"Or kidnapped," suggested Hazel.

"Oh, go sharpen a pencil," snapped Carole.

"Well, Oscar Levitt is certainly getting a

lot of mileage out of Lydia's disappearance," said Hazel. "A day doesn't go by that *Darkness in Hollywood* doesn't get a mention in the papers."

Clark asked wisely, "But has it gotten him a distributor?" Independent producers were always scrambling for a studio to distribute their product. The more fortunate ones, such as Walter Wanger, Hal Roach, and Edward Small, were under the umbrella United Artists provided. But it wasn't that easy for a Johnny-come-lately like Oscar Levitt, who had yet to land some sort of star name to decorate his marquee.

Carole said, "Why do I suspect Oscar has offered Mike Lynton a piece of the action if he'll put up the money to pay a couple of half-assed names?"

"Don't be rude, honey," cautioned Clark. "One of these days we may be listed among the half-assed."

"Not me!" insisted Carole. "Not me ever. I rose from the ranks of the half-assed and I have no intention of ever returning. My God, Pappy, doesn't it just kill you when you're doing a party scene and among the extras are once-famous names grateful for a day's pay when once they earned millions? Oh, this is such a cruel business!" Her eyes misted and she yelled at Gable, "Well, the

least you can do is offer me your handkerchief."

"I forgot to bring one." Hazel handed
Carole a tissue.

"No handkerchief! No gun! Honest to
God, Pappy, what's happening to you?"

"And I don't have a ham and cheese on
me, so?"

"You old poop!" sniffled Carole as she
dried her eyes, blew her nose, and then asked
Hazel if she wanted the tissue back.

"No thanks," said Hazel, suppressing a
shudder. "I have more in my handbag."

Clark asked Villon and Mallory, "When
are you guys going to go hunting with us?"

Villon fixed him with a stony stare. "What
do you think we're doing now?"

Carole snapped, "Put *that* in your pipe."

Groucho said, "He also forgot to bring a
pipe. Gable, you're hopeless."

"You lay off Pappy!" said Carole angrily.

Villon said firmly, "Ladies and gentlemen, I'm not upset that you have to leave
now."

Carole said, "Herb, you've been a dear. It
was nice of you to let us take up so much of
your time."

Groucho said to Herb, "Come on over to
my place and take up some of my time.
Because my time is your time and your time

is my time and whatever became of Rudy Vallee? That cheapskate! Do you know he has a pay telephone in his living room? If you need to use it you have to have a nickel. I have fed it many a slug in my time. So hello, I must be going!" He went gliding out of the office.

Carole clucked her tongue. "Poor Julius, trying so hard to shield his aching heart. Oh my God! Those poor boys!"

"What poor boys?" asked Herb.

"Our bodyguards!" said Carole brightly. "Roy and Sammy. They're sitting outside protecting the desk sergeant. Well, we'll show them a good time at the party."

Clark froze where he was standing. "What party?"

"Miriam's. Have you forgotten? How could you forget? Miriam doesn't give parties very often. She's always too broke. Now she has a new contract at Warner Brothers and this one's by way of celebration."

"Miriam Hopkins?" asked Gable.

Hands on hips, Carole said, "Well the only other Miriam I know is Miriam Rabinowitz, the masseuse. And she's not doing so hot these days because she's started to rub people the wrong way. Bye, Herb. Bye, Jim. If you boys get any fresh leads, be sure to tell us. Hazel, you coming or staying?"

"I need a word with Herb." Herb's eyes crossed.

"So long, kids," said Clark, and he hurried Carole out of Villon's office.

Hazel shut the door after them and said to the detectives, "Now how about that Loretta Lynton story?"

"You're not going to try and sell it?" queried Herb ominously.

"Of course not," said Hazel, "I can't think of who might buy it. Now you listen to me, Herb Villon, you haven't forgotten you're taking me to the Hopkins party."

"I didn't say positively!"

"Well, I did, and Jim is my witness."

"To what?" asked Jim, feeling slightly addled. Hazel always moved too fast for him and at the moment he was not about to get himself into one of their imbroglios.

Hazel said, "I'm going home to change and I'll be back in an hour."

"Hazel!" Herb yelled her name. "I'm not sure I can go!"

"Well, be sure by the time I get back!" She put her notebook in her handbag and left.

Herb leaned back in his chair and exhaled.

Jim asked, "You going to the party?"

"Probably."

"Can I come too?"

"Sure, Jim. There's bound to be lots of pretty girls for you to flirt with. But you never get serious about any of them."

"Sure I do. But the ones I like are never available."

"You should be grateful for that. I've seen a lot of the ones you like." Jim didn't remonstrate. Herb shuffled some papers on his desk. "I hope he doesn't."

Jim, perplexed, asked, "I hope who doesn't what?"

"Gable. I hope he doesn't knock Lombard around."

"She'd beat the crap out of him!" said Jim heatedly. Why, the very thought of anyone laying a hand on one of the many actresses he secretly loved and idolized was enough to send him charging into battle with a fixed bayonet.

"Ida Lupino didn't beat the crap out of him."

"Come on, Herb. He didn't beat up Lupino!"

"It was pathetic. They were having a very quiet romance, never appearing in public together. He was afraid Ria would find out. Don't look at me like you suspect I'm betraying my country."

"I like Gable. Now you're making me not like him. You're making it up."

"No, that's straight from the horse's mouth — Hazel."

"There was never anything about it in the papers."

"For once Hazel decided to keep a civil tongue in her typewriter. Gable's the king and you're asking for trouble when you try to dethrone a king. Lupino's mother told Hazel because she wanted Hazel to do something about it. Hazel went straight to Gable. Bearded the lion in his den. He didn't deny it but he also warned her to squelch the item. His boss is Louis B. Mayer and Louis thinks very little of destroying anybody who crosses him. He wrecked John Gilbert, Francis X. Bushman, and Mae Murray, to name a chosen few. Clark warned Hazel that Mayer would think nothing of having her erased." He drew an index finger across his throat and Mallory felt his mouth go dry. "So Hazel pigeonholed the story until she decides to write her tell-all book."

Herb sat back in his chair. "Hazel called on Lupino to get her side of the story. It wasn't pleasant. Lupino was sitting and staring at her phone, her fingers twisting a handkerchief, bruises on her face, one eye blackened. And when Hazel asked her, 'What about Gable?' her eyes never left the phone. When she finally spoke, Hazel said it spooked her. The voice wasn't Lupino's, not the Lupino voice that Hazel was familiar with. Lupino said, 'He doesn't phone, he doesn't write . . .' and burst into tears. Damn it!" Herb exploded. "Ain't some women something?" He was lighting a cigarette while staring at Jim, who looked as though he had just discovered his parish priest was a Nazi spy.

"Jim," said Villon softly. Jim looked at him. "Kid, there are a lot of closets in Hollywood, and they're all filled with skeletons. I've seen a lot of those skeletons. Gable is still playing around. He has a harem at Metro. Lana Turner, Virginia Grey, Judy Garland . . . yeah, yeah, yeah . . . he's been over her rainbow too."

Jim gulped and said, "I guess that's why she sang 'Dear Mr. Gable.' "

"She was paid for doing that one. Enough of this, let's get back to our missing people. Seven Japanese, three Caucasians and Lydia Austin." He tapped on the desk with a pencil. "Nathan Taft fascinates me."

"Export and import is fascinating?"

"It is when he zeroes in on an innocent little Eskimo tootsie. Except I don't think she's all that innocent."

"She chews blubber."

"That's just a filthy habit as far as I'm

concerned. I think she knows more than she's been telling."

"Herb."

"What?"

"Nathan Taft zeroed in on Nell Corday. It was Takameshuga who dated the Eskimo. Funny you should get them mixed up."

Herb looked at the notes he had written down after interviewing the three girls. "Funny, I've got Mala Anouk written down next to Nathan Taft. Now why the hell did I do that?"

"Maybe you were suspecting the Anouk kid had also played around with Taft."

"And none of them mentioned Oscar Nolan, the third missing man." He got out of his chair and started pacing, hands laced together behind his back, a frown on his face. "Nana Lewis seems smarter than all of them. I'd like to talk to her alone." He unlaced his hands and folded his arms in front of him, briefly the picture of a stern headmaster. "Jim, phone Nana Lewis and invite her to Miriam Hopkins' beach party."

"But I'm not even invited!"

"I invited you. And you decided to bring a date. And that date is Nana Lewis. You've got the phone number."

Jim brought out the pad on which he scribbled notes and found the number. He crossed to his desk, sat, and dialed. It rang five times and Jim was about to hang up when he heard "Hello?" and recognized Nana Lewis's voice. He cleared his throat and responded.

"Hello? Nana Lewis?"

"Yes?"

"Er . . . this is Detective Mallory. Jim Mallory."

"Oh sure." She was reclining on the couch, wearing shorts and a halter, a sexual vision it's just as well Jim couldn't see. "Should I be glad to hear from you or not?"

"I'm not calling on official business. This is a social call."

"Oh yes? Well, there's social and there's social." She was being careful. She was suspicious and wondering what he was after.

Jim cleared his throat again. Herb was amused at the way he was floundering. Jim said, "Well, it's like this. Herb Villon, my partner, and I were just invited to a cocktail party Miriam Hopkins is throwing on the beach at Malibu. You see, she has this house in Malibu and Herb's girlfriend is Hazel Dickson, who knows all the stars, and I said to Herb I don't have a date and he said why don't you ask one of Carole's girls and I thought about you and here I am."

Nana Lewis smiled. Both detectives were

attractive. She'd had the opportunity to size them up; if she had her druthers she'd select Herb Villon, but his liaison with Hazel Dickson was a Hollywood legend and one of these days she might need Hazel Dickson, so she wasn't about to step where angels fear. On the other hand, Jim Mallory was handsome and healthy, she assumed, and why not? She spoke into the phone, "You know, it's very funny. When you phoned I was doing my yoga lesson, and frankly, I was hoping some nice guy would phone and ask me out to dinner."

Jim said hastily, "Oh yes! Dinner too!"

Villon was thinking, Smart girl, Miss Lewis. If I was Carole Lombard, I'd put my money on her.

"I need some time to get ready," said Nana. "Why don't you pick me up in about an hour. I'm sure you haven't forgotten the way here?"

"I haven't forgotten. I'll be there in an hour. See you." He hung up and there was a silly grin on his face. "That was too easy."

"You handled her beautifully," said Herb. "Hazel knows the girls. Carole got her to interview them, so while Nana Lewis will come as a bit of a surprise to her, she won't be a shock."

Jim said, "Nana was hoping for a date

while she was practicing her yoga."

Herb's shoulders slumped. "One of those. We had a case once where some broad practicing yoga was raped in the lotus position."

"What's *that?*" asked Mallory.

"Convenient."

"I wish you wouldn't sulk when you're driving," Clark said to Carole.

"I'm not sulking. I'm thinking about the girls. Call it intuition, call it a hunch, but I think they know more about Lydia's disappearance than they're telling. When four young kids are living together under one roof it isn't easy to keep many secrets. I knew Mala Anouk was dating Takameshuga and Nell Corday was dating Nathan Taft. I wonder if they ever double-dated." She bore down on the horn as a DeSoto went whizzing past and then cut in front of her. She lowered her window and let loose a stream of oaths that the driver of the DeSoto couldn't hear but which gave her satisfaction.

"One of these days I'm going to wash your mouth out with soap," said Clark.

"I wouldn't try it, Pappy, not unless you want a certain appendage shortened, which it can ill afford."

"One of these days I might decide to wallop you."

"Don't even think about it," she warned him. "Bill Powell once took a swipe at me and I kicked him where he lived." She chuckled. "He didn't have much savoir-faire while he was screaming and holding his crotch." She raised her window and said, "Pappy? If I was kidnapped, how much ransom would you offer to pay?"

"The studio would offer the ransom."

"And you wouldn't offer *any?*"

"Louis B. Mayer loves me. He hates Wally Beery but he loves me."

"He hates Wally Beery? Why does he hate him? His pictures bring in as much money as yours."

"The hell they do!"

"The hell they don't. We have the same accountant and he tells me how much everybody makes and he also tells me which stars are hygienically unsanitary. Hee hee hee!"

"I don't believe it."

"You better. John Barrymore takes a bath maybe once a month, if even that much. When I did *Twentieth Century* with him, by the fifth day of shooting I couldn't stand the smell and I went to Harry Cohn and read him the riot act, Harry had three of his hoodlums throw Barrymore into a bath and they rubbed his skin raw. Poor bastard. Look at him now. So pissed out of his skin he never knows what day it is and that Elaine Barrie and her mother bleeding him dry. I'd invite him over but I don't think I can face it." She remembered someone else. "And what about Crawford?"

Gable stormed, "What about her?"

Carole rose to the challenge. "When she first came to Metro, the wardrobe women would pick up her clothes with a stick, they were so filthy."

"Now that's nasty!"

Carole agreed. "That's why they used a stick. Come on, Pappy, admit it. Weren't there times when you banged her she smelled a little ripe?"

"She perspires a lot!"

"So do we all, but we've heard of deodorants. Oh, the hell with Crawford! I want to talk about Lydia Austin. Did she really look like Loretta Lynton or were you just making that up?"

He said softly, "Loretta Lynton wasn't someone you made up. She was a living, breathing creature who could take your breath away."

"And how often did she take yours?"

"There you go again!" he raged.

"Come off it, Pappy. When you talked about her in Herb's office, clearly you were describing a woman you once went batty over. It wasn't a description, it was a eulogy. Don't get mad. I'm not jealous. I mean if she were still alive I'd track her down and kick the shit out of her, but she's dead and I don't believe in competing with the dead. I hope she's resting in peace." Afterthought, "Unless there's an afterlife and she still gets horny. Hee hee hee hee!"

Clark slumped in his seat, folded his arms, and said, "I don't want an afterlife. This one's been tough enough."

"I know, sweetheart," said Carole sympathetically, "all those old ladies you screwed to try and get someplace."

He jumped up with a fist clenched. "You're asking for it!"

Carole said threateningly, "Get rid of that fist or I smash into that truck coming in the opposite direction. Oh look! Riding horseback! It's Margaret Lindsay and Janet Gaynor! I thought *that* affair was finished."

"Maybe they meet once a week to reminisce." He was back to slumping in his seat.

"Now that's funny, Pappy. Meeting once a week to reminisce, hee hee hee. I'll have to tell that one to my mother."

"For crying out loud, it's not all that funny!"

"Pappy, believe me, coming from you it's funny. And not many funny things come from you. You're dear and loving and comforting, but face it, witty you ain't." She laughed and freed one hand from the steering wheel to chuck him under the chin. "You're so adorable when you're mad." She mouthed a kiss at him and he smiled weakly. She sure knew how to handle him, bless her heart. None of the others even tried. His first wife wanted him to be a star and his second wife thrived on his celebrity. And now, thank God, Carole.

Carole had gone back to Lydia Austin. If Carole was anything, thought Clark, she's tenacious. Why didn't he fall in love with her back in 1932 when they made *No Man of Her Own?* He gave voice to the question and Carole put Lydia Austin to one side, albeit reluctantly.

"I was still in love with Bill Powell and you were making believe you were in love with Ria. Anyway, I thought you were having it off with Dorothy Mackaill." Mackaill, a former star at Warner Brothers, was on the skids, but she had saved her money and invested wisely and now occupied the penthouse of a hotel in Honolulu. She gladly accepted the second lead to Lombard in *No Man of Her Own,* thinking it would lead to better roles in secondary films — a very wise decision that kept her in the spotlight until 1935 when she went to England for some films there.

Clark pooh-poohed the idea of an affair with Mackaill, who was at the time too busy with her affair with Lothar Mendes, a second-rate director who was now largely forgotten. "Dotty's a nice gal," said Carole. "And so was Lydia Austin. And . . ." She went silent.

"What?" asked Gable.

"It just came over me. I think she's dead." She pulled up to the side of the road and turned in her seat to Gable. "It's weird, but I think she's dead. Dear God, I hope not. It would kill her mother. She dotes on Lydia. The family has no money and they're betting all their hopes on Lydia. That's why I was so pleased Oscar Levitt decided to star her in the movie."

Clark could see her on the verge of sinking into a Lombard depression. Her depressions were famous. She would mope about for days on end and then strangely enough turn to the Bible. He remembered the first time he asked her if she read the Bible and she said, "Yes I read the Bible. It needs work."

"Who would want to murder Lydia?" Gable's brows were knitted and he truly could not understand why Lydia would be a target for murder. "She's a nice girl. She keeps her nose clean." Carole was now seated face forward staring through the windshield at the lush San Fernando Valley greenery. It was so placid, so peaceful, so beautiful. How could thoughts of murder dare intrude on this sylvan setting?

Carole finally spoke. Her voice was now soft but insistent. "She was Mike Lynton's girl before Groucho."

"So we're back to Mike Lynton."

"Yes. It seems that lots of roads lead to Mike Lynton and yet I still don't think he's capable of murder. He's got too good a sense of humor to be a murderer."

"Oh? And how many murderers have you been familiar with?"

"Only Lansing Brown that I know of. And he was a gloomy Gus if ever I knew one. Russ and I were always laughing while Lansing clucked his tongue in disapproval. That bullet hit the wrong man." She switched on the ignition and headed the car toward their ranch.

"You okay, baby?"

"I wish we could skip Miriam's. I want to sit and think."

"You can think at the party."

"Sure." Carole brightened. "Sure I can. I like Miriam a lot. She's all surface but that's what I think I like about her. She's sincerely superficial. Like when she disappeared to Palm Desert for four months and returned with a baby she said she had adopted."

"Meow."

Carole hee-hee'd. "Well, that's what she said. I even played along and gave her a baby shower. Oh God!" she howled as she turned into the road that led to their house. "Who the hell had it in for Lydia? I bet Herb Villon is asking himself the same question."

Little did Carole realize how prescient she was. Herb wondered aloud in his office, "Why would anybody want to kill Lydia Austin?"

"I wish I knew," said Jim Mallory. "Then we'd have our murderer."

There were times Jim Mallory reminded Herb of Stan Laurel and his occasional dim-witted insights and he hoped Nana Lewis was up to coping with Jim's non sequiturs and the frequent derailment of his thoughts.

"Mike Lynton?" Herb shook his head. "I'm with Carole. He's not the killer type."

"Doesn't mean he wouldn't hire one to do the job for him."

"That's Louis B. Mayer territory." He leaned back in his chair, scratched his cheek, and stared at the ceiling. "Not Mike Lynton. Certainly not Groucho. W. C. Fields?"

"Nah," dismissed Herb. "If he ever tried to kill someone he'd bungle it." He remembered something concerning Fields and chuckled. "Remember some years ago when Paramount kept pairing Fields in some pictures with Baby LeRoy?"

"Sure. Baby LeRoy Winebrenner. That was his full name."

Herb said with a sigh, "You have more garbage stored away in your brain. Baby LeRoy what?"

"Winebrenner."

"Winebrenner. Well anyway, the execs knew Fields loathed children and he especially grew to loathe Baby LeRoy. But strangely enough, the kid adored Fields and innocently stole every scene away from him. I mean he was so cute and Fields wasn't. So one day Fields got hold of the kid's baby bottle and filled it with gin." He roared with laughter at the perverse memory. "It almost killed the kid! He was sick for days!"

Mallory suggested, "You think maybe Fields gave Lydia Austin a baby bottle filled with gin?"

Villon stared at Mallory until there was a glaze over his eyes. In his mind he was hearing. "The March of the Cuckoos," the Laurel and Hardy theme song. He finally said, "I can't quite envision Lydia Austin accepting a baby bottle loaded with gin without voicing some suspicions." And then he asked himself, Why do I bother answering stupid questions? Because Jim Mallory is so ingenuous and doesn't recognize it. He was only a few years older than Mallory but felt like a father to him. He asked Jim in a friendly voice, "Kid, what do you want to be when you grow up?"

"Older."

Villon laughed. "I wish this was Christmas so I could ask Santa to deliver me a ransom note."

"It's useless. You said her family has no money. So why bother kidnapping her?"

Said Villon grimly, "To shut her up." He met Mallory's eyes. "She wasn't kidnapped for ransom. I think she's been erased. She knew something she shouldn't have known and her killer was afraid she'd talk."

"Oh God," said Jim, "what a terrible thing to do to someone so beautiful. She had so much to look forward to."

"Yeah, she had a great future behind her." He hit the desk with a fist. "But what was her connection to the Japanese and the other guys? Jim, I don't think she has any connection to them at all. Her going missing the same time they did is purely coincidental."

Jim asked eagerly, "You got proof?" He

ducked the pencil Herb threw at him.

"You don't have to get sore at me!" said Mallory as he retrieved the pencil from the floor. "Sometimes you treat me like I've got nothing in my attic. We've been working together a long time now, Herb, it's about time you showed me a little respect."

"I absolutely respect you, James. But there are times when I have to resist the urge to throttle you."

"I think I'm a hell of a lot smarter than Gable," said Mallory defiantly.

"Believe me, Jim, you most certainly are. I don't know how he landed Lombard, but land her he did. Luckily she's got enough brains for the two of them. She's the highest paid actress in Hollywood. Remember when she recently had her press agent plant the item in the newspapers that it was an honor to pay income taxes for the privilege of living in the United States?"

"A very noble statement."

"Noble indeed. And it brought her a million dollars worth of publicity plus a commendation from President Roosevelt and an invitation to visit him at the White House. Of course, he didn't tell her she was as cute as a button, which he told Janet Gaynor when she visited."

"I think Lombard has class," said Jim,

"and what a body."

Villon looked at his wristwatch. "You better get started for Nana Lewis. And I shall pick up Hazel." He crossed himself. He now stood at the mirror that hung over the sink and examined himself and then recited a verse he had composed earlier that day.

"Mirror, mirror on the wall, Before I start heading for a fall, Please deliver me a note of ransom, Even if you have to toss it over the transom."

"That's real cute, Herb, you write it yourself?"

Villon didn't answer him. He was praying for a break, a badly needed break.

While Herb Villon was praying for a ransom note, Carole parked the Cadillac in the driveway of the ranch and said to Clark, "I hear strange noises." Clark jerked his thumb in the direction of the back seat. Carole turned and looked and saw Roy Harvey and Sammy Rowan fast asleep. Their snores sounded like a harmonica duet. "Why those darlings, I completely forgot about them." She now assumed what she hoped was a motherly look. "Roy is adorable. He looks like a naughty little boy with his blond hair curled over his eyebrows. And look at Sammy. He's so enchanting with his mouth open, wheezing and dribbling." She puckered up her lips and whistled what she hoped was "Reveille." No response. Clark leaned over and first shook Roy and then Sammy.

"Come alive, you sleeping beauties!" shouted Clark. Roy's eyes opened slowly and then Sammy shook himself awake while drying his mouth on a jacket sleeve. It took them a few seconds to acclimate themselves and then Roy grinned sleepily at Carole. "It's been a long day," Roy said through a yawn.

"It's going to get longer as soon as I change into a beach outfit. We're going to a party at Malibu."

Sammy and Roy exchanged a look. Sammy said, "But we're not dressed for a beach party."

Carole said smartly, "You don't dress for a beach party. You undress." Clark and the young athletes followed Carole into the house. Carole yodeled for the help. "Albert! Agnes! Ada!"

Albert and Agnes hurried in from the kitchen while Ada, the maid, appeared at the top of the stairs. Carole said to Albert, "Where'd you stash Mr. Gable's old bathing trunks?"

"They're in his closet on the top shelf. I was thinking of heaving them out."

"For Pete's sake don't. They're still usable. Take the boys to Mr. Gable's room and, boys, you pick yourselves a pair of trunks. You can change in the guest bedroom."

Roy remonstrated, "But Mrs. Gable, we don't plan to go swimming. We're body-guards!"

Carole patted his cheek. "You dear sweet thing. This is Hollywood, the Gomorrah of the West Coast. Just about everybody will be shedding their outer garments and plunging into the Pacific." The blood drained from Roy's face and Carole could see he was trembling slightly. "My God!" said Carole. "You've got nothing to be ashamed of. I can tell you're both built beautifully. Aren't they, Pappy?" Gable ignored her, taking the stairs in his ascent two at a time. He didn't like being reminded that he was almost forty and a bit flabby to boot. He'd never had a specta-cular physique, even when he shed his shirt in *It Happened One Night* and single-handedly destroyed the underwear industry because he was barechested. Lately, when he had to bare his chest in a film his skin was tightly taped back to give an illusion of muscularity. These boys were genuinely muscular, beautifully proportioned, and Carole privately thought they looked good enough to eat, but she kept the thought private lest Gable throw a tan-trum.

Carole recognized that both the young men were uncomfortable. "What are you afraid of? This isn't going to be an orgy." Somebody snorted and she assumed it was Agnes, who had come to them after an unpleasant stay with Lionel Atwill and his wife. The Atwills were celebrated for their weekend orgies, which almost destroyed Atwill's career.

Sammy was suddenly all bravery and bravado. "Orgies don't frighten us, Mrs. Gable."

"I should hope not," said Carole. "You don't get bitten at outdoor orgies unless there are mosquitoes. Hee hee hee. I can assure you you'll be perfectly safe. Really, you don't have to go in swimming if you don't want to. In fact, I'm not so sure I will. I just had my hair done yesterday and Pappy goes bananas if I spend too much money at the beauty salon." She shouted up the stairs. "I'm coming, Ada. Get out that purple number I wore in *True Confession*. The one trimmed in monkey fur." She said over her shoulder to the boys, "I just adore monkey fur! I just adore monkeys. I did a jungle movie once, *White Woman* opposite Charles Laughton. Poor bastard. Such a slob." She clapped her hands sternly like a headmistress gone berserk. "Come on up, boys! Pick out your trunks." Roy and Sammy reluctantly climbed the stairs, Roy thinking, How can you be a bodyguard in swim trunks?

Jim Mallory had gone home and changed into tan slacks and a Hawaiian beach shirt that was a kaleidoscope of surfers, divers, porpoises, and general dubious taste. It was his favorite shirt. Herb and Hazel had bought it for him when they were on holiday in Honolulu last year. Driving his sports car to the house Nana shared with the other girls, his mind was a jumble of unconnected thoughts. There was Gable abusing Lupino, and Herb wishing for a ransom note. Jim briefly entertained sending him one just for the hell of it. There was Carole Lombard watching in horror as Lansing Brown shot Russ Columbo dead, though it was never proved she was present at the tragedy. He also saw Mike Lynton pouring himself another Drambuie, while waiting in the wings of his very active imagination was Groucho Marx doing a laugh-clown-laugh bit. He saw Loretta Lynton seducing any number of men that Mallory had never met and probably never would meet. And here was Lydia Austin trussed up like a holiday turkey revolving on a spit and being basted by a phantom. Mallory replaced that vision with Mala

Anouk chomping down on a square of greasy blubber while Takameshuga offered her a damp towel. Takameshuga was faceless because Jim had never seen a picture of him.

Come to think of it, he'd never seen a picture of any of the missing Japanese. None were ever reproduced in the newspapers because apparently none existed. Then something else rang a bell in his mind. These men were reported missing by their business offices, not by their families, because as Herb had commented a few days earlier, "It seems they've left their families behind in Japan. And what about the three non-Japanese? They too were reported missing by business associates. Apparently they too had no families."

Jim pulled over to the side of the road just a short distance from his destination and made notes in his pad. His heartbeat had accelerated and he knew he was on to something. He wasn't sure what, but he knew he was on to something. He couldn't wait to tell Herb. He'd have to choose his time carefully. Not speak in front of Hazel. He wondered if Herb had given this situation any thought and not discussed it with Jim until he was sure of what he was talking about. Herb was always careful, sometimes too careful, thought Jim.

And then, as he placed the pad back in his pocket, gunned the motor, and proceeded on to pick up Nana Lewis, Jim thought, suppose these men never existed? What a crazy thought, but still, it nagged at him.

The little men who weren't there. But they had been there, all right, and now they had vanished, presumably into thin air. Didn't anybody ever vanish into fat air?

He pulled up and parked, got out of the car, crossed to the door, rang the bell, and waited. The door opened and Nana Lewis, a striking vision in white dress and white beret, made him catch his breath. "Something wrong?" she asked.

"Hell no," said Jim, "something very right."

FIVE

Herb Villon didn't plan on it, but he would be late picking up Hazel. He told her so on the phone. He was entertaining a late caller, freshly arrived from Washington, D.C. It was important he spend some time with him. From the tone of Villon's voice, Hazel knew better than to give him an argument. She would make her own way to Miriam Hopkins' house on the beach. Herb told her he'd get there as soon as possible. The man sitting in the chair opposite Herb introduced himself as Carl Arden. He was with the Federal Bureau of Investigation. A fed. His credentials were in order. Herb had respect for government seals and in turn he expected respect from Carl Arden. Arden was prepared to give him that. Before flying to L.A., he had done a thorough check of Herb Villon and what he found out impressed him. Herb was something rare in the LAPD, a good, honest cop. He didn't always play by the rules, often bending them to his own specifications. But he was respected by just about everyone in Los Angeles. His record for breaking cases was impeccable. Carl Arden knew about his relationship to Hazel Dickson and had also read up on and approved of Jim Mallory. He questioned Jim's whereabouts.

"He's picking up a very beautiful actress who he's escorting to a party in Malibu Beach. The hostess is Miriam Hopkins." Carl Arden was impressed. "The lady I was speaking to on the phone is my girlfriend, Hazel Dickson." He told Arden about Hazel's proclivities — sniffing out gossip and frequently very important information. "I'm meeting Hazel at the party." He smiled. "She didn't kvetch about my not picking her up. She could tell something important was the reason for the delay. So, you're here about the missing men?"

"This case didn't interest us until we noticed the names of Nathan Taft and Ito Takameshuga."

Herb had lit a cigarette and narrowed his eyes when the smoke attacked them. "Am I wrong in suspecting they're enemy agents?"

"Go to the head of the class, Herb."

"I don't want to go to the head of the class, I want to go to the party. I need some laughs, though I had Groucho Marx in here a couple of hours ago. He depressed me." He told Arden about Lydia Austin and Arden advised him she was not linked to the missing men. "You're on your own with her." Herb told Arden about Lydia, the three other girls, and their involvement with Carole Lombard.

Arden shrugged and said, "Every story should have a little sex appeal. The only thing that interested me about Bonnie and Clyde was Bonnie. Then we found out she was a lez and he was impotent and I live in dread of the day I hear Mae West is really a man in drag."

Herb laughed. "That's a nasty rumor I think Mae started herself. I was on a case involving her five years ago and believe you me, she's got everything in the right place including a hair-trigger brain."

Arden was lighting a pipe, which Herb decided was FBI stock in trade. A legal background was essential to becoming an FBI agent and legal backgrounds and pipes seemed to go hand in hand. "Anyway, what I've got to tell you about Takameshuga and Taft and their supporting cast won't take too much time. They're enemy agents, Takameshuga for the Japanese and Taft for the Russians."

Herb was surprised about Taft. "No Nazis?"

"He could be a little of both. We only know his Russian connections."

"You know he was friendly with Pola Negri in Berlin?"

"Miss Negri came to see us in D.C. on the advice of her very smart lawyer. We cross-examined her for hours and the result was we gave her a clean bill of health and let her stay in the U.S." He sucked on the pipe but it was dead. He applied a match to the bowl and it soon glowed. "I might add she had some valuable information to give us about Hitler, Goering, Goebbels and the rest of the all-star cast but I don't think she knew how valuable it was. She was chock full of gossip about the Nazis. Did you know Rudolph Hess painted his toenails?"

Herb feigned shock. "No!"

Arden nodded gravely. "The whole gang of them is perverted. It seems they're all dopers too."

"I guess it takes their minds off pressing matters." Herb crossed one leg over the other. "Carl, I have a suspicion what you're really trying to tell me is we're heading toward war whether we want to or not."

"Oh, it's inevitable. We were closing in on Takameshuga, Taft and the others, but they were tipped off and high-tailed it. To get us off the scent they cooked up this mass kidnapping crap, which I gather has all of Hollywood in a panic."

"There isn't a free-lance bodyguard available in this town. They're all booked and at very fancy prices." Arden chuckled. "There's an Eskimo actress in town named Mala Anouk. She was occasionally dating Takameshuga. Funny, I kept thinking she was dating Nathan Taft. I guess my subconscious was suspecting Taft and Takameshuga of the same perfidy. Perfidy! Ha! And where the hell did that word come from?"

"Your subconscious, I guess."

"No, I think it came from the last Charlie Chan movie I saw. Anyway, you want to talk to the Eskimo. She's got a hot stash of whale blubber in her cold refrigerator."

"I'll talk to her but I doubt she'll have much to tell me. Takameshuga's a clever bastard. He doesn't talk very much and that's because there isn't very much he dares say."

"How much danger have we to fear from Japan right now?"

"We know they're building a stockpile of arms and ammunition from the scrap iron we sell them."

Herb said with indignation, "We should stop selling them scrap iron!"

"What? And make them suspicious we know more than they want us to know?" He sucked on the pipe. "Very vicious circle. We put an embargo on scrap iron and we've tipped our hat. Anyway, that's not why I'm here. By the way, I've got some associates with me. They're off on other related assignments. We're all staying at the Ambassador." He suddenly exploded. "That Victor McLaglen is certainly one big pain in the ass!"

"Very stupid too," added Herb. "Investigating his private army, the Black Shirts?"

"The Black Shirts! Sons of bitches. They cribbed that from Mussolini's Black Shirt army. McLaglen doesn't worry you?"

"His cockamamie army is mostly Hollywood's Irish has-beens and boozers. It's another excuse to get drunk and whoop it up on Sunday. They only meet on Sunday because most of the rest of the week they're too busy making movies. No, McLaglen and his McNamara's band don't worry me. They'll soon get bored with playing soldier and disappear back in the woodwork."

"I hope so. They've got some big-timers in Hollywood worried and we have to pay attention to them because Roosevelt pays attention to them. He needs their very valuable support."

"So he's going to run for a third term."

"You got it."

"What about Nathan Taft? He was dating

a young actress named Nell Corday." Herb filled him in on Carole's four protégées and what he knew of their extracurricular activities. "Taft took Corday to a party at Pola Negri's."

"All their social circles overlap," said Arden knowledgeably. "In Europe our boys go near berserk trying to figure out who knows who and who's doing what to who and they end up in Switzerland for whatever cure the Swiss offer. Well, I don't want to keep you from your party. You can spread the word there's no phantom kidnapping gang on the loose and put a lot of bodyguards out of work. You can step up your search for the missing lady —"

"Lydia Austin."

"Right, Lydia Austin."

"She was Groucho Marx's girl, and before that a gambler named Mike Lynton. And somewhere she found time and space for W. C. Fields."

"Likes the fatherly types. Especially funny fatherly types. You know Lynton?"

"Pretty well. I like him. He's a square shooter. If you want some words on him, Clark Gable's the man to see. He goes back to the twenties with Lynton."

Carl Arden was deep in thought for a few moments while Herb wished he would get a move on so Herb could get to Malibu Beach. He was even looking forward to Hazel but more important he was looking forward to a nice cold vodka martini on the rocks. Arden asked, "Will Mike Lynton be at the party?"

"Possibly. Probably if he holds any markers on Hopkins. He seems to hold them on everybody in this town. Herb paused. "Ever been to a Hollywood party?"

"No. They don't give them in D.C."

"Want to go to this one? Come on. The beach is big. The party can sprawl out."

"Lots of beauties and lots of 'moom pitcher' stars?" Arden laughed. "I have an eight-year-old daughter. She's stuck on 'moom pitcher' stars. When I told her I was going on assignment to Hollywood, she begged me to try and get Clark Gable's autograph and to shoot Deanna Durbin. She can't stand her. Professional rivalry. Sybil — that's my daughter — also sings. Not too bad at that. My wife's a professional. A few months back she left on a tour of a new Shubert production of *The Student Prince*. Haven't seen her since. The Shuberts think they're lost someplace in Greenland. The Shuberts are always losing touring companies. Last season they misplaced *Maytime*." He laughed. "That look on your face kills me, Herb. Sybil and I are used to my wife's disappearances. She'll turn up sooner or later. There's no rush. Sybil's staying with my sister Ethel and her family. Ethel's into the occult." Herb, refreshing himself at the office sink, wondered if Carl was pulling his leg. He hadn't had a good leg pull in a long time. "Sybil loves to stay with her aunt Ethel. She conducts a séance every night of the week. Now Sybil's on speaking terms with Rudolph Valentino but she has a hard time understanding him. Very thick Italian accent. He sings to her too. Usually 'Pale Hands I Love Beside the Shalimar.' Sometimes when he's in a really good mood he sings a tarantella. He's been teaching Sybil how to tango."

Herb couldn't resist asking, "When she's dancing with a ghost, who leads?"

"Oh, Sybil always leads. She's a control freak."

Jim Mallory offered to put the top of the convertible up but Nana Lewis, to his surprise, preferred it down. "I love the wind in my hair," she said lightly. "It's so balmy out and you're my first convertible in weeks." Jim was dying to know who owned her last convertible, someone like Cary Grant or some hotshot producer like Hunt Stromberg, but he didn't like the idea of her comparing him to them. Grant had lots of class and Stromberg had lots of money and Jim didn't feel their equal on either score. "Oscar Levitt has a convertible. We drove out to Marina del Rey for brunch one Sunday. Very charming, very well mannered for a big hunk like him. You must have met him. Unfortunately he's got this gambling sickness."

"I hear he's in to Mike Lynton for a lot of markers."

"Probably. I know he doesn't dare set foot south of the border. He owes a bundle in Tijuana. And don't correct me," she cautioned him. "It's Tijuana, not Tia Juana, which means Aunt Jane."

"You speak many languages?" Jim asked innocently.

"My Spanish is very hazy and my French equally so." After a pause she asked, "You guys think Lydia's dead." It wasn't a question. It was a positive statement, as though she had a direct line to Herb's office.

Jim said, "You sound as though you know she's dead for a fact."

"If she's alive, we would have heard something by now. Lydia's clever, very clever."

Jim got the uneasy feeling Nana Lewis wasn't very fond of the missing Lydia and said so.

"It's not easy to be fond of Lydia. She's

135

so competitive."

She's also won the part you were after and will get if Lydia turns up dead, that is if Oscar Levitt holds to his promise. And if he took her out to Marina del Rey for brunch, thought Jim, he'll hold to his promise. Lots of motels en route to Marina del Rey and Nana wondered why Jim was blushing. He cleared his throat and asked, "Don't you girls all get along?"

"Sure we do," said Nana. "We take turns cooking and washing dishes. Lydia's specialty is corned beef hash, straight out of the can. She remembers to top it with an egg fried sunny side up. So tell me, old pal, are we three ladies under suspicion of kidnapping and murdering Lydia?"

"To tell the truth, we haven't considered that possibility." Jim glanced sideways at Nana. Her hands were holding her hair back to keep it from flying in her eyes and he asked her again if she'd like the top up and again she said she preferred it down.

"I'll bet you boys have."

"You'll bet we boys have what?"

"Considered we three might have ganged up on Lydia."

"Do Mala and Nell have a reason to kill Lydia? You're the only one who would profit. You're next in line for the lead in

Levitt's picture."

Nana said with a small laugh, "The next one up in the succession to the throne." She stretched her arms above her head and asked, "Why do we do it?"

"Do what?" asked Jim.

"Make asses of ourselves struggling for a break in films."

"You've got a toehold. You seem to work fairly often at Columbia."

"I've got a stock contract. Seventy-five bucks a week. I'm on call to do everything except scrub floors and I keep waiting for the day when I'll be handed a mop and a pail and directed to a ladies' room. And you know, I'm one of the lucky ones. My contract has three more months to go so I'm assured of a weekly check until then." She lowered her arms. "Who knows. Maybe I'll stay lucky. Maybe they'll renew me for another six months. Christ!" She practically spit the name. "More Three Stooges comedies. Probably another Charles Starrett western. At least he's good to look at. Say! I'll bet you don't know I tested for *Gone With the Wind*."

Jim didn't want to be cruel and remind her that the only female who didn't test for the movie was Eleanor Roosevelt. And for all he knew maybe she did, sub rosa, the way

137

it was rumored Dietrich did as a possible Belle Watling. He could hear her saying "Wet Butler" and strangled a giggle.

Nana said, "That was the week Selznick was thinking of casting an out-and-out unknown and to hell with names. I hope I'm not shocking you when I tell you Selznick expected me to go down on him." The words emerged so blasé, you might have thought Selznick had asked for a chocolate malted. Jim knew she was eyeing him and he hoped to God he wasn't blushing again. He blushed easily. It was a family trait. His father told him his mother blushed throughout their honeymoon. Every time he saw a Mae West movie he blushed. Nana continued unfazed. "I reminded David O. that that was Paulette Goddard's specialty. You should have seen the look of absolute bliss on his face. Obviously he had experienced her specialty. Then I remembered she had the second lead in his *The Young in Heart.* Cute picture. Don't you have a steady girl?"

He almost drove off the road. "Sorry. My hands slipped." Sure, thought Nana. The palms are sweating with embarrassment. Jim Mallory. Good-looking if you liked them clean cut and unblemished, tall without stooping his shoulders, and could probably burst into tears at the slightest provocation.

She repeated the question.

"No steady girl," he said, and then added lightly, "and no unsteady one."

My heavens, thought Nana, he's getting frivolous.

About half a mile ahead of them, driving one of his three Model-T Fords with the top down, was W. C. Fields. He sported a straw boater that threatened to disappear in the wind, except that the left hand of his live-in lover, Carlotta Monterey, was holding it down. Carlotta was a pretty, self-styled actress of extremely limited talent who found a much needed meal ticket when Fields found her. She worked her behind off to hold on to that meal ticket. In her right hand she held a parasol above her head. Her hat was a Mr. Frederick original and her dress was a charming pink organdy trimmed with fake roses, daisies, petunias and, as Fields described it, "one stinking hollyhock."

Between her and Fields on the seat rested a doctor's bag. It held what Fields called his plasma. Scotch plasma, gin plasma, vodka plasma. Fields was a lousy driver even when sober. Every other car on the road was a challenge that he was eager to meet. He fancied himself behind the wheel as Don Quixote tilting at windmills, Teddy Roosevelt charging up San Juan Hill, General Meade leading his men into the decisive battle at Gettysburg. He muttered as he drove, "You forgot to pack chasers."

Carlotta reminded him there was no room for chasers. They'd been displaced by a large carafe of rum. Fields said with unusual assurance, "Miriam will have chasers. I was at her house once when all she served was chasers. She was on the wagon so she didn't stock any booze. These women who yield so easily to temptation. That one time I went on the wagon I kept a wide variety of bootleg booze in the apartment. I wasn't afraid. I wasn't tempted. I was in a coma for six days but that was because of the medicine I was taking for a head cold. Brutal affliction, a head cold. Carlotta, you never seem to get a head cold."

She didn't attempt to answer him. He didn't expect her to try. Monologues were his specialty and she actually enjoyed them. She expected to outlive him, hoped he would leave her something to remember him by, and prayed it would be cash and not the rhinestone-studded truss given to him as a gift by comedienne Fanny Brice one very damp Christmas a decade ago. She would then write her reminiscences of her life with William Claude Fields.

She knew somewhere there was a Mrs.

Fields and a W.C. Junior and she had no idea if they were divorced or still married. Fields referred to them with studious infrequency and when he did called them his "familial impedimenta." She sometimes had a feeling Bill wasn't sure if he was divorced or still married but she knew he mailed a check diligently every month. She admired him for living up to his responsibility. Many was the time he admonished Carlotta, "You must never submerge in a sea of debts, Carlotta. Never! Buy only the best and never buy on time and always demand fifth row center when buying seats for the theater. I think of going back to the theater from time to time. Maybe I'll revive *Poppy*. Or maybe I've done it too often. I did it as a silent called *Sally of the Sawdust*. Sally was Carol Dempster. I called her Carol Dumpster. Couldn't act for beans but she was D. W. Griffith's girlfriend. Also in the cast was a young Alfred Lunt. I forget whose girlfriend he was at the time. I just did *Poppy* in 1936 for Paramount, those scumbag blackguards. Fie on them for dropping my option with a thud heard round the world." And then came the non sequitur. "Do you suppose she's dead?"

"Lydia Austin?"

He cast a suspicious look at her. "Are you

a mind reader? How do you know I meant Lydia Austin? I could have been alluding to Amelia Earhart."

"You've been talking about Lydia Austin ever since she disappeared."

"Why shouldn't I talk about her? It's a free country. Lydia was a pretty tootsie. The apple of her mother's eye, though I remember Lydia saying her mother wasn't partial to apples. Chomping down on them made too much noise and unnerved her." He looked up at the parasol. "It's getting cloudy." Then, "Damn David O. Selznick and full speed ahead. I just found out *Gone With the Wind* is finished and here I spent an hour demanding he test me for Rhett Butler." He bristled for approximately thirty seconds and then reached into his inside jacket pocket for a cigar. Thus began the familiar production of opening the cigar case with only one hand off the wheel, biting off an end, and spitting it out the window into the wind, which swiftly carried the cigar end back into Fields' eye. Fields did imaginary battle with the cigar end while Carlotta's hand abandoned the straw boater and grabbed the wheel. He slapped her hand. "Get that appendage off my wheel. I'm driving this car, not you."

"You'll kill us both!" shouted Carlotta.

Fields said softly, "Why, my little red corpuscle, I wouldn't dream of leaving you behind when I shuffle off this mortal coil." He started singing "Coil of My Dreams, I Love You" and Carlotta realized he needed a drink. He had lighted the cigar and his hands were back on the wheel. Carlotta had opened the doctor's bag while Fields trumpeted, "My raspberry popsicle, since when have you taken to drink?"

Carlotta rattled off, "Scotch? Gin? Vodka? Rye? Rum?"

"You sound like we're in a department store elevator! I'll have a little of each."

"Now really, Bill!"

"Aha! Not up to the challenge!" Carlotta fished a paper cup out of the doctor's bag and determinedly met the challenge. She measured out equal portions of the liquors until she had a concoction of no recognizable color. He took the paper cup from her with a trembling hand, but as always succeeded in not spilling a drop. He downed the liquid in one long swig and then said sadly, "We lack two objects I would most like to see. A ginger ale chaser and a ginger peachy Lydia Austin. Don't be jealous. We didn't have an affair. I liked to hear her read me the Sunday comics. Her 'Dick Tracy' was a wow. A wow, I tell you, a wow!"

"And tell me, beloved. How else did she wow you?"

"Your tone of voice abrades my senses. One of these days, my hapless courtesan, I shall beat you!"

"At what?"

The Gable and Lombard Cadillac was the only impressive motor car on Sunset Boulevard, heading in the direction of Malibu Beach. Clark now handled the wheel while Carole, seated next to him, worked on her fingernails with an emery board. "You boys okay back there?" Little did Roy and Sammy suspect this would be their last day as bodyguards. Tomorrow they'd be back posing for beefcake photos with a selection of MGM starlets.

"We're fine, Mrs. Gable," Roy assured her, though his swim trunks were so tight he feared strangulation.

Carole was thinking, How tender, how sweet, how courtly. *Mrs. Gable*. Never Miss Lombard. Such darling boys. She said to Clark, "Take the right turn dead ahead." She lowered the window and inhaled deeply. "How delicious! Boys! Roll down your windows and smell the Pacific Ocean." They obeyed immediately. "Pappy!" Her voice commanded attention. "Inhale, Pappy, inhale! Smell the Pacific Ocean! It's so clean, so virginal, so out of this world."

Unexcited by the prospect of what the Pacific's aroma promised, Clark said, "When I was making *Mutiny on the Bounty* I had my fill of the Pacific Ocean. Give me the smells of horseflesh and bay —"

"And manure," Carole interjected swiftly. She said to the boys, "Pappy dotes on manure. He can't get enough of it."

Gable's eyes were narrowed as he clenched his false teeth. Does Carole ever know when she's gone too far, or does she go too far deliberately? He cast a glance at her. She was staring ahead, looking almost beatific. She probably wasn't even aware she had annoyed Clark. Her mind was already at the beach. She was thinking of a day several Saturdays ago when she accompanied Oscar Levitt and the four girls for publicity shots, which she had offered to stage and supervise. She had done all that bathing beauty posing for Mack Sennett, she and another aspiring actress named Madalynne Fields, who was destined to become her best friend, confidante, and private secretary. Carole called her Fieldsie. Fieldsie was now the wife of the celebrated Twentieth Century–Fox director Walter Lang but whenever Carole sent her a signal Fieldsie hurried to her side.

That Saturday Fieldsie was on hand with the four girls and helped the photographer set his lights. Despite the glorious sunshine, the photographer insisted they needed the lights.

Carole remembered Fieldsie saying to her, "Lydia doesn't need more lights. She has enough of a glow all her own. Egad she is beautiful. What's that mess the Eskimo is chewing on?"

"Blubber."

"What the hell's blubber?"

"Whale fat."

Fieldsie had paled. "I just may throw up."

"Well, if you do, keep it out of the wind."

Oscar Levitt sauntered over to Carole while the girls bounced a beach ball and the photographer took some candid shots. "God, but these babes are knockouts." He was also a cigar smoker, and was working on one that Carole thought looked like a miniature baseball bat. "How'd you find them?"

"I had all my casting director friends on the lookout. It was tough picking these four out of what turned up. There's so much young beauty available in this town. It's almost sacrilegious. Think of all the beauties who will never make it. They'll grow frustrated and then bitter and get swallowed up in disappointments and then they're old and unwanted . . ."

Oscar said, "You're a barrel of joy, Carole."

"I know how I felt when I was disfigured in the automobile accident. I thought my world had come to an end. No future, no money, no hope. Until that blessed saint of a plastic surgeon smiled at me and said, 'Don't worry, I won't let you go to waste.' " Her eyes were misting and Oscar put an arm around her shoulders. Carole sniffed and asked with the notorious Lombard voice of suspicion, "What are you after, Oscar?"

"I desperately need a kind word."

"What's the word?"

"Mike Lynton's leaning on me."

"How much you into him for?"

Oscar mentioned a sum that brought a low whistle to Carole's lips. "No wonder he's leaning on you. And you can't pay up."

"I got him Lydia."

Carole turned to him angrily, her eyes ablaze. "That's filthy, low, and cheap. I'm ashamed of you and now I'm ashamed of her."

"For crying out loud, she told me she liked him. Come on, Carol, for some girls he's one hell of a catch. But now Mike's sure she's thrown him over for Groucho. So he's making my life miserable again."

Carole saw that Lydia was watching them, and probably suspecting she was the subject under discussion. Carole said to Oscar, "And I'm to put in the kind word that'll get Mike off your back."

He said earnestly and heatedly, "I'm cutting him in on the picture!"

"A cut of zero is zero." She didn't like the script but as a showcase for Lydia, she knew it would serve its purpose.

"Come on, Carole. Give me a break. Mike's got me up the creek without a paddle."

Carole studied Oscar. He was tall and broad and homely, a neanderthal who'd worked his way up from Brooklyn by way of bootleg liquor at which he'd made and soon lost a fortune. But he'd nurtured some good connections and soon was at work in Hollywood assistant-producing what were known as Poverty Row pictures, cheap features that served as the second half of the then growing practice of double features. They usually starred fading silent film names on their way down or promising young hopefuls on their way up. Carole had been in several as a teenager and she was thankful that most of them no longer existed. When she worked in the Sennett shorts, the old man was hanging by a thread himself.

While working on the Poverty Row cheapies, Oscar won the eye of Harry Cohn, whose Columbia Pictures was located in an old studio on Gower Street smack in the center of Hollywood. So many low-budget westerns were churned out there that Gower Street became known as Gower Gulch. Cohn was desperate to remove himself from this identity and so had backed a talented young director of Poverty Row comedies, Frank Capra. Capra scored big and Harry Cohn, thanks to him, was a respected name in films at last. He was equally hated. He was a cruel man, a sadist, but he certainly knew how to make good pictures. He put Oscar Levitt in charge of a unit and Levitt's first three films garnered respectful notices, ending up on the black side of the ledger. Oscar was soon overimpressed by his success, found backers who also shared Oscar's admiration of Oscar, and backed a handful of features for Oscar's company. They bombed and Oscar was now scrounging around for the money to keep his company afloat. He found enough suckers to put together *Darkness in Hollywood*, a script he wrote himself because he couldn't afford a writer. Carole suspected this but kept her suspicion to herself, especially when it looked like one of her girls would snare the lead.

God, but he's huge, thought Carole. He would better serve clinging to the top of the Empire State Building swatting at airplanes. Carole finally spoke against a background of squealing and shrieking actresses who were tossing a beach ball at each other in the flimsiest swimsuits the censors would allow. "Has Mike threatened to get your legs broken unless you pay up?"

"He threatened to get a kneecap smashed."

"Just one? I suppose he thinks you'll need the other one to get down on when pleading for mercy. Mike can't be all that sore. He's a two-kneecap man."

"If that's supposed to be funny, I'm not laughing."

"And if I don't try to intervene with Mike, Lydia's out of the picture, I suppose?"

"Of course not! Would I do anything so low and cheap?"

Carole resisted answering him in the affirmative. Oscar, like his former boss Harry Cohn, had made a fine art of things low and cheap. Oscar was now wallowing in the area of lower and cheaper and just conversing with him made Carole feel unclean. She watched Lydia as she thrust her bosom toward the camera, and thought to herself, She

150

not only knows all the tricks, she's inventing a few new ones.

Oscar's insides were churning. Lydia out of the picture? God no. He'd raised most of the money by showing photographs of Lydia in which he'd convinced her to pose in the nude. Lydia didn't object as long as he gave her the negatives. He gave her the negatives as promised, but kept a set of copies in his safe. If she truly became a major name in films, those negatives would be worth a fortune.

Somebody, reckoned Oscar, might even kill for them.

Carole said, "I assume Mike has banned you from the casino."

Oscar said, "He doesn't have to ban me. I'll never set foot in there again as long as I live." Probably the very words spoken by Julius Caesar in the Roman Forum as his assassins' daggers sent him plunging into the nevermore.

Carole persisted. "Can't you raise some money to give him to keep him passive for a while?"

"I've drained my last resource."

If he thought she'd offer to help him with cash he was off in cloud cuckoo land. She'd buy him a meal if he was hungry — she'd do that for anybody as she had often done in the past — but contribute to the welfare of a gambling czar like Mike Lynton, not now and not ever.

Carole said, "I'll talk to Mike."

"Talk to Mike about what?" asked Clark. "What?"

"You just said 'I'll talk to Mike.' "

"You're crazy!" She had been so deep into her memory that she had no idea she'd spoken those words aloud. Oh God, suppose I talk in my sleep. The things I dream about! I can't possibly talk about them, Pappy would have a conniption!

"I'm not crazy. Boys? Did you hear Mrs. Gable say 'I'll talk to Mike'?"

Both insisted they hadn't. She'd spoken so low they would have had to kneel to hear her.

"Oh for crying out loud!" yelped Carole, always a fast thinker. "Hee hee hee," she giggled. "I promised Fieldsie I'd get her husband an item in Mike Connelly's column." She asked the boys, "You've heard of Mike Connelly?" They hadn't, they were that new to Hollywood and its mores. "He's the publisher of the *Hollywood Reporter* and writes a daily column. He and it are very powerful. Compared to him Louella Parsons is Little Bo Peep. Though she doesn't lose her sheep, she sells them. Hee hee hee. 'I'll talk to

Mike.' Why Pappy, I didn't realize I said anything. Sayyy? Do I talk in my sleep?"

"You know I'm a heavy sleeper. I don't hear anything once my head hits the pillow."

Carole had never been sure of that, but now breathed a soft sigh of relief.

Gable asked her, "Did you talk to Mike?"

"No," she said truthfully. "I left a message."

She didn't add, I didn't speak to Mike Lynton either. He was away in San Francisco that weekend and by the time he got back, Lydia had gone missing. And when I heard that, I didn't want to talk to anybody. "Damn it! Look at all those effing cars! Pappy! It'll take forever to find a parking space!"

"Why don't we drop you," volunteered Sammy, "and we'll find a parking space and join you at the party."

"Oh you darlings," gushed Carole, "you're such treasures."

Under his breath Clark said, "Cut the crap."

Roy asked, "We don't have an invitation. Will we have any trouble joining the party?"

Carole stated flatly, "With your looks and your physiques, you don't need any invitations. If I know Miriam, you'll be getting an invitation. I did her first movie with her. *Fast and Loose.* And nary truer word was ever spoken." She and Clark left the car. The boys climbed into the front seat. Clark warned them about dents or any other damages. Sammy was behind the wheel and assured Clark they'd take good care of the Cadillac. Front doors shut, Roy whispered, "Let 'er rip!" The wheels screeched in agony as Sammy pulled away.

Gable went white while Carole yelled with joy, "Oh, look at him go! Barney Oldfield heading down the stretch!" She took his hand and pulled him after her, "Come on, Pappy. Sounds like they're having one hell of a swell time." They descended a wooden staircase at the side of the house that led to the beach. There was an eight-piece orchestra on a bandstand Miriam had had constructed for the occasion. Under a huge tent, numerous tables were covered with food and drink. There was a dance floor constructed overnight by engineers on loan from the Warner Brothers studio and Carole and Clark watched jitter buggers having a hell of a time.

"It looks like such fun!" squealed Carole. "Come on, Pappy, let's mingle. We haven't mingled in ages. Look, there's David and Irene! The Selznicks never look as though they're having a good time. Yoo hoo! David!

Irene!" They couldn't hear her over the cacophony from the orchestra. "Isn't that Johnny Davis leading the orchestra? It is!" He was under contract at Warners. "Yoo hoo! Johnny!" He couldn't hear her either.

There were numerous waiters and women servers in proper uniforms. "I need a drink," said Clark. He stopped a pretty server and asked for a scotch and soda and a wine spritzer for Carole. The server recognized Gable and said with underlined insinuation, "Oh Mr. Gable, you can have anything you want."

Carole said, "He doesn't want 'anything.' He wants a scotch and soda and a wine spritzer for his wife, *capish?*" The girl hurried off. Gable smiled at Carole.

"We better stay right here," Gable said to Carole, "or she'll never find us again."

"With any luck," said Carole grimly.

"My dahlin's, my dahlin's!" Miriam Hopkins was coming at them with outstretched arms. "I was so afraid you wouldn't come! I was afraid you heard I invited Ria and I swear it was all a mistake!" Carole didn't bat an eyelash on hearing Clark's most recent ex-wife was on the premises. She could handle her if anything cropped up that required handling. She cast a glance at Clark and there was his professional fixed smile

155

pasted across his lips.

Carole recognized the gamine expression on Miriam's face, the one she used behind your back when in front of the camera and trying to steal a scene. As far as Carole was concerned, stealing a scene in a Paramount picture was petty larceny. "Now, Miriam, just you calm down. I'm not upset, Clark's not upset, and Hollywood's such a small town really, it's almost unavoidable running into exes of all kinds. How are all your exes, darling? Are they all here?"

"If they are, it's under false pretenses!" Her southern accent got thicker when she was under stress, and Carole thought she could cut the accent like she was carving a block of halvah. Their cheeks sideswiped in the usual phony show of Hollywood affection. Then Clark kissed Miriam's cheek and she giggled and said, "Your mustache still tickles!"

Keep it up, Hopkins, Carole said to herself, and you'll be eating a knuckle sandwich. Clark was amused. Years ago, long before Carole, he would angle for an invitation to Miriam's. She was then "labeled" hot stuff, but she was also benefiting from the pleasures of Maurice Chevalier's lower lip.

"I don't see any bodyguards, Miriam. I had no idea you were that brave or self-assured in this kidnapping mess."

"Brave? Self-assured? Me? Are you mad?"

"Only slightly," said Clark and Carole raised a foot to kick his shin and then thought better of it.

"There are bodyguards all over the place. The men are either waiters or disguised as guests. I auditioned each and every one of them. Did I say auditioned? I meant interviewed."

Carole said wisely, "You auditioned and I'm sure you're exhausted."

"Carole, you can be so wicked. That's why we all adore you. Don't we, Clark?" The waitress brought the Gables their drinks and then smiled her way back into the crowd.

"What quick service! That girl's a fast worker," said Carole.

Miriam's tone of voice turned lethal. "So you've noticed. She's been working on Darryl Zanuck but I advised her if she thought she'd bag him, she'd better affect a French accent." She did a French accent very badly. "Monsoo Zanook he prefairs the likes of Simone Simon and Annabella, Nesseepa?"

Carole said, "I'm sorry, Miriam, but I don't speak German."

"Oh you are so funny!" laughed Miriam. "Oh my God, there's Kay Francis. Warners dropped her and signed me and what do I say to her?"

"Try 'hello' for starters," suggested Carole. "Kay's a lady. She'll take it from there. We just did a movie together. I like her."

"Miwiam, Miwiam, Miwiam!" Kay Francis didn't worry about her *r* trouble when not in front of the camera. One Warners writer once got so mad at her in a script he wrote he named her leading men Robert, Richard, Raymond, and Reginald. Unfazed, Kay referred to each of them as "dahling" and audiences went berserk trying to figure out which one she was referring to.

"Kay darling, you look ravishing!" While Kay and the Gables greeted each other, Miriam continued gushing and they let her continue gushing as there was no stopping her.

"Thank you, so do you, sweetie," said Kay. She looked over her shoulder. "I seem to have lost my escort. He's supposed to be my bodyguard." She spotted what she thought was her bodyguard. "I wonder if that's him?" asked Kay.

"You mean the tall drink of water with a ribbon in his hair?" asked Carole.

"If he's wearing a ribbon in his hair, I suppose I should be guarding him." Everyone laughed politely. "No, that's not him. It doesn't matter. What could happen to me in a crowd this huge. Miwiam, how do you afford a party this size?"

"I just had to celebrate my new deal with Warners and . . . oh Kay. I'm so sorry."

"About what?"

"Warners dropped you."

"That's right. I'm on that list of box-office poison along with Hepburn, Dietrich, Garbo, and some eminent others. I'm in superb company, don't you think?"

"The Warners are a bunch of shits," said Carole. To Miriam she said, "You'll soon agree."

"Now really, Carole, I've been involved with a lot of shits in my time and I can handle them. My deal with Jack Warner isn't life-threatening. It's just for six pictures. One's with Bette Davis."

Carole exclaimed, "Well, talk about life-threatening! Whoops! Talk of the devil! Bette, sweetheart, you're not alone, are you?"

Davis gestured with her right hand, which held the always present cigarette. "No, he's somewhere out there picking pockets."

"Oh Bette!" exclaimed Miriam. "You're so unkind!"

"Oh? You think so? I just think I'm honest.

It's my Yankee upbringing. I caught the bastard going through my pocketbook when he picked me up. I should have dumped him right then and there, but it was too late to snare a substitute."

"Hee hee hee!" giggled Carole. "I'll bet you're going to marry him."

"I may as well," said Bette, "I'm not busy next week." She said to the Gables, "You two look positively glowing. You're the only newlyweds in town who are still married."

Carole said, "And we intend to stay that way." She transferred the spritzer to her left hand and put her right around Gable's waist. "We're going to stay married until he throttles me to death. Hee hee hee. Sometimes I get on his nerves."

"Enough of that. Now get on mine!" Groucho had joined them. "Miriam, this must be costing a bundle."

Miriam leaned into the group conspiratorially, "Warners is paying for a lot of it. It's the only way Jack could talk me into doing *The Lady with Red Hair*."

"Oh God, Miwiam, they're not still flogging that chestnut!" Kay told the others, "It's supposed to be based on the life of Mrs. Leslie Carter." Carter had been a celebrated stage star at the turn of the century. She had blazing red hair and a fascinating personality

160

that camouflaged a noticeable lack of talent. "Miwiam! Don't you know how many of us turned that down — and flatly."

"You're being a bitch!" hissed Hopkins.

"Oh Miwiam. I mean you no harm!" She said to the others, "Ruth Chatterton wouldn't do it, Bette wouldn't do it, and I wouldn't do it. They tried to borrow Sylvia Sidney from Paramount and even she wouldn't do it."

Miriam drew herself up with a splendid display of hauteur. "Well, I'm doing it and I shall do it proud! I know I have a feel for Mrs. Leslie Carter."

"Oh yes?" asked Groucho. "I have a feel for her too. Where is she? Point her out to me."

"Be still, my heart," they heard Miriam whisper as she stared past them at Sammy and Roy, who were approaching them.

"Hee hee hee!" Carole was enjoying herself enormously. "They're our bodyguards. Metro assigned them to us."

"I should have signed with Metro," said Miriam.

"Did they want you?" asked Clark.

"No, but I should have signed with them anyway."

"Here's the car keys, Mr. Gable," said Roy as he held them out, "or should I give them to the boss?" Gable snatched the keys out of Roy's hand while, convulsed with laughter, Carole buried her face in Clark's chest.

"They certainly are adorable," said Bette Davis. "I never get anything like them. All we've got at Warners are Humphrey Bogart and one of the Rover boys, Ronald Reagan." Bette introduced herself and the others to Roy and Sammy, both of whom were boyishly overwhelmed facing all this celebrity.

Groucho undiplomatically asked Bette, "I thought you also had George Brent."

Bette fixed him with a venomous look and cobra eyes. "Several times." Bette spat both words.

"Well," persisted Groucho, "it's a good thing you never married him. It would look like hell on a marquee."

"What would?" asked Kay.

"Bette Brent." Even Davis roared with laughter, realizing at last that Groucho was kidding her.

Said Bette, "It would more likely have been George Davis!"

Kay gave the warning. "Evwybody shut up. Here comes Hazel Dickson."

Bette chirruped, "Hello, Hazel. Have you come alone? Where's your dick?"

"What?" screeched Carole.

"Oh my God! I meant where's your detective. I'm so sorry, Hazel!"

Hazel hoped she was smiling affably. "He should be here soon. He couldn't pick me up."

"I couldn't pick you up either," said Groucho, "and you're not as heavy as Margaret Dumont."

Hazel continued, "He was in conference with someone from the FBI."

"FBI. That's what Selznick's always asking his new Swedish star. FBI? 'Feeling Better, Ingrid?'"

Kay said, "Well, it's about time the feds got involved in these kidnappings. It's all so tewwible. Those missing Japanese. If my gardener disappears I'll have a conniption."

"Have two," suggested Groucho, "in case they're on the small side. But seriously, Hazel — has the FBI been brought in to find Lydia?"

"Who's Lydia?" asked Bette Davis.

Carole explained about Lydia Austin. "It's been in all the papers."

"I only skim the papers," said Bette, "if I bother reading them at all."

"She's been in Louella's column twice since she disappeared."

"Maybe that's where she disappeared to," suggested Kay Francis. "Louella's column." She said it with humor, not intending bitterness. Now that her star was slowly fading, Louella no longer sought items from the actress. Francis seemed to be taking it in her stride.

"I'd better look for my escort," said Bette. "There are a lot of spider webs around here he might get entrapped in. See you later." She left them and was promptly swallowed up in the crowd.

Kay asked Hazel, "Who's this Arthur Farnsworth it's rumored Bette might be marrying?"

"He manages a hotel in New England. Bette met him on vacation a couple of months ago."

"Is it serious?" asked Kay.

Carole said, "The hell with Arthur whatever. Hazel, did Herb send for the FBI?"

"So help me Hannah, I haven't the vaguest idea. This guy just materialized from out of nowhere. Herb didn't say much because I think he couldn't say much. In fact, he often doesn't say much. And you can ask him yourself. Here he comes now accompanied by a perfect stranger who I assume is with the FBI."

SIX

"He looks like a department store floor walker," said Carole.

"He can walk my floor anytime he likes," said Kay.

"He's wearing a wedding band," said Miriam, toying with the pearls hanging around her neck.

"That could be camouflage," said Carole. "Maybe he was warned about the predatory ladies of Hollywood."

"He has nothing to worry about here," said Miriam. "I didn't invite Norma Shearer and Joan Crawford." She now wore her gracious hostess and movie star smile as Herb Villon returned her greeting and introduced Carl Arden to everyone. Arden didn't hear Miriam Hopkins say "He should be played by Errol Flynn."

"Not at all," disputed Kay Francis. "The FBI don't carry concealed swords." She extended her hand and said to Carl Arden. "How nice to meet you, Mr. Arden. Have you come to our wescue?"

"If it's kidnappers you're referring to, I'm happy to tell you it's a false alarm. The men

165

who vanished from Los Angeles did so of their own volition." He didn't elucidate and trusted neither would Herb. "You can send your bodyguards on their way."

Roy and Sammy looked stricken. A tear trickled down Carole's cheek. "Oh Roy! Oh Sammy! I'll miss you terribly."

Clark went into his hail-fellows-well-met routine. "There's no reason to miss them. They can come visit us anytime. They're like family." He smiled at the boys, flashing his trademark dimples and his set of very expensive dentures. "Phone first."

Carole said, "Where're you going?" The boys had turned to leave. "You stay and enjoy the party. Have a good time!"

Miriam had her arms intertwined with one each of Sammy's and Roy's. "I wouldn't dream of letting you boys go!"

Kay said sotto voce to Carole, "I'll give you odds before the evening's out she'll have them both chained in the basement."

"Hee hee hee."

Groucho boomed, "How can you all forget Lydia Austin? The poor sweet innocent girl has been missing for days!" He asked Herb, "Haven't you any new leads? Any new supporting players? And speaking of nobody in particular, here comes Oscar Levitt lumbering over the horizon. Hey Oscar, come meet

Carl Arden. Any relation to Eve Arden, Carl?" Arden didn't get a chance to speak. "She was in my movie, *A Day At the Circus*. You're not as good-looking as she is." He turned to Hazel. "And neither are you."

Hazel ignored him. She was too busy badgering Herb to join her on one side away from the others and give her the scoop on Carl Arden. Herb knew better than to do battle with Hazel when she wanted information. "We'll be right back," said Herb, hoping he knew what he was talking about. The day had been a long one of questions with few answers and he was in no mood for more. As Hazel walked him away down the beach, he looked around for any sign of Jim Mallory and Nana Lewis and briefly had a sinking feeling that they might have detoured to a motel for a let's-get-acquainted quickie. Hazel had her pad and pen at the ready and shot question after question at Villon beginning with, "Is this Arden guy for real?"

With practiced eye and years of FBI training, Carl Arden sized up Oscar Levitt swiftly. He was especially interested in him when told his was the film in which Lydia Austin had been promised the lead. Carole said with a wicked grin, "All that's missing to make this circle complete is Mike Lynton." She explained to Arden who Mike Lynton was but Arden was ahead of her — he already knew.

"Of course you know," said Carole. "There are so few surprises for the FBI."

Carl Arden favored Carole with a smile. She thought he ought to be modeling toothpaste ads. Carroll Righter, Hollywood's favorite astrologer, came swooping down on them like a bird of prey. At his side was a tiny wisp of a woman sporting garish orange hair. She wore a gossamer dress that reached her ankles, and the bracelets on her wrists jangled ominously. Her mouth was an orange slash and her eyelids were a vivid shade of purple. Her cheeks were magenta, carefully applied. In her left hand she carried a cigarette holder that was decorated with chips of jewelry. The holder held a Turkish cigarette which from the odor of the smoke Carole thought had been rolled in camel dung.

Righter asked the group, "Are you exclusive or can anyone join in?"

Carole was wondering if he was the little lady's friend or keeper. Carroll introduced her as Lola Kramm. "*The* Lola Kramm," he emphasized. "The famous British psychic."

Groucho asked, "Who needs a sidekick?"

"He said psychic, Groucho, and stop being such a pain in the butt." Lola Kramm froze in position.

"What's wrong with her?" Carole asked Righter.

"Hush! She's getting a vibration."

Lola Kramm was breathing heavily. "We are in luck," whispered Righter. "She's getting a vision. A message. I've seen this before. I think she's trying very hard to concentrate."

"*Death,*" said Lola Kramm. Her voice was ghostly and Carole's flesh began to crawl with goose bumps. Herb and Hazel had rejoined them and Carl Arden explained what was going on. Hazel began scribbling in her pad. Lola's eyes began circling the group like a klieg light at a movie premiere. "Death is not among this group, but it's nearby."

"I think she's right," Clark said to Carole. "I see Ria at the buffet."

"Don't look for trouble," said Carole. "Be charming. Your divorce is in the past. Has she seen us yet?"

"No, she's too busy piling her plate. Uh-oh. The woman with her sees us." Carole squinted in Ria's direction.

Ria was very subtly moving her head in their direction. "She sees us," said Carole.

"*Death,*" repeated Lola Kramm.

Groucho whispered to Carl Arden, "Her needle's stuck."

"This is her usual routine," said Arden.

169

"You've met her before?" asked Groucho.

"Psychics are a way of life for us. Some of them are good. Most of them are phonies."

"What about this one?" asked Groucho.

"Actually, Lola's pretty good. She pinpointed the Lindbergh baby. Wait. She's onto something."

Lola Kramm's eyes flew open as Jim Mallory and Nana Lewis arrived on the scene.

Nana spoke as though she was struggling to stifle a yawn. "So *she's* back in town."

"You know her?" asked Jim.

"We've never been officially introduced but I've seen her do her parlor tricks. She's staring at you, Jim."

"No, she's staring at you."

"Maybe she likes my outfit. I'm not crazy about hers." Lola Kramm moved slowly toward Nana. When Lola reached her, she stopped and stared up in Nana's face. She put Carole in mind of Daphne Pollard, the tiny comedienne with whom she had worked at the Sennett studio, but there was nothing amusing about Lola Kramm. Carole clutched Gable's arm.

"Need another drink?" he asked.

"No, but I think she does."

Lola said to Nana, "Death has touched you." Nana betrayed nothing. Carole heard a gasp and without looking attributed it to

Miriam Hopkins, who was given to frequent gasping. Kay patted Miriam's hand. Miss Francis was an old hand at this sort of thing. She had met several Hollywood witches, real ones, not actresses. She'd also met a warlock, a male witch. He was a dear old soul in West Hollywood who adored hexing enemies for you. There was also the writer Sally Benson whose penchant was stealing gloves and placing them in a drawer, where they presumably worked their black magic. Some years in the future she'd be famous for stealing Ingrid Bergman's gloves and consigning it to her drawer. Ingrid then met Roberto Rossellini, had an affair and a baby, and was on a blacklist for several years.

Groucho was thinking, Nana is Lydia's housemate. And Lola Kramm says death has touched her. Groucho edged his way to Herb Villon. "She said death has touched Nana. Lydia lives with Nana."

"Quiet, Groucho," said Herb as one of Lola's hands moved to her forehead and rubbed it.

Carroll Righter asked Lola, "Is that all?"

"Isn't that quite enough?" She said to Nana, "We've met before, but we've never been introduced."

Nana replied, "Hallowe'en two years ago. At Bela Lugosi's."

"I was there," said Lola, "but I don't recall you."

Oscar Levitt was standing behind Nana. Large as he was, he now seemed smaller compared to Nana. Lola addressed Oscar. "We've met before too."

Oscar said, "I don't think so."

"Possibly it was on an astral plane."

Groucho went to Lola Kramm. He pointed at Nana and said, "This young woman shares a house with three others. One of them's my girlfriend, Lydia Austin. She's missing."

"I know," said the psychic.

"You got any leads?"

Lola smiled. "Mr. Marx, I can't tell you anything without feeling an article of the young woman's clothing."

"Can't you feel one of mine? We've necked a lot."

Jim Mallory was asking Herb, "What the hell's going on?"

Herb explained, "The lady's a psychic, a friend of Carroll Righter's. She's apparently had a long run on the Hollywood party circuit." Then he introduced Jim to Carl Arden. Lola Kramm moved away from Nana and Groucho and looked at Carole and Gable without speaking.

"Pappy, she's giving me the willies. I don't

like the way she's looking at me."

"Party tricks," scoffed Gable. "Come on, sweetheart. We need a drink. I'm getting bored holding an empty glass." He took her hand and led her away. Carole could feel the psychic's eyes boring into the back of her head. In a sudden rage, Carole turned and shouted, "Keep out of my head!"

Lola said, "I'm sorry. I meant you no harm."

Hazel now stood in front of Lola. "Why do I get the feeling you're holding something back?"

Lola asked, "Are you also a psychic?"

Hazel said, "No. I'm a gossip saleswoman."

"Tell me. Do you know that man?" She indicated Oscar Levitt.

"His name is Oscar Levitt. He produces films."

"Oh."

Hazel said, "What have you got on him?"

"What do you mean?"

"You're getting vibrations on Oscar."

"I get vibrations on everyone," said the psychic, "but it takes time to sort them out. Excuse me. Carroll is gesturing he wants me." As Lola Kramm drifted in the direction of Carroll Righter, Herb, Jim, and Nana joined Hazel.

"She's quite a spook," said Herb.

173

"Don't sneer, Herb. She's pretty good," said Hazel. "She's been written up in several magazines who take this psychic stuff very seriously. Aldous Huxley swears by her. He's a pretty damned good writer. His opinions are highly respected. When I interviewed him a couple of months ago while he was writing the screenplay of *Pride and Prejudice*, he told me Lola saw this ectoplasm over his head and it materialized for a few seconds into Jane Austen, who wrote the book."

"Oh come on," scoffed Herb. "That's a lot of superstitious bullshit."

Hazel said nothing. She was staring at Oscar Levitt, who was dabbing at his forehead with a handkerchief. It was warm but it wasn't uncomfortable. Something was bothering Oscar and she intended to find out what it was. But her eye had caught the figure of Ria Gable, and Ria was standing facing Carole and Clark. It looked very civil.

Ria was saying, "You both look so handsome, but I'm not jealous."

"You've no reason to be," said Carole with a fake smile. "The divorce was so many months ago."

"I bear no grudge, my dear. I meant what I said. You both look so handsome."

"We're on our way to get a drink. Do you want one?"

"A waiter's bringing me one, if he can find me in this crowd. Don't let me hold you up."

Said Carole, the memory of the enormous settlement Ria received burning in her memory, "You already have."

Clark pulled her away and when he felt they were safely out of Ria's earshot, he burst out laughing. "Okay, baby, score one for you. That was beautiful!"

"Hee hee hee hee. She left herself wide open for that one. You're not mad at me?"

He kissed her cheek. "I'm mad about you."

"Uh-oh," said Carole.

"What?"

"Loretta Young."

"She's here?"

"Heading straight for us. Haven't you seen her since *Call of the Wild?*"

"No, damn it, I haven't. And I don't want to see her now."

Too late. "Carole! Clark!" trilled Hollywood's leading Catholic. "How nice to see you!"

Oh boy, thought Carole, Hazel Dickson's spying on us. If she makes an item out of this, I'll crack her skull. It was an open secret in Hollywood that when co-starring in the movie version of Jack London's *The Call of the Wild*, Young and Gable had a torrid affair while on location, which resulted in a daughter, Judy. When you saw Judy there was no mistaking the Gable ears.

Carole admired Loretta's beach pajamas. "They're so *you*," said Carole. "I bet they cost a bundle."

"I like to pamper myself every now and then. Clark, I see Ria's here."

Clark said nothing. Carole said vivaciously, "Why, it's just like old home week."

There was a beatific expression on Loretta Young's face. Saint Loretta, thought Clark. He and Spencer Tracy had traded notes on her one drunken night at a saloon near the Metro lot. They had finished a tough day's shoot on *San Francisco* with Jeanette MacDonald, who both agreed should have become a nun. Spencer and Loretta had an affair back in 1933 when they were filming *A Man's Castle* and Spencer's drinking was truly getting out of hand.

Carole was also admiring the expression on Loretta's face. She was either seeing the second coming or planning a trip to Rome to scold the pope. "Share it with us, Loretta," said Carole with a rare sweetness of tone.

"Share what?"

"Whatever's brought that expression on your face."

"And what kind of expression do you see?" asked Loretta, prepared to do battle should Carole take aim and strike Loretta with one of her famous barbed remarks.

"It's as though you've had a vision of the holy mother."

"Oh, I get those all the time."

"All the time? Don't they sort of crowd into each other?"

"You can scoff all you like," said Loretta, in a voice of steel.

"I'm not scoffing. I admire you. I'm not terribly religious. I'm terribly superstitious, aren't I, Pappy?"

Said Gable affably, "I think Carole was born to be a witch. She can read palms."

"And the bumps on your head. Do you have bumps, Loretta? I'll read them. I don't charge. I've read Pappy's bumps." She smiled. "They're obscene."

Clark grabbed Carole's arm. "There's Edna Mae Oliver. I haven't seen her in months."

"You're not missing a thing. I ran into her at Max Factor's salon on Monday. She was having a facial. With Edna Mae the before and after is the same thing. Let's go talk to the old dodo. She looks like she's having a

177

terrible time. See you later, Loretta!"

She hightailed it after Clark, who impatiently headed toward the elderly character actress with the horse face. He was afraid Carole would unsubtly bring up the subject of his and Loretta's bastard daughter. Carole caught up with Clark and held on to his arm. "You didn't say goodbye to Loretta. It suddenly occurs to me how she gets those beatific expressions out of mothballs and plasters them to her face. It's those immaculate conceptions she's had."

"Oh shut up!"

Nana Lewis was on the verge of losing her cool. Lola Kramm was trailing her with a quizzical expression on her face, and Nana was wondering if the psychic was getting a premonition about her. Jim Mallory thought Lola was connecting Nana to Lydia Austin, and Nana saw Oscar Levitt lumbering toward her and Jim. Maybe he'd made up his mind to hire her as Lydia's replacement.

"I hope I'm not interrupting anything?" said Levitt when he reached them. "This Kramm broad has me spooked. A little while ago she said to me something about my boat being clouded in darkness. And I said it's my new movie, *Darkness in Hollywood*, and she said no, it's your boat."

Nana said to Jim, "Oscar has a reconditioned sloop he bought in Baja a couple of financially successful movies ago. It's moored just past Mike Lynton's casino. We've been to Catalina on it a couple of times. The last time the boat sprang a leak. For crying out loud, Oscar, don't let the Kramm thing haunt you. That look on your face!"

"Well, damn it, Lydia Austin was with us the last time." The way he said "the last time," it sounded so final. "Do you suppose that's the cloud the Kramm dame sees?"

"Careful," cautioned Jim, "she's staring at you."

Nana said, "Maybe she sees a couple of financial backers playing with your ectoplasm."

"She doesn't see a damn thing," exploded Oscar. Then calmly, "I'm sorry. But I don't enjoy being haunted."

Carroll Righter had brought Lola a drink and the psychic said, "I'm making that man nervous."

"Which one? Oscar Levitt?" Lola nodded. "Lydia Austin is to do the lead in his new movie."

"She won't." The voice was eerily self-assured.

Righter was celebrated for his cockeyed prognostications, mostly brought on by an

179

overdose of scotch whiskey, but he didn't make anyone's skin crawl the way Lola made his. A typical Righter reading consisted of his suggesting to a client that she spend Saturday cleaning her closet or that she take a drive out to the desert and meditate but beware of sunstroke and Gila monsters. Lola Kramm was something else again. She had once told an elderly actor there'd be a death in his family, which prompted him to keel over from a heart attack, and Lola said to his newly created widow, "See?"

"Lydia won't do Oscar's movie?"

"There won't be a movie."

"Aren't we being a bit fanciful, Lola?"

She drew herself up to her full four foot eleven inches, looked into Righter's face, and said, "The movie will never be made."

"Just as well," said Righter. "I hear the script's a stinker." Now he waxed whimsical. "I dare you to tell this to Oscar Levitt."

The psychic said, "He's had an affair with Lydia Austin."

"If you say so. You're the psychic."

"Don't mock me."

Righter said soberly, "Yes, they were an item not too long ago." He scratched his nose. "Now let me see, in Lydia's life there was also Mike Lynton, W. C. Fields . . ."

Lola shuddered. "That dirty old man."

"Lola, Hollywood has cornered the market in dirty old men. Surely you've heard of Louis B. Mayer, Jack Warner, Harry Cohn, John Barrymore, et cetera et cetera et cetera. Lydia's most recent is Groucho Marx."

"The lady had quite an eclectic taste."

"Had? Had? Past tense?" Righter's eyes narrowed with suspicion. Hazel Dickson had come up behind the psychic, the soft sand muting her approach. "You're positive Lydia Austin's dead!"

Hazel echoed, "You're positive?" Lola yelped and turned to see Hazel and scold her.

"You frightened the hell out of me! Don't sneak up on people like that."

Hazel couldn't resist asking, "Couldn't you feel me coming?"

Lola said haughtily, "All the noise on the beach is playing havoc with my reception."

Hazel was back to business. "You sense Lydia is dead?"

"Either dead or unconscious."

"She's been missing over a week," said Hazel. "Maybe she's in a coma. I better tell Herb and Jim." The psychic and the astrologer watched as Hazel scurried away in search of Jim and Herb. She passed Clark and Carole conversing with Edna Mae Oliver.

Edna Mae was saying, "I hate parties. I don't know why I go to them. I don't drink very much. I don't nosh very much. And I absolutely loathe most of those in attendance."

Carole jollied her. "Come off it, Edna. You love to go to parties so you can make some evil comments about anybody and everybody."

"That's not true. That's a canard. I only speak my mind. And when I speak my mind I speak the truth. Take that utterly offensive Lola Kramm. She's over there" — she pointed blatantly — "yonder, with the equally offensive Carroll Righter. The man's dangerous. He's a lush. He should be drummed out of the regiment."

"What regiment?" asked Clark.

"Mr. McLaglen and his odious Black Shirts. They're fascists and racists and they should be investigated."

"Maybe they are," said Clark. "See that gentleman talking to W. C. Fields? He's Carl Arden of the FBI."

"Oh, is he indeed?" She wore pince-nez suspended on a chain around her neck. She positioned them on the bridge at her nose for a better look at Arden. "Rather a handsome man, Mr. Arden. What could he possibly have to discuss with that old reprobate

Fields? Years ago when we were both on Broadway, Bill dated me a few times. We were both working for Flo Ziegfeld. Bill was in one of the Follies, I think, and I was doing Parthy Ann Hawks in *Showboat*. I must say with all those beautiful Follies girls I was rather flattered that Bill selected me for a date. He later explained they were all of a kind and I was a novelty."

"Hee hee hee," giggled Carole. "Did he try to rape you?"

"Damn it, no."

Carole asked, "What do you think of Lola Kramm's ethereal getup?"

"I like the dress," said Edna Mae, "but not what's in it. Lola and Mr. Righter are quite right for each other. They both specialize in empty gestures. Ten years ago Righter told me to give up trying to make it in Hollywood. Not with my face."

"I love your face," said Carole kindly.

"You do? Make me an offer. As we all know, my dears, this face is my fortune. Thanks to it I'm a very rich woman and I can afford my bodyguards. Where the hell are the brutes?"

"You don't need them," said Clark.

"Why? Do you think my face would scare off any kidnappers?"

Clark gently pinched her cheek. "No,

babe. There are no kidnappers. It's a false alarm. Carl Arden told us."

"Well, I'll be hanged! But what about the Austin child? Isn't she kidnapped?"

"My poor darling has certainly disappeared. But now we're not so sure it's a case of kidnapping." Carole shuddered.

"What's wrong?" asked Clark.

Carole was embracing herself. "Somebody just walked over my grave."

"Oh stop that! Stuff and nonsense!" fumed Edna Mae.

"Fancy meeting you here, my stuffed Hungarian cabbage!" W. C. Fields had lost Carlotta somewhere but decided Edna Mae would be a likely substitute.

"I'm neither Hungarian nor a cabbage," said Edna Mae in her most ladylike voice. "What have you done with Carlotta? I thought I saw her with you a short time ago."

"Well, I've either lost her or misplaced her. I've been thinking of trading her in for a new model." He asked them, "Anybody interested in Carlotta? I'm entertaining all offers. I'm certainly not entertaining Carlotta." He had his cane under one shoulder while lighting a cigar. "Do any of you know if I've had an affair with Miriam Hopkins? She looks so familiar. An animated powder puff. I've been talking to the FBI. We were discussing the missing Japs. He thinks they're probably miles out to sea by now. Knots to you. Smuggled out of the country on a Japanese fishing boat. Why didn't they fly out, I asked him in my most genteel voice, and he said because they wanted to avoid going through customs. So I said they're probably spies and he just gave me this strange look that makes me think I guessed right." He looked hard at Carole. "Why of course! You're Carole Lombard! What's become of you? What have you been up to lately? Trying to make a comeback?" Carole winked at Edna Mae. Fields stared hard at Clark. "Why you varlet! You mountebank!" He raised the cane over his head. "You stole my part! You did Rhett Butler!"

Carole reached up and pulled the cane out of Fields' hand. "You might hurt someone with this pig sticker."

"How dare you! Unhand me! Return my weapon or I'll crush you to a pulp. Are you two still married? Ah, the joys of wedded bliss!" He retrieved the cane and focused on Edna Mae Oliver. "Why, as I live and struggle to breathe, it's my old partner in crime Edna Mae Oliver!" Delicately he took her hand and kissed it. "Been deflowered yet?"

"Oh Bill," said Carole. "What a terrible thing to ask."

"Why, I ask you, why? I'm as concerned about it as she is. You know, Eddie Sutherland, who's trying to direct my current opus, tells me I'm an institution."

Edna Mae said with a sniff, "You're an institution who belongs in one!"

Carole's eyes found Hazel Dickson and Herb Villon. Jim Mallory and Nana Lewis were with them, but apparently engaged in a conversation of their own. Carl Arden joined Herb and Hazel as she was telling Herb about the conversation with Lola Kramm and Carroll Righter.

Herb mulled over Hazel's words carefully. He was a master at sifting through information and placing it in the right perspective. Hazel, at Herb's insistence, repeated what she'd told him and Carl Arden said, "Lola Kramm is right in there with the best but that doesn't mean she's infallible."

Herb said to Arden, "I have to admit I'm so desperate, I've been entertaining some pretty wild thoughts as to what fate has befallen Lydia."

"Let me hear some of those wild thoughts," said Arden. "Maybe I can help tame them."

"Maybe she went off with Takameshuga and the six other dwarfs."

"Why would she do that?" asked Arden.

Herb explained. "Lydia gets around. We know she met him through Mala Anouk, whom he dated several times. So maybe on the sly Lydia played footsie with Takameshuga and he liked her feet and invited her back to Japan."

"To do what?" asked a skeptical Hazel. "Study to become a geisha girl?"

From her tone of voice, Carl Arden could tell that Hazel, like so many other Americans, had geisha girls all wrong. "Hazel, I think you're under the misconception that geisha girls are whores. No such thing. They are carefully trained to give satisfaction but sex rarely rears its pretty head. Oh, maybe here and there from time to time one of the girls succumbs to the blandishments of a hot and bothered male, but if they do and they're caught out, they're finished. It's a great honor to be selected and trained as a geisha. Most of them make very good marriages."

"Oh really?" said Hazel. "Maybe I should start giving Japan some careful consideration." Carl Arden didn't have the heart to tell her she was a bit long in the tooth for a career as a geisha. He also didn't tell her that highly trained informants had alerted Washington to the possibility of a conspiracy entered into by Japan and Germany. He also refrained from sharing the information that

American spies in Japan had been apprehended and executed. And Washington was helpless to retaliate. That is why he sought Takameshuga and the six other Japanese who had vanished and cursed the higher-ups for waiting too long to send him out on a mission that might now prove to be fruitless. He pinned his hopes on the American spy ships patrolling the Pacific waters under various camouflages seeking Japanese boats that were not registered, such as the *Sarita Maru*, the one that had sailed from Long Beach at the time Takameshuga and the others disappeared.

The sun was starting to set and some of the guests were departing for other venues or to other engagements.

"Miwiam," Kay said to Miriam Hopkins, "you've given a superb party. Elsa Maxwell couldn't have done it better." Maxwell was the celebrated society party thrower. She choreographed them for wealthy clients at very eye-popping fees. She was short and obese, and played the piano brilliantly. A product of the Midwest, she had invented herself magnificently and was an international success. She had few rivals. Of these, one was Syrie Maugham, ex-wife of author W. Somerset Maugham, and another was Elsie De Wolfe, who married Charles

Mendl, who was a lord, and now De Wolfe was Lady Mendl and never let anyone forget it. It was Elsa who comforted Lady Mendl when she bemoaned the thought of few people showing up at a party she had arranged for the same night Maxwell was overseeing one. Maxwell phoned Lady Mendl and said magnanimously, "Elsie darling! My list is overloaded! I'd be delighted to lend you some of my guests!"

Though her party had been packed with guests, Miriam bemoaned several who hadn't shown up. "No Garbo! No Dietrich! No Stanwyck!"

"The hell with them," said Kay. "Did you tell anyone they were invited?"

"Oh of course not," said Miriam. "It's bad luck to share a guest list!"

Kay didn't question where Miriam had heard that one. Miriam did come up with some lalapaloozas. "And anyway," Kay said, "just because the sun and some of your guests are setting doesn't mean the party's over! Everyone's having a marvelous time! Look at the ones in the water! They're splashing and playing games and mark my words: I predict there'll be many an abortion as a result of this party!"

"How cynical!"

"My eye cynical! Cawwoll Wighter's had

a snootful. I hope he's not driving!"

Kay followed Miriam, who led her to Righter and Lola Kramm. Miriam said to the psychic, "Carroll's not driving you home, is he? He's in no condition."

"Don't worry," said Lola, who herself had had a fair share of liquor. "Two lovely young men have volunteered to drive us home. Their names are Roy and Sammy and until this evening they were bodyguards for the Gables, but the Gables don't need them anymore since the FBI person told them the kidnapping scare is a false alarm, But of course!" She waved her right hand and said airily, "Those mysterious ten men who are gone were here under false pretenses."

"Oh weally?" asked Kay. "You know this for sure?"

"Not for sure. Just take it as a qualified assertion by a great psychic!"

Miriam whispered to Kay, "What an ego. She puts me to shame!"

Kay was watching Nana Lewis and Jim Mallory, who had stripped down to bathing ensemble and swim trunks as they ran into the ocean.

"Ah, youth!" Kay said with a faraway look in her eyes. "They say youth must be served. Now I understand why. They'll take it anyway."

"Take what?" asked Miriam, somewhat confused as well she should be. Kay was getting morbid.

"What they want. What they feel they are owed. Miwiam, we're contemporaries. In our youth, did we make unweasonable demands?"

Miriam said stoutly, "My demands were never unreasonable despite my reputation for being difficult. I knew what I wanted. I went after it and I got it. And so did you, Kay."

"If I had my life to live over again, it would all be so different."

"How would it be different?"

She favored Miriam with a small laugh and said. "I'd have children."

"Didn't Kenneth McKenna," Kay's ex-husband, an actor, "want children?"

"He did. I didn't."

"Oh." She put an arm around Kay's waist. "No use crying over spilt offspring. Anyway, you're too old to bear children."

Kay bristled. "Who says so?" She thought of Maurice Chevalier, who had once so desperately wanted to marry her. "I'd have a child wight now except Maurice is back in France. I'd have a baby at the drop of a hat."

"And did Maurice take his hat with him?"

In the water, Sammy and Roy were entertaining some guests with their acrobatics. Jim Mallory and Nana Lewis were dog-paddling and vastly enjoying the exhibition. Roy balanced Sammy on his shoulders, and then Sammy reciprocated. They acknowledged their damp applause, enjoying their reception.

On the beach, Hazel was trying to lure Herb Villon into the water, but Herb was having none of it. As far as he was concerned, bathing should be confined to the bathtub.

"Come on, Herb. Nobody'll notice your knobby knees."

"They are not knobby!" he said flashing her a slightly filthy look. Hazel knew better than to continue arguing the point. She had seen him in the buff often enough to know his knees were knobby, just as she knew that Dietrich was knock-kneed and posed her legs very carefully for the camera.

Herb was staring out at the water beyond where Sammy and Roy were cavorting. He shaded his eyes with his hands for a better look. "What's out there?" asked Hazel. "Johnny Weissmuller looking for a lost vine?"

Suddenly Herb was stripping. First his shirt, then his shoes and trousers, and Hazel gleefully unzipped her dress to join Herb in a dip. Without a word to Hazel, he ran into the water, unmindful of the late afternoon chill.

"Wait for me!" shrieked Hazel as she gave chase.

On the beach, Carole saw Hazel chasing after Herb and had the urge to join them. "Come on, Pappy! Let's show them the Australian crawl!" She was quickly out of her costume.

Edna Mae urged Clark, "Go on! Have some fun! I might wade in up to my knees. Haven't done that in ages. Not since the Dark Ages."

Herb was a strong swimmer. Jim Mallory saw him go past Sammy and Roy and sensed something was wrong. He left Nana and swam quickly in Herb's direction.

Carole screamed with delight as Clark shoved her head under water. When she surfaced she yelled, "Now it's my turn to try and drown you!"

But Clark had seen what Herb had seen and headed toward him. "Hey!" shouted Carole. "Where're you going, Pappy?" Now she saw what they saw. She saw Jim Mallory joining them. Then she yelled at Sammy and Roy, pointing in the direction Clark and Herb had taken. Roy, standing on Sammy's shoulders, shouted something unintelligible to Carole but which Sammy understood. Roy dove into the water and with beautiful precision he and Sammy swam toward Herb and Clark, Jim meeting them from another direction. Nana Lewis followed Jim. Her intuition drove her.

There was a body floating out there. Nana feared it might be Lydia Austin. It was floating face downward and it was hard to recognize the gender.

Herb reached the body and turned it over on its back.

"Oh my God!" sputtered Carole. "Oh my God!"

Hazel Dickson had joined them and remembered she had left her pad and pen on the beach, so she hurried back. What a scoop!

There was a gaping knife wound in Mike Lynton's chest.

SEVEN

Hazel was doing her best Chicken Little impersonation, not proclaiming the sky was falling, but announcing to Louella Parsons that Mike Lynton's body had been found floating in the Pacific off Miriam Hopkins' private beach. She gave Clark Gable and Herb Villon equal billing while on the other end of the wire Louella cooed like the pouter pigeon she resembled. She kept repeating what Hazel told her, while on an extension in Louella's mansion her assistant, Dorothy Manners, listened and took everything down in shorthand.

"Go on, Hazel, Dorothy is taking it all down. Clark and the detective pulled the body to the shore."

That wasn't quite accurate, but Louella Parsons was never noted for accuracy. She strewed facts through her column like a farmer gone berserk placing seed in the ground. Hazel yelled into the phone, "Not just a detective! Herb Villon! *My* Herb Villon! Dorothy, have you got that?" Dorothy assured her she had. Hazel continued with more facts because the more she delivered the fancier her price and Hazel was determined to own a chinchilla wrap, which she knew Herb Villon would never buy for her.

Hazel rattled off the names of Miriam's guests and threw in the names of several stars who hadn't attended the party but to whom she owed a payback, and an appearance in Lolly Parsons' column was indeed quite a payback.

Then she added, "Carole Lombard gave Lynton artificial respiration when the body was hauled out of the water but whether artificial or genuine the respiration didn't help. Carole gave it her all and we're all proud of her. Groucho Marx made some snide remark that he didn't know Lynton had been invited to the party and Lola Kramm, the psychic, insists she warned Lynton days ago to stay away from water as it boded ill. Now let me see." She scratched her head. "Oh yes. There was a gaping chest wound in the body, which I noticed before I did a fast swim to the shore to phone you *exclusively*, Louella."

On the beach, Miriam's butler had brought a blanket with which to cover the corpse until the police and the coroner arrived. Kay Francis was feeding Miriam Hopkins brandy and pleading with her to be brave. "Brave! Brave!" exploded Miriam.

"The body of a man I detest washes up on my beach and wrecks my party and you want me to be brave! Really, Kay!"

Kay and Carole exchanged a look, knowing Miriam would dine out on this for weeks to come.

In addition to the blanket to cover the body, Miriam's household thoughtfully provided towels and soon those who had been in the water when the body invaded their high jinks were dried and dressed again. Herb advised the guests that no one was to leave until his backup arrived and took their names and addresses. Oscar Levitt was throwing up into the Pacific, resembling a whale depositing ambergris. Nana Lewis was at his side with a wet towel, which she applied to his face, and Carole was pretty positive she'd be replacing Lydia Austin in Oscar's movie. Carole shared her supposition with Clark who said, "Poor bastard. Lynton was supposed to go hunting with us this weekend."

"Pappy," said Carole sweetly, "you're all heart."

Edna Mae Oliver looked at the blanket covering Mike Lynton's body and said, "Miriam will have a conniption. That blanket's cashmere. Terribly expensive."

Jim said to Villon, "Should I phone the

casino and tell them about this?"

Herb said. "What's the rush? They won't close for the night. The show must go on." He could see Oscar Levitt squatting on the beach, gasping for breath, being fanned by Nana Lewis.

Carole said, "Poor Oscar. He's having a hard time breathing. He's asthmatic. On the other hand, with Mike Lynton dead, he should be breathing easier." She said to Clark, "I don't see why Herb is detaining everybody. Mike didn't float in from the party, he floated in from someplace out there." She gestured vaguely out to sea.

She heard Groucho ask no one in particular, "And what was he doing somewhere out there? Digging for clams?"

Carole said to Herb Villon, "I've got some ideas as to who might have killed Mike."

Herb decided to take her seriously as there was little else to do until his group arrived. It had been trouble enough getting Hazel off the phone so Mallory could phone for backup. She had threatened to divest Jim of an essential part of his anatomy but he was brave and took his chance. Hazel was soon in command of the phone again but didn't call Louella back. If she had to, she'd explain that the police had commandeered the phone. Hazel phoned the second most notorious and unpopular Hollywood gorgon, Hedda Hopper, who lapped up Hazel's story like a camel that had wandered in after weeks without water in the Sahara desert.

Herb had walked Carole away out of earshot of those milling about the body. Clark was curious but knew better than to interfere. Carole told Herb, "Lydia Austin told me a few choice things about Mike and I hope they'll be of some assistance."

Herb had always found Carole's honesty irresistible in a town where, along with loyalty, honesty was little practiced because most of the movie colony found loyalty and honesty too expensive. Herb did Carole the honor of jotting down what she said in his notebook. "Mike was mixed up with the Chicago mob. Before he came to the coast, he wanted to open a casino near Chicago, but he wouldn't play ball with Al Capone."

"Capone's behind bars."

"Don't be so naive. Even from behind bars, Capone rules with a fist of steel." She sighed. "Capone's behind bars. Mike's dead."

"What you're saying is Capone had a contract out on him."

"You know as well as I do Capone gave out contracts with the alacrity of a Louis B. Mayer. In case you don't know, alacrity means speed —"

"Oh shut up." Villon had a college degree and he knew Carole knew it. Hazel Dickson had shared the knowledge with anybody in Hollywood who would take a minute to listen.

Carole ignored Villon's admonition and continued. "Mike tried to get into Las Vegas but Bugsy Siegel and his deadly *mishpocha* kept him out."

College or no college, Herb was now in a bind. "Spell *mishpocha*."

"I'm an actress not a genius. Substitute 'family.'

"Then of course I don't have to remind you of Mike's numerous cruelties to a lot of people who owed him money. Broken kneecaps, broken arms, cracked skulls. As you must be well aware, he treated skulls like walnuts. And there are a lot of ladies in the territory who would be happier knowing Mike Lynton is dead."

"Poison is a ladies' weapon," reminded Herb.

"Tell Agatha Christie to go soak her head. You ever see a Hollywood lady tearing into a T-bone steak?"

"You've got a point there." He had gestured to Jim Mallory, who joined them somewhat reluctantly. Nana Lewis was now attached to Oscar Levitt's hip, or so it seemed, and Jim was anxious to restake his territory. Herb asked Jim, "Did you check the tides?"

"I spoke to the precinct on my car intercom. The tides were going in an westerly direction at about the time Mike Lynton dropped in."

"That's cute," said Carole.

Jim resumed talking. "That means he was dumped in the drink from anywhere in the vicinity of Marina del Rey. It would take the body a couple of hours to float here."

"Just because the casino is in Marina doesn't necessarily mean he was killed there."

"No, but it's a start," said Jim reasonably.

"I'm with Jim," said Carole, "and don't tell me to shut up or I'll sic Pappy on you. And where the hell is he?" She looked in the direction of the body and the guests milling about. "There he is. He's furious Mike was murdered. They had a date to go hunting this weekend."

"Gee, that's tough." The irony in Villon's voice didn't escape Carole. She had liked him when she met him six years earlier, investigating the Russ Columbo shooting. She found him terribly gentle and understanding for a Los Angeles detective. He refrained from any snide remarks as to the relationship

201

between Russ and Lansing Brown. When she told him she wasn't present when the shooting occurred, Villon made a comment that made Carole realize she was lucky she wasn't there or there might have been two victims instead of one.

Carole said, "For Pappy, it's tough. It isn't easy finding a hunting companion in this town unless it's a publicity shoot set up by the studio."

Villon asked Carole, "Anything else you want to tell me?"

"Your hair needs combing."

Villon smiled and then they heard sirens. "The gentlemen of the ensemble are arriving. Let's go." They trudged back to the center of activity.

Groucho Marx asked Edna Mae Oliver, "Tell me, gorgeous. Do coroners give coronaries?"

"Perhaps they don't," said Edna Mae with her trademark sniff, "but I do."

From a short distance they and others who were waiting to be dealt with by police officers watched the coroner, kneeling at the corpse's side and reciting to an assistant who took notes. The coroner's name was Edmund Weber and rather than examining Mike Lynton's body, he wished he was examining Kay Francis's body. He worshiped her and this was the first time he'd seen her in the flesh. At the first opportunity he planned to recite the titles of all her films that had given him pleasure. A bachelor, he was free to indulge in as many fantasies involving her as he cared to, with no wife or girlfriend to be guilty about. Kay and Miriam stood a bit beyond him and the corpse, Kay simply curious and Miriam quite indignant her party had been brought to such a gruesome finale. They were oblivious to the reporters and photographers swarming all over the place, and they didn't hear the coroner say under his breath, "Kay Francis, I dedicate this corpse to you," a toreador in the arena gifting a señorita with a bull's precious ear. At one point he caught the actress's eye and he smiled. She smiled back and supposed he'd be asking for her autograph when he finished. He was wondering if he dared ask her to dinner. He thought of himself as a pleasant chap with average good looks. When he shaved in the morning, he admired and respected the distinguished-looking gentleman he saw in the mirror and kept wondering how come he was still single, a sentiment shared by his mother, who was in her early seventies and wanted a grandchild before her departure to that other world she hoped awaited her.

"He certainly seems to know what he's doing," said Kay to Miriam of the coroner.

"Well, I should hope so!" said Miriam, wondering if she'd be doing Kay a favor by asking the coroner to join them for dinner. She was sure the cook had enough for the three of them.

W. C. Fields stared down at the coroner, who recognized him and was flattered to see the great man in his audience. Fields indicated the others watching the coroner's preliminary examination, the more thorough one to take place in the morgue. "A bloodthirsty lot. Every man and woman a vampire. Can you tell me how many times he was stabbed or is that privileged information? I have a bet on with my paramour" — he indicated Carlotta who stood with her back to him, a handkerchief at her mouth — "my paramour who I found at Paramount. We've a bet on as to how many stab wounds you've found or will find."

Herb Villon intervened. "Hello, Ed. How's your mother?" The coroner didn't say he wished it was his mother's body he was examining, thereby dispelling the myth he was a devoted son. He had almost murdered her when she discovered his cache of pornographic magazines at the bottom of his dresser drawer and consigned them to a fiery demise. In case the coroner didn't know or hadn't been told, Villon identified Mike Lynton.

"Well, what do you know," said the coroner with a pleased look. "I never dreamed I'd ever meet him. Imagine dealing with a Hollywood legend on the beach at Malibu." He got to his feet. "Two stab wounds. Probably a butcher or a bread knife. One severed his aorta, which is the body's major blood vessel. That killed him instantly."

"No few minutes to writhe in agony?" asked Herb.

"Didn't you like him?"

"I liked him well enough. When you've done it thorough, phone me and send me a memo. Ed, you're not listening. Who're you ogling?"

"Kay Francis. Behind you. Don't look now!" he said hastily. "She'll know we're talking about her."

"She expects to be talked about. She's a movie star."

"But she's unique. She's not like all the others. She's a lady." Herb said to himself, Oh Edmund, if you knew what I knew. "I mean I've autopsied Jean Harlow, Thelma Todd, and the other floozy types."

"You've got the girls all wrong. Jean came

from an upper-class Kansas family and Thelma was a respected schoolteacher."

"Do you know Miss Francis?"

"We've been introduced."

"I'm dying to meet her." He looked from the right to the left and then from the left to the right and Villon had to strain to hear what the coroner was saying. "She's my secret passion."

"No kidding." Villon was savoring the moment and the sharing of the confidence.

"Ever since *Girls About Town* with Lilyan Tashman. I also adored Tashman but she's dead so why waste my time. And that delicious comedy, *The Jewel Robbery* and *Trouble in Paradise*, which she did with our hostess, Miriam Hopkins. And so many others."

"Tell your boys to remove the body and then I'll introduce you."

"My God!" His mouth salivated with anticipation. "My cup runneth over." He gave an instruction to his assistants and then followed Villon to his goddess.

Herb said, "Kay, I'd like you to meet our coroner, or at least one of them, Edmund Weber."

Kay extended a hand. "I'm charmed. I really am. You're my first cowoner. Miriam, meet Edmund Weber."

Miriam said hastily, "Would you care to

join us for dinner?"

"Miwiam," said Kay Francis, "you're so impetuous!"

Kay had other plans for the evening but saw no reason to reveal them. She was having dinner with an old flame, Herbert Marshall, who had been Kay and Miriam's leading man in *Trouble in Paradise*. He had a wooden leg, which Kay found very convenient when she felt the urge to knock on wood. "I can't join you for dinner," said Kay graciously, "I'll take a waincheck."

"And of course so will you, Mr. Weber," said Miriam with a lovely smile. She'd be damned if she'd be saddled with a man she didn't know and didn't care to know.

Edmund Weber's ecstasy at the prospect of dinner with the two stars dissolved into chagrin and disappointment. He said he too was busy. Dinner with his mother. A roast chicken and of course he was elected to dissect it. He excused himself and hurried to the precinct's meat wagon, which would transport him back to the morgue. He scrubbed Kay Francis as a secret passion and went back to an earlier romantic fantasy, Eleanor Powell. The dancer twirled about in his vivid and active imagination and soon he was clicking his tongue, simulating the sound of her busy tap shoes.

The beach was swarming with photographers and reporters having a field day. For them, Miriam's guests were a banquet and they couldn't be happier feasting. David O. Selznick, never one to let an opportunity for publicity to slip by, took command of the press. He reminded them that Clark and Carole would be departing for Atlanta for the world premiere of *Gone With the Wind* along with himself, his wife, and Clark's co-stars in the movie. No, Leslie Howard wouldn't be with them; the British patriot was back in England helping with the war effort. He deftly sidestepped questions about why the Negro actresses Hattie McDaniel and Butterfly McQueen had been exempted from the junket.

"They're not going to be with us," said Carole pointedly, "because the mayor of Atlanta couldn't come up with decent accommodations for them." Selznick started to turn purple and his wife rummaged in her handbag for his glycerin capsules. Selznick's heart was in the right place but it occasionally malfunctioned. Gable chuckled at Carole's bluntness. He would miss the two actresses. They had been great fun on the set, filming a movie he loathed participating in.

Mike Lynton's body was strapped to a stretcher and before the attendants could lift it into the ambulance, a photographer pulled the sheet back revealing his head and no longer handsome face. Somehow, Nana Lewis had edged her way toward the stretcher and stood staring down at the corpse, a sad expression on her face, and she even squeezed out a tear for added effect. Oscar Levitt had made a miraculous recovery and informed any press and photographers within earshot that Nana Lewis was to star in his new production, *Darkness in Hollywood.* Carole, now annoyed and angry, mouthed a vicious epithet but Oscar was deaf to everything except the popping of flashbulbs. Roy and Sammy were insinuated into the photograph by a woman photographer who had enjoyed a three-way with the boys the previous Saturday night and her ears were still ringing. Jim Mallory saw Nana Lewis with different eyes: just another actress on the make. Clark Gable looked upon the spectacle with disgust. He pulled up the sheet to mask Lynton's face and Oscar Levitt was about to pull the sheet back down when a look from Clark warned him to back off. He was not about to curry Clark's disfavor. He was a member of Clark's upcoming hunting party and was also hoping the star would have some influence in getting MGM to distribute his film.

Lola Kramm weaved her way to Herb Villon's side and gestured for him to bend down so she could whisper in his ear. "The murderer is among us." She reeked with alcoholic fumes but Herb bravely didn't move his head away. Pissed as she was she might be onto something.

"Where?"

She waved her right hand airily. "Someplace." She was not very steady on her feet and Herb caught her under the arms as she was about to fall forward atop the corpse. Soon another pair of hands took charge of the psychic and Herb thanked Carroll Righter for coming to his rescue.

Righter said with slurred speech, "I'd marry her if I liked women." He gestured to Sammy and Roy who hurried forward and took charge of Lola. They literally dragged her across the sand and up the stairs to the road, then had a slight misunderstanding as to where they might have parked.

Hazel said to Herb Villon, "I heard what Lola told you."

"I thought I noticed you crawling around."

"Don't be mean. How could the murderer be among us if Lynton was killed miles from here?"

"A cinch by automobile, Hazel. And a

ghastly surprise seeing the victim washing up in the middle of the party."

Hands on hips, challenging Herb, Hazel demanded, "You got any ideas?"

"I've always got ideas," said Herb, "but they're not necessarily connected with murder." Clark and Carole had watched as the corpse was lifted into the ambulance. Edmund Weber sat in the front seat next to the driver. His window was rolled down and he waved goodbye to Kay and Miriam.

Miriam said to Kay, "I think you've broken his heart."

"How ridiculous," scoffed Kay. "Imagine being romanced by a cowoner."

"Well," said Miriam, "it would be a novelty." They watched the ambulance pull away, bell clanging. The butler had retrieved the cashmere blanket from an attendant who had replaced it with a sheet.

"Egbert!" yelped Miriam. "Is that my best cashmere blanket?"

Egbert told her it was, explaining, "It has developed moth holes, Miss Hopkins, totally useless now except for covering a corpse."

Said Kay, "Sounds weasonable to me."

"Moth holes can be mended!" exploded Miriam.

"Not even in the best of families," said Egbert haughtily, having seen service years earlier with Lady Astor in London. He continued on his way back to the house. Kay heard Miriam mutter, "His days are numbered."

Groucho Marx was haunting Herb Villon. "I suspected Mike Lynton was responsible for spiriting my Lydia away. He was still in love with her. Lydia told me." He hopped in front of Villon. "Who do you suspect did this dastardly deed? You must suspect someone. Go ahead. Suspect me. I'm available. I haven't been a suspect in ages."

"Cut it out, Groucho!"

Groucho said to Hazel, "I'm sure it's dangerous when he uses that tone of voice. I know one person who'll be glad to hear Mike is dead. My brother Chico. There's a suspect for you. But Chico doesn't knife people to death. He bores them to death. He bores me, but don't tell him I said so. He'll pelt me with rocks. I'll go hunting with Clark if you'll go hunting with Clark. How can you go hunting if you have a murder to solve? How can you solve a murder if you haven't any suspects?" He snapped his fingers. "I've got it. Look for a disgruntled employee. Is there ever a gruntled employee?"

Miriam's party was disintegrating rapidly. Guests sought her out and told her it was a *marvelous* party. W. C. Fields said to Miriam,

"Lovely party, my southern sassafras. Clever climax. Who but you, Miriam, would think of a corpse in the water?"

Miriam stifled a rising scream. Kay held her hand tightly. Death wasn't funny, murder even less so. Mike Lynton's murder was beginning to sink in. Kay was thinking of calling Herbert Marshall, canceling their date and spending the evening with Miriam. She suggested as much to Miriam, but suddenly Miriam's eyes sparkled. "That's so sweet of you, Kay, but the boys are coming back after they get rid of Carroll and Lola."

The boys? thought Kay. And then she remembered, Of course. Sammy and Roy, those superb examples of young masculinity. "Why Miriam, you sly puss you!"

"We're going to read some Shakespeare together. Isn't that sweet?"

"Isn't what sweet?" asked Carole as she joined them. "I could use some cheering up after the recent unpleasantness. Clark's phoning the casino to tell them the boss is dead. I doubt if it's been on the radio yet, Pappy is so thoughtful that way. Look at David O. and Irene. Probably still seething over my remark about Hattie and Butterfly. We've seen a screening and the ladies just about walk away with the picture."

"Not weally!" said Kay.

Carole said, "Hattie should be nominated for an Academy Award. I bet she will and I hope she wins. I'm going to vote a lot of times for her."

"Shame on you, Carole," said Miriam.

"Why? You know the studios rig the awards. When they first began in 1928 Janet Gaynor won for *three* pictures. Can you beat that? And then Louis B. Mayer and Irving Thalberg saw to it that Norma Shearer won for *The Divorcee* the next year. Did either of you see that stinker?" She saw Herb Villon and Jim Mallory with their heads together. "Herb Villon is such a dear man, the poor guy. First the kidnapping scare gets blown to bits by that FBI fink. Look. He's joining Herb and Jim, like they need his great mind. Hee hee hee."

Herb said to Carl Arden, "I've been ignoring you. Sorry. I didn't expect a murdered man to put in an appearance."

Arden responded, "Quite a show! You didn't arrange it just for me, did you?" He said to Jim Mallory, "Your girlfriend must be pleased as punch."

"What girlfriend?" asked Jim innocently.

"I hope I'm not speaking out of turn. I assumed the young lady you escorted to the party was your girlfriend."

"Nana Lewis isn't my girlfriend," said Jim. "She's just a young lady I escorted to the party. And it looks as though Oscar Levitt is taking over." Nana came up to them, out of breath.

"Jim, I hope you don't mind. Oscar wants to talk about the movie and he's asked me to dinner. You don't mind, do you?"

"No. Good luck with the movie."

"You're so sweet! Good night, all!" She hurried off to rejoin Oscar Levitt, kicking sand as she passed Carole.

Carole asked the three men, "Who's chasing her?"

"Oscar Levitt," said Jim.

The men winced as Carole bombarded the air with a string of Lombard expletives. "The picture doesn't start shooting for weeks! Lydia could still turn up! Damn it, she's not dead! She can't be dead! She's the liveliest one of my protégées!"

Herb explained Carole's protégées to Carl Arden who said to Carole, "That's very generous of you, Miss Lombard."

"Yeah," said Carole, still smoldering over Levitt's hasty decision in announcing Nana's replacement of Lydia, "beats hell. Pappy! Over here!" Gable trudged through the sand to Carole's side. "Who'd you talk to at the casino?"

"Mike's manager. He was shocked. Nobody had heard yet."

Carole asked, "Does Mike have a stand-in?" Clark chuckled at hearing a replacement for Mike Lynton referred to in typical Hollywood jargon.

Herb spoke up. "You can be sure Mike trained somebody to replace him. Mike was very thorough about his operation. You can also be sure there are several mugs who'll be looking to move in on the operation. There's going to be a lot of *Sturm and Drang* erupting soon."

"Do you mean a gang war?" Carole's eyes seemed to be on the verge of popping out of her head. Wearily she said, "Just what we need. Pappy, you in the mood for Romanoff's? I don't feel like going back to the ranch yet. Okay?"

"Sure, sweetheart. Mike'll cheer us both up. Here's Kay. Should we ask her to join us?"

Kay Francis found an enchanting smile for Carl Arden when they were introduced, but turned down the offer of dinner.

"What about Miriam?" asked Carole with genuine concern. "We can't leave her alone in that big mansion. Knowing our Miriam, she'll be seeing ghosts."

"Oh no she won't," said Kay piquantly,

"she's having Sammy and Roy for dinner."

"Raw?" asked Carole, her eyebrows shooting up.

"They're going to read Shakespeare."

"Hee hee hee. That's a new one on me. Boy, Miriam sure works fast and under cover."

Clark said, "I've heard Miriam has done some of her best work under cover."

"Oh Pappy! You're such a bitch!"

Kay said, "I don't want to be the first one to leave this bunch!"

"After dinner, I've got to work on the guns," said Gable. "Carl? If you've nothing special on for Saturday morning, why don't you join us hunting. I'm providing the guns and the ammunition."

"And I'm providing lunch," said Carole. "Our trailer truck is outfitted with a kitchen. Very unpretentious and serviceable."

Herb said to Gable before Carl could come to a decision, "If the invite is still open, Jim and I will join you."

"That's swell! The more the merrier!" Clark said. To Carole he added, "How about that, sweetheart? There'll be venison for Sunday brunch!"

His eagerness at the prospect of slaughtering animals dismayed Carole. Because she so deeply loved him, she had altered her lifestyle to suit his needs. He needed to be a hunter, a he-man. It was macho, of which Carole had once said, "Macho do about nothing." Now she urged him to hunt. It was one of the few sports that provided him with pleasure. He didn't have many close pals, not like Jim Cagney and Pat O'Brien and their Hibernians. Ronald Colman ruled the British set, which included David Niven and Patric Knowles. Every Sunday they either played cricket or rode to the hounds while their wives gathered at somebody's home to bitch about non-British wives.

What friends Carole and Gable had now were Carole's friends: Fieldsie and her husband, Walter Lang; her press agent Otto Winkler and his wife. Carole was still fond of her ex-husband, William Powell, and invited him often to the house. When his beloved mistress Jean Harlow died in 1937, Powell fell apart mentally and physically. Physically because he was syphilitic, a condition that led to a colostomy that kept him off the screen for almost two years. It was the syphilis with which he had infected Harlow that killed her, not the cock and bull stories put out by the studio. The knowledge that he was responsible for her death would haunt Powell for an eternity. In 1936 Carole and Powell agreed to co-star in *My Man*

Godfrey, a brilliant comedy in which their chemistry resulted in two matchless comedy performances. They almost fell in love again, but each kept a tight rein on their emotions. Powell had Harlow, and Carole, like everyone else in films, adored Harlow, who was known then as "Baby."

After mulling over Clark's invitation for a few moments, Carl Arden said he'd be delighted to join the hunting party. Hazel Dickson piped up, "I'll come along to keep Carole company." Carole made a mental note to bring cotton for her ears. Herb didn't exactly whoop with joy at the prospect of Hazel joining them, but she'd overheard him telling Clark he and Jim would join the blood sport caravan. Herb had something else on his mind than the slaughter of animals. Once as a teenager he'd killed a rabbit and as it lay dying, writhing in agony, struggling to rise from the ground, he burst into tears. His brothers never stopped razzing him for being a sissy.

Hazel asked Carole, "What do you wear when you go hunting?"

Carole said, "A look of determination."

Mike Romanoff's restaurant was in the heart of Beverly Hills Village, right behind the chic Beverly Wilshire Hotel. Romanoff's was a culinary rarity in Hollywood. The food was exceptionally good and what's more, Romanoff's also catered and delivered to one's home. Mike crowed that his menu was derived from several created in the royal palace in St. Petersburg. Groucho said the closest Mike ever got to St. Petersburg was when he saw the movie *Rasputin and the Empress.* Mike Romanoff was a bogus prince and Hollywood was notorious for taking anyone and anything bogus to its heart. Mike carved his niche quickly, thanks to endorsements from the likes of Clark and Carole and Humphrey Bogart and his wife Mayo Methot, with whom he was constantly embroiled in battle. Mike's restaurant was Mike's palace and he lorded over it like an emperor. He was not known for any romantic entanglements and it was rumored he had mob connections. Where else could he have gotten his financial backing?

Romanoff greeted the Gables effusively as they walked in, followed by Herb, Hazel, Jim, and Carl Arden, who feasted on the celebrities he recognized. Though they hadn't phoned for a reservation, there would be no problem accommodating the Gables and their party. Romanoff always kept several tables available and free of reservations though on each of these tables was a placard that read Reserved. Hazel cursed herself for not going home and changing into an evening dress, though she was aware Carole didn't share her feeling. If anybody didn't like what Carole was wearing or found it too sporty for the evening, they were welcome to take a running jump for themselves.

They were hailed by W. C. Fields who, with Carlotta, occupied one of the front booths where the VIPs were always seated. Bogart was with them, nursing a gin martini.

Carole asked Bogart, "Where's Mayo?"

"At home in the kitchen with a piece of steak on her eye," said Bogart, flexing his fists.

Carole wasn't sure whether to believe him or not. It was usually Mayo who got the best of Bogart in battle. She packed a mean punch as Bogart himself freely bragged. Well, decided Carole, if it was Mayo nursing a black eye, Bogart must have snuck up on her and taken her by surprise. She said this to Bogart and he erupted with laughter. Then he admitted, "She's in the ladies' room fixing her face. You know her face. That'll take hours."

"Now, Bogey, don't be ungallant. Carlotta? What's that you're drinking? It looks delicious."

Fields spoke for Carlotta. "That's a pussy

café. It's French."

"It's *pousse* café," said Carlotta, and it came out purse cafe and Carole immediately lost interest.

The Gables' table was next to the Fields' booth and Bogie asked them about Mike Lynton's murder.

Herb asked, "Is it already being noised abroad?"

"Oh yeah," said Bogart, "it's all over town. Didn't you tune in Louella? It was her big item on tonight's broadcast. Hey, Hazel, you give her the scoop?"

"If I'm blushing, the answer is yes," said Hazel while examining her face in the mirror of her compact.

"Knifed in the chest, eh?" said Bogart. "Hey, Herb, shouldn't you be out sniffing for suspects?"

Herb said, "After dinner. I've sent a crew to the casino to interview the employees. They'll get nothing out of them, but I like to go through the motions."

Bogie persisted, "You don't think he was knifed on the premises?"

"If he was, we'd have the suspect in protective custody. Mike's men would have made hash of him."

"He? Him?" repeated Carole. "Couldn't it have been a woman?"

Gable asked her, "Offering yourself as a suspect?"

"Don't be silly, Pappy. I have an iron-clad alibi. I was with you and the boys until we left for Miriam's. Poor Mike. I don't suppose a woman could have made that awful wound."

"If she was angry enough," said Herb. "Don't underestimate the strength of your sex, Carole. An uncontrollable temper can turn any woman into a killing machine."

"And here she comes now," said Bogart as Mayo arrived from the powder room, greeted everyone, and was impressed to hear Carl Arden was an FBI man.

"Where's my drink?" she demanded of Bogart.

"I guess the waiter didn't think you were coming back. You usually don't when you take a powder for the powder." He winked at Gable.

"I saw that wink! What was that all about?"

"Just an innocent flirtation. Here, have my martini. I haven't touched it."

"I don't want your goddamn martini, I want my own."

Carole said with a sigh, "Here we go again." She yelled at Romanoff, who was at the bar conversing with a director, James

Whale. "Hey Mike, bring Mayo a martini or send for the riot squad."

Mayo said, "I don't find that funny."

Carole accepted the underlined challenge. "If you activated a sense of humor more often, you'd find it funny."

Mayo knew better than to lock horns with Carole Lombard. She had a nasty tongue and the sharpest nails in town. Anyway Mike Romanoff was hurrying to them with Mayo's martini. A waiter followed him. Mayo wisely changed the subject. "The powder room's abuzz with Mike Lynton's murder. It seems to have taken everybody by surprise."

"You weren't surprised?" asked Herb Villon.

"I'm never surprised when a man has as many enemies as Lynton had. I liked him. I'll miss him. He had manners, unlike a lot of hoodlums in this town."

Carole rose to the defense of the so-called hoodlums of Hollywood. "My pappy and my ex have perfect manners. And right here at this table so do Herb and Jim." The waiter was busy scribbling everyone's order but drank in every word that came popping out of the Lombard mouth. "I don't know what I'm carrying on about. Mayo, why are you so cantankerous? You're a lovely broad and a damned good actress. You're married to a sweetheart —"

"Ha!" interjected Mayo.

"Anyone who has the good taste to flirt with my husband is a sweetheart! Hee hee hee." She couldn't ever imagine Gable locked in the arms of another man, except for his father when Gable was an infant.

"Cut that out!" said Gable.

"Now Pappy," cautioned Carole, "don't start suspecting you're losing your masculinity like the dykes often do." She noticed Mayo didn't thank Romanoff for dutifully and swiftly delivering her martini. Thought Carole, Talk about a lack of manners.

Herb had Mayo on a hook and he enjoyed the thought of her wiggling. "Mayo, what do you know about Mike Lynton's enemies?"

Mayo was unruffled. "It stands to reason he has them. There's half the population who can't pay up their gambling debts."

"Which half?" asked Bogart. He said to Herb, "I suppose it's a matter of separating the riff from the raff."

"He most certainly had enemies," Herb confirmed. "There was never a reason for me to ask him who they were and he never called on me for help in the threat department. But he was involved with Lydia Austin . . ."

"Oh poor Lydia," moaned Carole, remembering again that one of her protégées was among the missing.

Mayo said, "I always thought he was kind of sweet on her."

"Lots of guys were sweet on her," said Herb. "Lydia got around and made no bones about it. The only guy that I know she slipped up on was Cesar Romero."

"Oh poor Butch" — Romero's nickname — "he must have dated her because he needed a beard. I'll bet that's when they went out with Ty Power." Carole asked the table, "Why do queer guys think if they're seen in public with a beautiful broad, that'll take the curse off the gossip?"

Gable hoped she wasn't going to dissertate on her short period as Russ Columbo's beard. He'd heard it too often and it had begun to nauseate him. Back in 1930 there had spread a rumor that Clark had permitted the once popular actor William Haines to service him in his dressing room at Metro. It was also rumored that Gable had caused George Cukor to be fired from *Gone With the Wind* because Haines, Cukor's close friend at the time, blabbed to Cukor, who in turn took up the blab slack and spread the ugly word.

Bogart asked Herb Villon, "Got any suspicions you can share with us?"

"It's too soon in a murder case to share

anything. Hazel, what the hell are you scribbling in that pad of yours?"

"Anything I think is usable," snapped Hazel.

"You mean salable," said Mayo.

Carl Arden's brain was whirling. The banter at the two tables was all too fast for him. This wasn't like Washington where the men dressed like floor walkers and had floor walker mentalities.

Carole asked Arden, "I think your mind's wandering. Don't let it wander too far, it might get lost."

Arden admitted, "You're all too quick for me."

Bogart said, "I think Lynton's killer was too quick for him. He wasn't murdered in his casino, eh? But he was found floating in the ocean. Doing the dead man's crawl?"

"Not funny," said Mayo. Carole resisted asking Mayo how she would know. The poor thing. Rarely gets acting jobs though she's damned good, and refuses to settle for the oblivion of marriage. Hell, Bogart's a great catch. She should be making the most of him.

Villon said, "Mike was probably on someone else's boat."

"Whose boat?" asked Carl Arden.

"Carl, if I knew whose boat, then I'd have

a promising suspect." Herb noticed that Romanoff and the drinkers at the bar were huddled around the bartender's small radio. "I wonder what's up at the bar?" Jim volunteered to find out. He had seen Oscar Levitt and Nana Lewis come in and ushered to no man's land, the tables in the rear of the restaurant. He felt the urge to gloat and could see Oscar trying to cajole a better table out of the headwaiter. The headwaiter was adamant. Oscar had no reservation. This was the best the headwaiter could do, also implying that Oscar was free to try his luck elsewhere.

Jim spoke with Romanoff and then returned to his group.

"What's up?" asked Herb.

"A Japanese ship was sunk. They think it was hit by one of the phantoms patrolling the area undercover. The *Sarita Maru*." Herb stared at Carl Arden. That was the name of the steamer transporting Takameshuga and entourage back to Japan.

"Any survivors?" asked Arden.

"There didn't seem to be any," said Mallory.

Carl Arden didn't try to hide his very pleased smile.

EIGHT

The radio never gave a latitude and a longitude when a ship was lost. Broadcasting executives assumed their listeners didn't know one from the other and they were probably right. The *Sarita Maru* was sunk in Japanese waters, at Japan's front door, and the Japanese hierarchy didn't like it. They didn't know for sure if it was an American phantom that had done the job but only U.S. phantoms were known to patrol the waters. The Japanese were equally derelict with their own spy ships. Earlier that year one had arrived at the North Shore of Long Island with engine trouble. The crew calmly went about repairing the motor despite knowing they were under the surveillance of the U.S. coast guard. The incident was kept from the media, and the submarine cast off, leaving behind only an oil slick.

Carl Arden shared this information authoritatively while some at the table worried about this vulnerability, the easy access the Japanese and probably the Germans had to America's coast lines.

"Sayyy!" cried Carole. "Do you suppose

the Japanese were spying on us when Mike Lynton's body cruised in?"

Carl Arden said simply, "Probably." The word gave Carole and the others cold comfort. The war in Europe was escalating. Poland had fallen to the Nazis, and France, it was predicted, was next in line despite their supposedly impenetrable Maginot Line, which one American general likened to a tinker toy construction. Carole worried about Clark. Though he was almost forty, she knew he wouldn't resist the lure of the air force and would enlist at the earliest possible moment should America be forced into the war. He had already been involved in several wars, the Civil War in *Gone With the Wind*, the World War in *Hell Below*, Chinese pirates in *China Seas*, to name the more prominent ones. She'd think by now he'd had enough of war. She looked at Gable with an expression reflecting a powerful love. Bogart saw the look and envied Gable. If Mayo looked at him that way, she'd be measuring the distance between him and the vase she was preparing to send hurtling in his direction. Mayo also saw the look on Carole's face and dismissed it as a foolish fancy. Only Clark was oblivious to the way Carole looked at him. He was too involved with Herb, Jim, and Carl Arden, going from the subject of the *Sarita Maru* to Mike Lynton's murder to the joys of hunting as though he were bobbing for apples. In between he attacked the T-bone steak he had ordered while Carole toyed with her chef's salad. She was scheduled to start shooting *Mr. and Mrs. Smith* in a few weeks and for the past month she'd been stuffing herself with everything placed before her.

Now her mind dwelt on the *Sarita Maru* and the watery grave of Ito Takameshuga. She sought Carl Arden's ear. "Carl, the sinking of the *Sarita Maru* doesn't end it for you, does it."

"Not by a long shot. There's a lot of investigating to be done out here." He leaned toward her and lowered his voice. "We have to avoid any possible sabotage."

"Oh?"

"It's no secret so I'm able to tell you there are a lot of Japanese agents and sympathizers at large in California."

She asked innocently, "How much of at large?"

"Do you have a Japanese gardener? A pool man? A laundress?"

"We have one of each." She felt a bead of perspiration trickling down her spine. Those three could be a threat? But they were lovely people. They had charming families. The

laundress frequently brought her grand-
children to the ranch. True, they were little
devils but a swift boot to their rear ends
calmed the imps down. She said to Arden,
"Are you telling me to trust no one who is
Japanese?"

"Of course they'll do you no harm. But
should you suddenly discover they've disappeared . . ." He said nothing further. Nothing more needed to be said. He speared a
slice of tomato, consigned it to his ample
mouth, and chewed contentedly, like one of
their horses.

Hazel had been eavesdropping and Carl
Arden reminded her of radio newscaster
Gabriel Heatter, who had been labeled a
warmonger. He was always warning the na-
tion to prepare because he knew the U.S.
was not prepared for any conflict should one
arise. Hazel said to Carole, "Carl makes
making movies seem very unimportant.
What's the matter? Still worried about Lydia
Austin?"

"I've got this feeling that there's a link
between her disappearance and Mike Lynton's murder. I wish those damn fools would
quit discussing hunting and think about
hunting enemy agents."

"Now calm down, Carole. The enemy
isn't in the lobby of Grauman's Chinese."

"Oh yeah?" Carole was feisty again. "You got inside information? And how will you feel when you see Herb marching to a new kind of cadence?"

"I'll feel very proud."

"Who writes your corny dialogue?" Hazel said nothing. Carole was sorry for what she said. Her voice softened. "I'm sorry, Hazel. Herb's too old for a war."

"He's no older than Clark. Jim's the youngest among them."

"Oh poor Jim." Carole stared at Mallory across the table and then thought that with his luck he'd have flat feet. She wondered if Clark had flat feet. He had never mentioned it. Well, when the time came, if he didn't have flat feet, she'd flatten them for him.

In the rear of the restaurant Oscar Levitt returned from a trip to the bar. He apologized to Nana for staying away so long. "I was catching up on the sinking, the *Sarita Maru*."

"It was a tub," said Nana while pouring sugar into an iced tea.

"You know the boat?"

"Was on it once. Just before Takameshuga made his fadeout. He took me and Mala Anouk down to the pier for some clams. The ship was docked there and Mala was curious about it. He said he knew the captain. He sure did. The captain invited us aboard. He gave us the five cent tour. Most of the boat was restricted to visitors, but I didn't care. It gave me the creeps. The crew looked as though they hadn't bathed and shaved in weeks. It smelled something awful."

"Strange the Japanese would make their getaway on a tub like that."

"What I didn't say was that it looked like a tub. You know the old one, looks can be deceiving. I had a suspicion there were arms on the boat, like maybe a couple of cannons and some depth charges."

"You actually saw this?"

Nana said, "I didn't see anything. Like I said, the boat had a lot of restricted areas, restricted especially to civilians like us."

Oscar Levitt looked away from her to Carl Arden. "I wonder if we should tell this to Carl Arden."

"Why?"

"He's with the FBI, for crying out loud. He might value information like this."

"What information? I only mentioned a supposition. That and a dime will get you a bus ride to Anaheim." Levitt made a motion to rise and Nana put a hand over one of his. "Don't crash their party."

"I just want to tell Arden —"

"It can wait. Carole and a few of the others

saw us coming in. If they wanted us to join their party, they would have waved us over instead of letting that snotty headwaiter consign us to Antarctica."

Oscar sat back. "You know, I really don't get it. Why would the sinking of a tub like the *Sarita Maru* be newsworthy?"

"It's a maritime disaster, Maritime disasters are very popular. The newsreels love them. And some Japanese who were working in L.A. were rumored to be aboard." Oscar questioned her with a look. "Well, does anybody know for sure?"

Carole was coincidentally asking Carl Arden a similar question. Arden said, "It's a good excuse to send newsreel planes into the territory. Like when Amelia Earhart disappeared. Our planes had a field day searching for her. They photographed the entire area in that region of the Pacific."

"And you're going to tell me they were very revealing."

"I'll say they were very useful and let it rest at that."

"You're sure you can afford to take the time off to go hunting?"

"I can afford as much time as Herb Villon can."

"Good man, Herb. He looks after us celebrities. He protects us when we need protection, and when don't we need protection. Hey! Here's Kay and, well I'll be darned. She's turned back the clock and found Herbert Marshall."

Carl Arden was impressed. "That's Herbert Marshall?"

Carole squinted. "Well, it used to be. Oh sure it's Herbert. Hey, come on over and have a drink. Herbert, this is Carl Arden, FBI."

"Very impressive," said Marshall dryly. "I suppose Kay's met everyone at Miriam's party."

Carole asked, "Why weren't you there?"

"Too much to do these days. No time for parties."

"But he found time for me," said Kay gaily. "Hasn't this been a day! A dead body and the sinking of a ship. I wonder if Lola Kramm foresaw any of this."

Herb said, "I wonder if she's foreseeing a brutal hangover tomorrow."

Carl Arden added innocently, "Maybe she's fighting off Carroll Righter."

"Why?" Carole was wondering if Kay and Herbert were picking up where they left off eight years ago. They both needed a shoulder to rest on. Marshall was recently divorced and Kay was doing the deadly free-lance bit. True, she'd landed some plum roles of late, not as a star, but as a supporting player. Still, the parts were good and her salary was as formidable as it had been at Warner Brothers. It took courage to swallow her pride and her ego and accept mother roles. By the same token she took to horseback in a Randolph Scott western, *When the Daltons Rode*, to be shown next year. Kay was one of Hollywood's shrewder actresses. She saved her money and invested wisely. As she had told Miriam earlier at the party, "They won't have to throw any benefits for me." Miriam wished she could say the same for herself. She was one of the smartest actresses in the business, but she had no money sense. She assumed she'd always be earning. Her Warners contract was very lucrative. And now she was to do *The Old Maid* with Bette Davis and was already plotting how to sabotage her co-star's performance.

Mike Romanoff came to personally escort Kay and Herbert to their excellent table in the center of the restaurant. They were two of his favorite people, highly civilized, highly intelligent, and he loved Kay for telling him when Warners had dropped her and he had commiserated, "Bless you, Mike, but don't wowwy about me. I'm a highly twained executive secretary," and she truly was.

Kay and Herbert took their leave of the

Gables and the others and followed Romanoff to the table he had prepared for them. It featured a bowl of gardenias and a grateful Kay kissed Romanoff's cheek. He always remembered her gardenias.

At the Gables' table, Hazel said to Carole. "I hope Kay's aware there's a very young lady in Herbert's life."

"Kay is aware of everything," said Carole. "They'll be singing no sad songs for Kay," little knowing that ten years in the future Miss Francis would be a hopeless alcoholic, and on her death would leave her millions to the Seeing Eye.

The Bogarts were having a heated conversation with W. C. Fields and Carlotta Monterey. Fields held sway, ignoring the corn flakes and milk Carlotta had ordered for him. "We have nothing to fear from Japan. My gardener, who is of the Oriental fraternity, assured me. He's in constant touch with his cousin, a samurai, whatever that is. Maybe it's a fraternal organization like the Elks or the Fallopians."

Mayo enlightened him. "The samurai are an order of ferocious warriors."

Fields pushed the corn flakes and milk aside with distaste. "I'll have an order of pot roast with very crisp potato pancakes, gravy on the side."

"You can't eat that sort of thing," Carlotta cautioned. "You must pay attention to your doctor."

Fields said to the Bogarts, "It seems I have this ulcer. When the doctor first told me I thought he said I had an ulster and I told him no I don't I have an ordinary overcoat. Waiter! Waiter! On the double." The waiter smiled at him. "You have lovely teeth," said Fields coldly. "Now bring me pot roast, very crisp potato pancakes, gravy on the side, and three cold bottles of Mexican beer." The waiter looked at Carlotta for corroboration, she having warned the staff a long time ago of Fields' odd and dangerous eating habits. Fields raised his cane and shouted, "I'll clobber both you conspirators. Fie and hie, varlet," he said to the waiter, "and be quick about it."

Mike Romanoff always cautioned the bartender about his radio. It was usually unnecessary, as the din in the room drowned the radio out. Every restaurant patronized by the movie crowd had a radio. It was a necessity because just about every columnist in Hollywood had a news program. Louella Parsons on Sunday night at nine was a must because she was followed at nine-fifteen by Walter Winchell's frenetic program. There was Jimmy Fidler's Hollywood, also a must, and numerous others. Now the habitués at the bar were engrossed in the news of Mike Lynton's murder.

Jack Warner, listening in his living room, was delighted the corpse had landed just off Miriam Hopkins' private beach. Just the mention of her name could stimulate box office for her coming opus, *Virginia City*, in which her sparring mate was young Errol Flynn.

Carole and Kay Francis joined the barflies and listened intently. The Mike Lynton item was followed by an update on the sinking of the *Sarita Maru*. While Carole was absorbed, Kay went back to her table. The news commentator seemed to relish his descriptions of limbless and decapitated bodies caused by the tremendous impact of a series of explosions. Nana Lewis's suspicions were right on the nose. There had been a tremendous store of explosives and ammunition in the ship's hold. Kay hurried back to her table to share the news with Herbert Marshall. Carole rejoined her group, eagerly sharing all the gruesome details.

Mayo Methot said, "Carole, you're so bloodthirsty!"

Carole rejoined swiftly, "That's something we have in common, hee hee hee!"

Clark asked Carl Arden, "Did you suspect

the ship was carrying all that ammo?"

"We didn't suspect. We knew." Arden crunched down on a stalk of celery. As he chewed, he spoke. "We had an informant on board. He was very good. We'll miss him."

"How cold-blooded!" said Carole.

Carl explained. "I didn't know him. I never met him. I never saw his photograph. To me he's just a cipher. I'm sorry he's dead, I'm always sorry when someone dies in the line of duty."

Carole asked, "Were you sorry for Amelia Earhart?"

"Amelia was a terrific gal."

Terrific gal, thought Carole, what a hell of an epitaph. She said, "I'll bet I'm right."

Clark patted her hand. "Sure you are, sweetheart."

"Don't you even want to know what I think I'm right about?"

"Sure, sweetheart, sure. You tell us."

Carole's temper was rising. "I'll tell you a lot of things if you continue patronizing me!" She zeroed in on Carl Arden. "Here's what I think! Blink once if I'm wrong, blink twice if I'm right. Earhart was following instructions when she landed on that island. There was nothing wrong with her plane. She feigned a crash landing so we'd have an excuse to send reconnaissance planes to look

for her. That's when they took all those pictures you people were so pleased with." Carl
Arden neither blinked once or twice nor
spoke. He continued munching away at the
celery while Carole folded her arms and sat
back. She knew she had scored. She knew
she was right and Carl Arden knew she was
right. Their eyes linked briefly and he
winked. She was grateful for that.

Herb Villon asked her, "Got any theories
as to who killed Mike Lynton?"

"Pulling my leg, Herb?"

He silently wished he could while he said,
"No I'm not. You've got a good, logical
mind. I have a feeling the solution to Mike's
killing would be a very simple one if I put
my mind to work. I know there's a connection to Lydia Austin's disappearance. It goes
back to when they were having an affair.
They both knew something then that was a
threat to someone and that someone decided
they were both expendable."

"You think Lydia's dead." Carole's voice
was hollow. Clark put an arm around her.

"Yes," said Herb, "I think she was killed
the day she disappeared."

Carole raged, "Why didn't you say so
then?"

"I was hoping I was wrong. I might still
be wrong, but why hasn't there been a peep

out of her kidnapper? It's a lot of trouble holding someone prisoner. There have to be accomplices."

Hazel spoke up. "Of course there are."

Carole snapped, "How do *you* know?"

"It's simple logic, Carole. If she's alive, she has to be fed. That calls for accomplices. Or at least an accomplice. Herb and I have discussed this at length."

"You also think she's dead." Carole's eyes seemed to be penetrating Hazel's skull. Hazel nodded. "And so does Oscar Levitt."

"Why?" It was so soft-spoken, the word seemed to have crept out of Herb's mouth as though it were on a clandestine mission.

"The way he told the reporters Nana Lewis would replace Lydia in the movie. There's still time before it starts shooting. Still time for Lydia to show up. But she's not going to show up. Everyone's so damn sure she won't." She said stubbornly, "Well, I think she's going to show up. So there!"

The waiter was clearing the table while waiting for coffee and dessert orders, not sure there would be any. The gaiety that had sparked the table earlier was gone. It's as though they had heard the studio system was about to collapse and with it their high styles of living, he thought. And also the generous tips he usually received. He agreed with his

mother, who phoned him frequently to remind him that life is not easy, don't take it
for granted.

Carole said, "I hate to be a party poop,
but I want to go home."

"Sure, sweetheart. I'll get the check," said
Clark. Carole kicked him under the table.
His eyes shut in pain. Carl Arden spoke up.
"Dinner's on me. I'm on an expense ac-
count. J. Edgar will be very impressed with
the guest list."

"He's always impressed by celebrities,"
snorted Carole, "that's why he's always investigating us, hee hee hee. Honest to God
the couple of times I met him when I was
in Washington, I marveled at the rate at
which he dropped names. Edgar's like an old
maid who checks under the bed every night
before she turns in. Afraid there'll be a bur-
glar under the bed and disappointed when
she doesn't find one. He still shacking up
with that what'shisname . . . Clyde Tol-
son?"

"They're the best of friends," said Carl
Arden swiftly while he selected some crisp
bills from his alligator-skin wallet.

"Hee hee hee. Why didn't you just say,
'No comment,' Carl?"

"Actually, I have a comment. Live and let
live, I say. To each his own."

The waiter picked up the bills and the check, thanked the FBI man politely, and then put a curse on him when the cashier pointed out Arden had left a meager tip.

Bogart looked at his wristwatch and said to Mayo, "Let's go home. I know it's early but we can spar a few rounds in the basement."

W. C. Fields was having a stomachache but didn't tell Carlotta. Jim Mallory was standing, looking to the rear of the restaurant. Nana Lewis and Oscar Levitt were gone. He hadn't seen them leave. For him, the day had not been a happy one.

In the beautifully appointed boudoir of her mansion, Miriam Hopkins reposed on the bed seductively, as she supposed Madame Récamier had done a couple of centuries ago in France. She said to Sammy and Roy, "Boys, it's better with your shoes off."

Before leaving the restaurant, Herb had a brief session with Mike Romanoff in Romanoff's booth near the bar. The Gables left shortly after the bill was paid as Gable could sense Carole was growing testy. He could see she was displeased with Carl Arden, upset by the unanimous opinion that Lydia Austin was dead, and very worried that there was another world war in their future. She wanted to abduct Clark and spirit him away and have him all to herself the way Paris had made off with Helen of Troy. But where could she hide with him? Where was safe? Desert islands were once romantic and remote but today they were infested with secret armies. She sighed. She supposed she could whisk him away to the offices of the William Morris Agency, the most powerful in the business. She'd been told often enough by Hollywood cynics nobody would find her there. Then realistically, she knew Clark Gable could never be sequestered anywhere by anyone. She spat out a nasty four-letter word.

"What was that for?" asked Clark, who had been enduring her unusually long bout of silence as he drove them home.

"That was for nothing," said Carole. She resumed brooding over Lydia Austin. She was one of Carole's kids. Carefully chosen along with the three others. And finally she was reminded of Mala Anouk.

"Oh God," she groaned.

"Now what?" asked Clark patiently.

"Mala Anouk. My poor little Eskimo. She must be very upset. She must have heard about the *Sarita Maru*."

"You're sure she knew Takameshuga was sailing on her?"

"I'm not sure of anything anymore. The only thing I'm sure of is we're legally married. We are, aren't we?"

"You're having a bad time, baby. I'm sorry."

"Don't be." She rearranged herself in the seat. "I've been too smug. Don't say I haven't. Smug smug smug. I knew in my heart Lydia was dead. She was just past twenty. Damn it! She was robbed of her lifetime! Like Dorothy Dell! Remember her? Nineteen when she was killed in that car crash. Paramount predicted big things for her. Oh, I can still hear her singing 'With My Eyes Wide Open I'm Dreaming.' " She burst into tears.

"Hey hey, kiddo. What is it? What's wrong?" He pulled to the side of the road and put his arm around her. Carole cried softly, unmindful of the damage to her mascara. She opened the glove compartment where there were tissues. She lowered her window, took some deep breaths, and cast a shy look at Clark.

"I'm sorry, Pappy. I've been holding it in too long. It's all piling up and heavy heavy lies over our heads. Thank God the kidnapping scare was just a scare. I'd been wondering for days how much I'd offer to pay if you were grabbed."

"Would you have offered much?"

"Don't you know to me you're worth double your weight in gold?" He kissed her gently. Then she was her old self again. "What would you have offered for me?"

"I'd have offered nothing until they proved you hadn't escaped."

"Hee hee hee; I'll bet I'd have escaped, but not until I was sure I was plastered on the front pages of every gazette from here to China! Oh, let's stop kidding around and go home." The car shot forward. "Well, I guess Nana Lewis gets her big break now."

"I wonder if she ever was mixed up with Mike Lynton."

"You know, from time to time I've been thinking the same thing. Remember that time we ran into her at the casino? She said she was alone. Stood to reason. She had no steady guy that I knew of. Lots of gals go places by themselves in this town. Pride goeth before a fall or some such crap." She stared out the window. "Nana always got around. She knew a lot of people. I once asked her jokingly could she spare some of her leftover contacts. And she said, 'Carole, I've got friends I haven't even used yet.' I'd have a talk with her, except I've had talks with her before. She talks but she doesn't offer much." She was thinking again. "It's still early, Pappy."

"What's on your mind?"

"I thought maybe we'd drop in on Mala and Nell Corday. Where does the idea grab you?"

It grabbed him. He headed for the Hollywood hills.

"So?" said Hazel to Herb Villon, who wasn't liking Jim Mallory's driving at all. Neither did Carl Arden, in the back seat with Hazel. She was hunched forward to hear what Herb would have to say if he said anything. To Arden, Hazel's position reminded him of girls when he was a teenager, girls who were expecting a necking session and frequently were disappointed. Carl wasn't highly sexed, which didn't surprise or disappoint him in the least. It was fine by his wife, who'd rather wrestle with a book than her husband. Both of them married each other because it was expected that they would marry each other. When his wife became pregnant her sister remarked snidely, "She's pregnant probably because neither one of them was paying attention."

"So?" said Hazel again, now insistent, bearing down on the word.

"So what?" he finally responded.

"Mike Romanoff."

"What about him?"

"What did he tell you?"

"When?"

Hazel was losing patience, and when lost, it would stay lost. She rarely went in search of it. "At the bar. Before we left."

"Now, Hazel, you know better than to expect me to share privileged information."

Hazel was bristling. "Privileged information is between lawyer and client, doctor and patient. Not between restaurant owner and detective."

"Hazel, when are you going to learn to think before you speak?"

A trace of a smile appeared on Jim Mallory's face and Herb felt better. Jim was obviously unhappy about the way the day had gone. Nana proves to be a washout, Mike Lynton is murdered, and Herb treats it so matter-of-factly, or seemingly so, that Jim was wondering if Herb was burned out. Herb was convinced Lynton wasn't murdered at his casino, but still he should have gone directly there to conduct the questioning of the staff instead of going off to Romanoff's. Herb had long ago mastered the art of reading Jim Mallory's mind and was prepared to pacify him if pacifying was still called for.

Herb was thinking that Hazel should have

known he preferred not to relay information in front of Carl Arden. Arden would find out what he wanted to know in due time, if there was anything he wanted to know. Meanwhile he preferred keeping the FBI man at arm's length. Herb didn't know who Arden knew in Hollywood and might deliberately or inadvertently relay information to. He then dwelled on Carole and her free-wheeling attitudes. She gave much better than she got and was a hell of a lot smarter than her husband. Anybody was a hell of a lot smarter than her husband. Herb didn't want to go hunting. He loathed hunting animals that weren't two-legged, but Clark was so anxious to round up a larger hunting party than was available to him, he decided to pitch in and offer his and Jim's company. Of course, Hazel had to shoehorn her way in. Carole will go berserk listening to Hazel while the men were away hunting. Hunting. What a laugh. The only one among them who would get an animal in his sight would be Gable. He wasn't sure about Carl Arden.

"You do much hunting, Carl?" Herb asked nonchalantly.

"Haven't stalked a wild animal in years."

"Then why'd you agree to join the hunt?"

"I couldn't turn down an invitation from Clark Gable." Arden didn't see Jim's jaw drop. Herb blinked his eyes like a semaphor out of control. Hazel concentrated on the scenery out her window. "Carl," said Herb, "you'd be surprised how many men have turned down Clark Gable's invitations."

"But aha!" cried Hazel, sounding like comedienne Fanny Brice doing one of her routines. "Few women have turned him down!"

"Yes, I heard about his reputation back in Washington. But I guess Carole has got him tamed now."

"Try telling that to Carole," said Hazel dryly. "Like so many married ladies in this town, she grins and bears it, a past mistress at the gentle art of biting the bullet."

"I think she's a great gal," said Arden.

Herb was thinking, There are squares and there are squares, but there are no squares like a square square.

Mala Anouk and Nell Corday were delighted by Carole and Clark's surprise visit. A pot of coffee was brewing in the kitchen and Mala Anouk hastened to serve blubber cookies from her grandmother's original recipe. Yes, they had heard about the *Sarita Maru* on the radio and Mala said the news saddened them both. Carole wondered why the strange look on Nell Corday's face, little knowing Nell loathed Ito Takameshuga.

Carole asked, "You knew Takameshuga had sailed on the ship, Mala?"

"Yes."

"Why didn't you tell the authorities when you knew they thought he might be kidnapped?"

"Tacky swore me to secrecy. He liked me to call him Tacky."

Carole told the girls that it was likely that Lydia Austin was dead.

"We decided that several days ago," said Nell. "Oops! The coffee's boiling over!" She fled to the kitchen.

"Nana's got Lydia's part in the picture. It's official."

"I'm very happy for her," Mala said unenthusiastically. Carole wondered if any of the girls really liked each other. Circumstances had brought them together under one roof and they were apparently making the best of it. Carole was sure Nana Lewis would find a place of her own once the picture was shooting. She was the only one of the girls making steady money at Columbia Pictures but what would have gone toward rent ended up on her back. That was no bargain basement number she was wearing tonight.

Mala said, "That must have been quite a shock at the party when Mike Lynton's body came drifting in."

"Yes," said Carole, "a macabre way of crashing a party."

They heard the unoiled wheels of a cart bearing coffee and blubber cookies. "Ah! I'll pour!" said Mala.

Carole was thinking of saying, And you take the first bite of a blubber cookie, but thought better of it. Everyone took their coffee black which made it easier for Mala. Nell passed around the plate of cookies.

Clark decided the polite thing to do was to take a cookie. Mala had told him a long time ago she was a big fan of his and the least he could do for a big fan was eat one of her blubber cookies. The cookies were shaped like bagels with a hole in the center. Carole examined her cookie with suspicion. She expected water to come spurting out at her as from a whale's funnel.

"They're so crisp and tasty," said Carole, despite the fact that cookie was flat and tasteless. There were so many things she wanted to ask the girls while fearing some of the answers she would receive. Why weren't their faces tear-stained, especially Mala's? Wasn't she affected by the deaths of Takameshuga and Lydia? Carole had wept, not for the Japanese whom she didn't know, but for Lydia. In for a penny, in for a pound. "How well did Lydia know Tacky?" It amused her to use what she was sure was a very appropriate nickname.

"I introduced them," said Mala.

"I assumed that. But how well did she know him?"

Mala placed her coffee cup on the saucer and set them aside. "What you're really asking me is did Lydia go away to be with him? Neither one of them confided things like that to me so I don't know."

"But you think they did." Clark had to hand it to his girl. She was as tenacious as a bulldog refusing to give up a bone.

"I've never given it any thought."

"Hee hee hee." Now the giggle was phony. "I'll bet you have. Weren't you sweet on Tacky?"

"Oh no." She said it too fast, making Carole even more suspicious. "Tacky was a friend of my aunt."

"Oh of course. Your aunt. The one who attended university in Tokyo. She taught you the tea ritual. How come we're not having tea tonight?"

"Because the coffee was already on the stove."

"Very practical."

"Would you prefer tea? I can prepare it in a jiffy."

"Goodness no, the coffee's just dandy.

Isn't the coffee dandy, Pappy?"

"Real dandy."

Carole insisted wickedly, "You haven't touched your blubber cookie."

"I had too much dinner." He said with menace in his voice, "I'll get to the cookie."

"Mala, it suddenly occurred to me. Is your aunt still in Japan?"

"Yes. She loves it there."

"Really? But aren't Japanese women subservient to their men? I read somewhere the men order their women around and if they get any backtalk, they belt them."

"Oh yes!" said Mala jovially. "It is the same with Eskimo women. We live to serve our men. After all, they do the hunting and the fishing and protect us from polar bears and other dangers. The least we can do is look up to and honor them. When my father's boots are frozen, my mother chews them until the leather is soft again and he can wear them to go hunting."

"No!" Carole looked at Clark. Fat chance he'd ever get her to chew his smelly boots back into condition. She hoped Mala wasn't giving him any ideas. "Are you still planning to go back to the Antarctic?"

"Oh yes. I will bring my money to my people and to my future husband."

"Husband? You got a boyfriend up there?"

Carole envisioned some poor slob stamping his feet and flagellating himself in a ferocious snowstorm to keep warm while waiting for his sweetie to get back with some cash and her strong teeth to gnaw away at his boots.

"I have lots of suitors!" said Mala joyously, making Nell feel like a perennial wallflower. "I will pick and choose when I get back."

"And once you've chosen and get married, or whatever's the custom, you plan to set up housekeeping in an igloo?"

Mala said haughtily. "Igloos are for peasants. We shall have a log cabin."

"How adorable," said Carole, "just like Abraham Lincoln."

"More coffee?" asked Nell. The Gables refused.

Carole asked, "Your aunt will be very upset when she hears of Takameshuga's death. In fact she's probably heard of it by now."

Mala said through a small smile, "We are not a very emotional people. We are taught as children to accept death as inevitable and beautiful. My people do not know of heaven and hell. When one shuts one's eyes forever, it is assumed there was a departure to a higher level."

"Oh of course," said Carole, "like going from Monogram movie cheapies to the lush surroundings at MGM. How cute. Is your aunt married?"

"Which one? I have a dozen."

Carole was awestruck. "I can see your grandmother never heard of birth control."

"Oh yes. The missionaries always lectured on birth control. My grandmother took them very seriously. Otherwise I would have two dozen aunts."

"Did you hear that, Pappy? Imagine having to cope with that every Christmas." Clark knew she was after something and wished she'd hurry up and get to it. He wanted to go home to the ranch and have a nightcap and then get to bed. Carole was saying to Mala, "Your aunt in Japan. Is she married?"

Mala looked into her coffee cup as though expecting to find the answer there. She said, "She is not married now."

"Oh. But she was married. That's why she stayed in Japan."

"What I meant was that she is not married."

"Mala?"

"Yes, Carole?"

"If you're a big success in America, making lots of pictures and lots of money, will you change your mind about going back up there?"

"Up there is the Arctic Circle. Down there is the Antarctic."

"Hee hee hee. I always get those things screwed up, don't I, Pappy?"

"Why baby, you're one of the greatest screwer-uppers in the business. And I'm tired." He said to Mala and Nell, "I hope you didn't mind our dropping in on you unannounced. But Carole was worried you'd be upset by all the bad news."

Mala said to Carole, "You're always so thoughtful. You're so good to us. How can we ever repay you?"

"Just have some success so I'll know I didn't work in vain. Now don't stay up all night chewing the rag." She stood up and followed Gable to the front door.

"Wait!" cried Mala. The Gables froze in their tracks. Mala rushed into the kitchen. Nell Corday had left her seat and stood against the wall near the front door. Mala was back with a paper bag, which she held out to Carole. "Blubber cookies for you to take home!"

"Oh marvy," said Carole as she took the bag. "We'll think of you with every bite we take."

Clark held the door open. It was a beautiful star-filled night, back in the days when stars weren't camouflaged behind the deadly Los Angeles smog. The Gables said their good nights and Nell closed the front door and leaned against it.

"Now what the hell was *that* all about?" she asked Mala.

Mala said nothing and sank into an easy chair. "They were just being thoughtful. Carole is always thoughtful."

"Yeah," said Nell, "it's like a hobby," and she set about clearing the coffee cups and saucers. "Gable didn't eat his blubber cookie." Then under her breath, out of Mala's earshot, "The coward."

Behind the steering wheel of the Cadillac, Gable listened contentedly to the purring motor, then asked Carole, "What was that all about?"

"What was what all about?"

"The third degree."

"Oh? Did it sound like I was giving Mala the third degree?"

"You weren't giving her a blood transfusion. Though for a while there she got so pale I thought a transfusion might be called for. Why are you so interested in her aunt?"

"Because I remember Mala telling us her aunt went to college in Tokyo. It occurred to me auntie fixed it for Takameshuga to meet up with Mala."

"And?"

"And so they spent a lot of time together."

"You trying to tell me they were a romance?"

"Not at all, Pappy. If old Tacky had a romance it was probably with Lydia."

"Possibly."

"Probably." Carole bore down on the word. "Orientals have a taste for Caucasian women. When Sessue Hayakawa was at Paramount making *Daughter of the Dragon*, he used to drive us nuts making passes."

"That's Sessue Hayakawa. That's not every Oriental."

"Making out with a Caucasian woman gives them status. Haven't you heard of white slavery?"

"Oh for crying out loud!"

"Don't you oh-for-crying-out-loud me. White slavery is still a thriving trade in the Orient. Booking agents ship American girl singers and dancers to the Far East all the time. The bait is great salaries in American dollars. Once the girls get settled in, there's no night club engagements, no American dollars, just good old prostitution. And there's no way out for the poor kids so they settle in and try to make the most of it. Some commit suicide." Gable snorted. "Well, that's what Anna May Wong told me and Anna May always has the facts. So there."

Anna May Wong was the only Chinese

actress to make it to the top in American films, yet occasionally she had to make do with work in England and France. She had terrific international connections as a result and frequently made use of them. When under contract to Paramount, she and Carole became good friends and lunched frequently in Carole's dressing room.

Clark sighed and said, "It seems your Lydia really got around."

"It seems she did," said Carole. "I get the impression Lydia wasn't too particular about where she placed her lips."

Clark chuckled. "You certainly have a way with words lately, baby."

"What do you mean 'lately'? I always say what's on my mind and you know it. Remember that line of Paulette Goddard's in *The Women*?" She mimicked Goddard perfectly. " 'Where I spit, no grass grows ever.' "

"Now what's really on your mind about Mala's aunt?"

"Ohhhh," said Carole, drawing out the word like she occasionally did with chewing gum. "I have a suspicion auntie is a very recent widow."

Came the dawn and Clark asked, "Takameshuga?"

"It's a possibility." She was very pleased with herself.

NINE

"I should have guessed that's what you were after, the way you kept harping on the aunt. Well, you did a damned good job."

Carole pinched his cheek. "Thank you, Pappy. And," she added with pride, "I had absolutely no preparation. You tell that to Carl Arden."

"So it's right to assume all ten of the Japanese were secret agents." He almost said "enemy agents." He thought that from the way things were shaping up "enemy agent" would very soon be the appropriate terminology.

"No matter how you slice it, agents of any kind are a crummy lot."

"I thought you were very fond of Myron." Myron Selznick, David O.'s brother, was a very powerful figure in the film world.

"Yes I'm very fond of him. He's rarely sober. His drinking is getting worse. He's up there in an exclusive class with John Barrymore and Bill Fields." And she sadly recognized it was a class from which none of them would graduate.

"You going to share what you suspect

about Mala's aunt with Carl Arden?"

"Of course. It's my patriotic duty. I hope he knows something about hunting. I'd hate to see you ending up with a bullet up your backside."

Gable laughed. Then he said, "There's something strange about Carl Arden."

"There usually is about government issue. Herb Villon seemed to like him." She groaned. "Do we have to take Hazel with us?"

"No point in shutting the barn door. The cow's already left."

"The older she gets, the pushier she gets."

"She's a frustrated spinster. She wants a ring on her wedding finger and a ring through Herb Villon's nose."

"If Herb Villon hasn't married her by now, he never will. I hope he and Jim Mallory know from which end of the rifle the bullet comes out. How come you didn't ask Otto Winkler?" Winkler was Carole's press agent.

"I did. He begged off. Too busy preparing for the festivities in Atlanta." After a moment he said heatedly, "Jesus, I wish we didn't have to go. Can't you think of some excuse to get us out of it?"

"I will not! I want to go to Atlanta. I want to see you feted and honored. And don't you dare let the ladies upstage you." The ladies were his co-stars, Vivien Leigh and Olivia de Havilland. "Pappy, we're not talking about Mike Lynton."

"Do we have to?"

"You go back a long ways with him."

"I go back a long ways with a lot of people. Do you hear me discussing them?"

"I wonder where Oscar Levitt all of a sudden raised the money for his budget. A few weeks ago he was having trouble. He put the touch on me. I'll think about it, I told him."

"And have you thought about it?"

"I'm still thinking."

"You'll have to give him something. He's given the lead to Nana Lewis, she's your girl."

"So's Lydia." She couldn't use the past tense referring to Lydia. She still had hopes the young actress would turn up alive.

"Now don't start crying again."

"I won't. I'm fresh out of tears. But Mike Lynton is nagging at me."

"Tell him to go away."

"I don't want him to go away. He was always good company."

"I thought you said your romance with him wasn't serious."

"That's right, it wasn't serious. But he was good company. He liked all the things you don't like. Opera, ballet, concerts, and good books."

"When I was a kid I read *Tom Sawyer* and *Treasure Island*."

"Big deal. What do you suppose could lure Mike Lynton to somebody else's boat?"

Clark said whimsically, "Cherchez la femme."

"Some broad, eh? In this town, there's a wide variety to choose from. Pappy, I wonder if Mike Lynton might have been onto something."

"What do you mean?"

"Like maybe he was getting wise to Takameshuga."

"Tacky's out of town. Way out of town. Try another theory."

"Not yet. I kind of like this one. Tacky might have left behind instructions to do something for him."

"Left instructions to do what and to whom?"

"Left instructions to get rid of Mike Lynton."

Clark was getting exasperated. "For what damn reason?"

"How the hell do I know? I'm not Philo Vance. Gee, Bill was great in his Philo Vance pictures." She thought for a moment and said, "Phyllis Vance. I could play a detective named Phyllis Vance! There haven't been enough women detectives on the screen!"

"Edna May was terrific as Hildegarde Withers."

"Name another one," said Carole defiantly. "Yah yah yah. You can't!"

"Phyllis Vance." Clark repeated the name a few more times. It was growing on him. "You know, it's not such a crazy idea. Maybe we can commission a script. Work up an independent deal. I really like the idea!"

He liked the idea and now Carole was sorry she broached it. He'd worry the idea for weeks, driving her nuts. Clark had no talent for following through. If there was any work to be done, it would be Carole who would have to do it. Why hadn't he worked that hard on Selznick to give her Scarlett O'Hara? She changed the subject. She went back to Mike Lynton. "Maybe Mike knew something that it was dangerous for him to know."

"Like what?"

"How the hell do I know? I'm just talking off the top of my head."

"It's real pretty."

"What is?"

"The top of your head."

After dropping Carl Arden at his hotel, Herb, Jim, and Hazel went to Mike Lynton's casino. Herb checked the precinct and they told him the men he had assigned to question the staff were still on the job. Herb was told they hadn't learned anything of much use, which stirred him to action. And when they got to the casino, it was as Herb feared. There were reporters and cameramen swarming all over the grounds. When they recognized Herb, he was under siege. He had nothing to tell them because he knew about as much as they did. All they got at the beach were shots of the dead man and of the numerous celebrities. The photographers who took close shots of Miriam were warned to airbrush them or else.

Herb led the way into the casino. His men were interrogating the employees in Mike's office and Herb led the way there. He learned very little from his fellow officers, who had learned very little from the staff except for one detective who had the hatcheck girl's home phone number. He was Jim Mallory's role model. Another detective informed Herb that Carole Lombard was trying to reach him. The message was relayed to the casino from the precinct. She must have called shortly after he checked in, Herb told Mallory. Hazel volunteered to phone Carole for him and Herb advised her he knew how to dial and she was to remember to stay out of police affairs.

There was another office next to Lynton's. Herb entered it, was satisfied it was unoccupied, sat at the desk, and phoned Carole. She told him about what she thought she had learned from Mala Anouk. Clark wondered if out there in Tokyo Mala's aunt's ears were burning, but not knowing the difference in time he couldn't be sure if she was awake or asleep. Herb commended Carole on a job well done. He assured her he knew one end of a rifle from the other and this eased Carole's mind somewhat.

Herb placed the phone back in its cradle. The few bits and pieces he had learned that day he could now weld to Carole's information. He couldn't shake his belief that Lynton and Lydia Austin were privy to dangerous information. Mala's aunt and the possibility that she was Takameshuga's widow added fuel to the fire in his mind. Carole's suspicion that Lydia and the Japanese had had a brief liaison also made sense. He wished he had met Lydia. There was a lot to do. He saw little point in continuing the questioning of Lynton's staff. There was no reason for them to know anything and Lynton didn't have a private secretary. Few racketeers did unless the private secretary in question doubled as mistress. There was a lot of that going around in certain circles, but not in

Villon's immediate vicinity.

He didn't relish having to tell Groucho Marx that all roads led to the unhappy fact that Lydia Austin was probably dead. It might have astonished Herb to find out Groucho had come to this sad conclusion on his own. While Herb sat in the office talking on the phone to Carole, Groucho Marx sat on a bench in a synagogue on Fairfax Avenue. He wore a yarmulke and in his mouth was an unlit cigar. There were a few other silent worshipers in the temple, and if any of them recognized Groucho, they didn't invade his private thoughts. He might be saying a prayer for either or both of his parents and so most certainly his privacy was to be respected. Groucho was now the Julius of his late teens when his gargoyle of a mother, Minnie, convinced him and three of his four brothers to form a vaudeville act. She could provide the foot inside vaudeville's door they needed. Her brother was Al Shean of the celebrated vaudeville team Gallagher and Shean, and they certainly had powerful connections. Groucho wished Minnie was alive and sitting next to him, though she had little use in her lifetime for *shuls* unless they were planning a gala and might hire her boys to entertain. Minnie would help with the prayer he was trying to formulate in his mind. It was little known that Groucho was a talented writer. He had recently completed a play, and the play had come easily to him. But he couldn't think of any words for the prayer. Minnie was terrific with prayers and curses, and even better with threats. Tough vaudeville bookers turned to aspic when she vented her wrath. What would she have come up with for Lydia, he wondered. And then what might have been her prayer began to circle his head like the revolving electric sign circling the Times tower in New York's Times Square. "She was a pretty girl with talent. She might have become a movie star or settled down to be a good wife and a good mother. The children would have favored her with their beautiful looks. They would have inherited the Marx brains. All in all, not too bad for Julius marrying the *shiksa*."

There'd be no marrying anyone in the near future. Groucho used his jacket sleeve to wipe his eyes. He was crying for Lydia. It made him feel good. It was nice to cry for someone. It didn't happen too often in his life.

Clark Gable was probably the only Hollywood celebrity who went hunting in a Cadillac. In the car with him he had Carl Arden at his side and Oscar Levitt in the back seat.

Jim was driving the van which held Carole, Herb, and Hazel. There were also three hunting dogs that Carole introduced as Patty, Maxene, and LaVerne, named for her favorite singing trio, the Andrews Sisters. This despite the fact that LaVerne (the dog) was a male and constantly sniffing around the other two. Carole explained to the others that it didn't matter if dogs were incestuous. They were keeping it in the family. In the van the Lynton case was discussed at great length. Herb had finally shared with Hazel Carole's suspicions about Mala's aunt being Takameshuga's widow. Hazel thought it made sense but was cautioned not to feed the information to any columnist. Herb wanted everything kept under wraps.

Jim Mallory admired the vehicle he was driving, which was more like a caravan on wheels than an ordinary trailer. It had once been Clark's dressing room suite at Metro but with the part of Rhett Butler came an even more opulent caravan and Carole insisted Clark commandeer and refit the one in which she was now riding. They were headed south to a heavily wooded area near the Salton Sea, California's inland body of water.

While talking with Herb, Carole checked and checked and then rechecked the food and liquor supplies. There were roasted chickens, a variety of pâtés, expensive cheeses, bread and biscuits, all forms of liquor, and cokes and other soft drinks. It would be a cold repast but a very sumptuous one. Nothing as spare and simple as what Daniel Boone brought along on a hunting trip.

In the Cadillac, Clark was wishing the weather was better. Clouds dominated the sky and he said if it was going to rain, they should have planned on hunting for ducks. But ducks meant rising at two or three A.M., setting out blinds near a marshy area, and then sitting in the damp and cramped blinds blowing on instruments that simulated ducks quacking and geese honking. Carl Arden was openly glad they weren't after fowl that morning. He passed around a flask of brandy. Clark warned him to go easy on the stuff. Hunting deer required a clear head and good eyesight.

The previous evening, while Clark prepared the weapons and ammunition, he and Carole had discussed in which direction Clark should lead the talk about Lynton's murder and the possibility of Lydia's having suffered a similar fate. Carl was prepared to be bombarded with questions and suppositions. He'd been advised by J. Edgar Hoover in Washington during a long conversation the previous day. Hoover was pleased with what Arden had learned from Carole and was impressed that a mere actress could have such an analytical brain.

"Tell me, Carl," asked Clark, "what are the laws governing the conduct of agents for hire by foreign nations?"

Carl cleared his throat and expostulated. The ball was in his court and he enjoyed running with it. "American agents in the employ of foreign powers must register with the Bureau. They must list in detail exactly what they've been contracted to do."

"They aren't looked upon as subversives? You know, acting against the best interests of the U.S.?"

"Professional agents, although they are always walking a thin line, do their damnedest to keep from being suspected as spies. These people are mostly hired to lobby business interests, investments, that sort of thing."

"What happens if they find out things they really shouldn't know?"

"They'd damn well better let us know about it or face arrest, a trial, and being stood up against a wall and shot."

Clark said, "A lot of people get away with it though, don't they?"

"Mostly those who defect or try to. We

haven't had much of that lately. I had a long session with Herb Villon yesterday." His laugh sounded like a gargle. "Good man, Herb, real good man."

"Yes," agreed Clark, "he's aces." It felt as though he was doing a scene in an espionage movie, with Carl Arden being played by Walter Pidgeon, the only actor in Hollywood who had the addresses of every important whorehouse and madam in the United States, Canada, and Mexico.

Carl said to Oscar Levitt, "Carole says you know how to keep your mouth shut."

Oscar said, "Carole should know. She's shut it often enough for me. She chewed me out on the phone for announcing Nana Lewis would replace Lydia Austin in my movie. Believe me, in my heart of hearts, I swear if Lydia turns up alive, she'll have the part again. I explained that to Nana and she's a good girl. She understands."

Clark said, "Also aces, eh? Sounds like a crooked poker game. Too many aces."

Carl said, "I don't know how Carole worked it, but the subtle way she pried that information out of the Eskimo girl about her aunt deserves an Academy Award."

"She'll take it. It wasn't all that hard. Mala didn't exactly blab at full speed, but she was helpful. I don't think she knew she was."

"That's the art of asking questions. Act innocent, matter-of-fact, and, boy, the things you can get out of people. Don't you find it that way, Oscar?"

"Find it what way?"

"How about that, Clark! He hasn't been listening. I have a feeling you'd be an easy mark, Oscar."

Oscar was annoyed at having been taken unawares. "I have nothing to hide," he said weakly.

Carl Arden said, "I'll bet you've got plenty to hide. Ha ha ha! Everybody has something to hide. Everybody's had their hand in the cookie jar at one time or another. Look at Oscar, Clark! Look! He's blushing!"

"It's very hot in the car." Clark rolled down his window.

"Mala's aunt?" asked Oscar.

"She has twelve of them," said Clark. "We didn't ask her about any uncles."

Carl said, "Carole suspects Mala's aunt is Takameshuga's widow."

"Her aunt's Japanese?" Oscar asked, looking a bit bewildered.

"Oh no," said Carl, "she's a true blue Eskimo. She went to college in Tokyo and decided to stay there. Carole thinks it was as Takameshuga's wife. That's how the man got to Mala, Carole says."

"Mala didn't deny it," said Clark. "Sweet girl, Mala. You ought to have a part for her, Oscar."

"I'm having one written in. One for Nell Corday too."

"Why Santa Claus, and it's months away from Christmas!"

Clark couldn't resist asking Oscar, "She fed you any of her blubber cookies?"

"Blubber cookies?" Carl looked at Clark. "What the hell are blubber cookies?"

Clark told him. "They're baked with whale fat. A couple of bites and you end up blubbering!" Clark found his joke terribly funny and roared with laughter. The others didn't join in. Clark was wondering what was going on in the trailer. They were somewhere behind the Cadillac.

In the trailer, Carole was holding forth on the sexual mores of Hollywood. Since she was a curious kid when she promised her brothers faithfully to show them "hers" if they'd show her "theirs," Carole took a deep interest in Tinseltown's sexual proclivities. Hers was a healthy attitude, unlike that of her peers who held up their hands in shock and looked aghast at the mere hint of who was doing what to whom and good heavens where do they learn such things? While expounding and not knowing she was making

Jim Mallory uncomfortable, Carole was doing all sorts of fascinating things with crackers and soft cheeses. Hazel admired a cracker slathered with camembert and two pieces of pimiento artfully, or rather daringly, placed so that they resembled two disembodied nipples. She suggested Jim might like to bite into this one and Hazel told Carole to behave herself.

Behave herself is what Carole had done in her many years in the limelight. Her mother was a loving and very moral woman and she inspired Carole, who was a good little girl and remained a good little girl until she found out why boys were different from girls, clapped her hands with joy, and began what in her high-minded way she considered scientific experiments. By the time she became a working actress and exposed to all forms of sexual aberrations about which she was tolerant but largely uninterested, Carole had only one objective, a man of her own. For a long time the title of the 1932 movie she did with Clark, *No Man Of Her Own*, was right on the nose. She would look back on that movie and wonder why she and Clark never cottoned to each other despite the fact each was married to other people. This at a time when most people at the studios were bed-hopping, cheating on their spouses, and crowing about their conquests in the studio commissary.

A lot of actors and actresses, it turned out, were what Carole termed "ambisextrous" and she dreaded ever having to count up the ladies of the charmed circle on the Paramount lot who took a stab at trying to wrestle Carole in her trailer. Fortunately, Carole's brothers had given her wrestling lessons when a child and she had since perfected a real mean hammerlock. There was one actress on the lot who persisted in paying court and Carole treated her with a soupçon each of patience and good humor. Gertrude Michael, it seemed, was headed for stardom after a few delightful films in which she played a jewel thief named Sophie Lang. Carole at one time suggested she reverse her name and be billed as Michael Gertrude. Carole spoke of the actress with kindness and understanding rather than rancor. "Poor Gertie," she said, "she's doing supporting roles on Poverty Row and she's become sadly alcoholic. Oh everybody! Look what I've done with the roquefort!" Only Hazel looked and clucked her tongue in dismay.

"Carole, how do you think of such things?" asked Hazel, slightly dazed by this talent of Carole's she never suspected existed.

"Hee hee hee!" giggled Carole, her only

throwback to her childhood that persisted into her adult years. It wasn't only a giggle of childish delight but a defense mechanism. It was one of the few things about Carole that could drive Clark into a frenzy. Carole recognized this and used it as an advantage when she felt an advantage was necessary.

Up ahead, Jim Mallory saw the Cadillac pulling into a clearing. Clark got out of the car and waved for Jim to pull in behind him. Carole was the first to leave the van and yelled, "Oh hell! It's drizzling!" Drizzle or no, the air was invigorating and the lush greenery gave off a delicious smell like none to be enjoyed in a studio. Clark was unloading the trunk of the car, assisted by Oscar Levitt, while Carl Arden put on a deerstalker that made him look like Basil Rathbone as Sherlock Holmes. Carole shouted to Clark, "It's better weather for ducks!" Clark flashed her a look that warned her to back off.

Patty, Maxene, and LaVerne were yelping with excitement. It had been many weeks since they had last gone hunting and they were prowling around with joy, sniffing for messages at the bottom of treetrunks, messages left by other hunting dogs. Dogs were always leaving messages for each other, a fact Clark had carefully explained to Carole the first time he took her hunting. Carole wanted to know, of course, why they didn't leave messages for other hunters and Clark said something about it being unsanitary. Carole said something that didn't bear repeating. She invited the men into the trailer for something to eat before starting off to worry the animals. Oscar Levitt didn't need to be asked twice. He was in the trailer and chomping on a chicken leg while Hazel, who had brought all the L.A. newspapers with her, settled onto a window seat and read aloud the news about Mike Lynton's murder, which remained fresh days after the murder because little else had happened to stir up a comparable frenzy.

There were photographs of Mike Lynton with Lydia Austin, with Bugsy Siegel, who was working hard to put Las Vegas on the map as the gambling mecca of the West. There was Mike Lynton's sister Loretta, dredged out of the files by a smart reporter who remembered there had been a sister who had committed suicide. There was a photo of Mike Lynton with Mae West at the fights, which were a Friday night must. There was Mike with Carole and Tyrone Power, who was looking lovingly at either Carole or Mike, and Hazel was positive the loving look was for Mike. Carole never mentioned any relationship with Ty Power, so there probably wasn't one, as Carole wasn't shy about mentioning her extracurricular activities. Hazel long suspected Carole had fabricated most of them, as she was not to be outfoxed by the competition. Hazel remembered a weak moment when for want of anyone better as an escort, Carole linked herself to Greg Bautzer, a well-known and well-liked Hollywood lawyer, who was very handsome, very wealthy, and very stereotyped. Carole called him "Any port in a storm Bautzer" because if an actress's romance was faltering, she called on Bautzer to pick up the slack until someone better came along.

Hazel said, "You've made the *L.A. Times,* Oscar." She handed him the newspaper. It was a picture of him taken several years ago when he had more hair and more promise and for a brief period dated a Mexican actress named Armida, who never was as successful as her sister, Raquel Torres, who made it as far as *Duck Soup* with the Marx Brothers. The photo caption implied that Lynton was a backer of *Darkness in Hollywood,* which Levitt neither denied or confirmed when Hazel questioned him.

Herb and Carl Arden were now in the van and Herb commented wryly on Carole's artwork with the crackers and cheese. Jim Mallory, who had been in the trailer's bathroom,

282

which Carole had decorated with pictures of herself and Gable, joined the others around the groaning board. He still harbored a curiosity as to whether Oscar had made it with Nell Corday. His instincts advised him Levitt had probably made it with most of the candidates for his picture. Years ago when Jim was Herb Villon's assistant, long before he was promoted to Herb's partner, Herb told Jim the quickest way to win candidates as bedroom partners was to announce he was producing a movie. Hollywood was notorious for announcing more movies than it produced. "That," said Herb, "is how most of the other guys make out." Jim not only did not have the courage to ask Hazel to place a come-on for him, he couldn't think of a title to use.

The smell of food brought the dogs back to the van, and Carole climbed in after them. "Don't feed the children!" she cautioned the others. "This stuff's too rich for them." Clark joined them and listened as Hazel read off headlines and portions of the story. Carole picked up a paper and flicked pages as she always did. She had a short attention span unless it was a story about an unsuspecting husband catching his wife *in flagrante delicto*. Carole thought that was a perfume and was chagrined when it was explained it meant an immoral act of sex. "Immoral my behind," snorted Carole, "it's a national pastime. Hee hee hee."

Carole commented that the *Sarita Maru* seemed to have bored the newspaper boys. There wasn't a line about it anymore. Herb suggested the papers had been cautioned to sit on the story. "How about it, Carl?"

"How about what?" asked the FBI man, while making a sandwich with cold cuts piled so high, Carole was positive when it came time for the first bite, Carl wouldn't be able to manage it. She was wrong.

"The *Sarita Maru*," Herb reminded him. "Is there a reason for you feds to drop a curtain over the story?"

"Not that I know of. I guess it's because there's no new information that's newsworthy."

"There's always the war in Europe." Carole had picked up another newspaper. "But you wouldn't know it if you read this rag. There hasn't been an offensive or a defensive in days. I think Neville Chamberlain is a shmuck. I'd like to tell him what to do with that umbrella of his." Her eye traveled to another photograph. "I know the king and queen have two daughters, but every time I look at them I can't believe they ever had sex."

Clark was impatient. "Come on, men, let's get going. It's after seven o'clock."

"Goodness!" exclaimed Carole. "The deer must be up by now." Early in her hunting career, in one of her wilder flights of fancy, Carole told some friends at lunch she had visions of the deer, upon hearing of celebrity hunters planning to pursue and destroy them, clapping their hoofs together and crying, "Goody gumdrops! The Gables are coming after us! We must set the alarm and get up bright and early to greet them!"

Their eyes haunted Carole. She thought that deer had such soulful eyes, like Fay Bainter, and she wouldn't dream of knocking off that lovely actress. Clark would try to assuage her by telling her the deer population was getting way out of hand all over the world. They were destructive. They stripped shrubs and trees bare. They were carriers of disease, in response to which Carole stormed, "So why do you lick your chops anticipating a venison roast for dinner! It could be fatal!" But still she accompanied him on the hunt, so deep was her love for him. Joan Crawford once remarked, "Carole is so in love with Big Ears that if he was sentenced to the electric chair, she'd sit on his lap." To which Carole, on hearing the crack, riposted, "I'd have a tough time getting her off it."

Despite the fact Gable was her very own, Carole fretted in silence about what she suspected was still an ongoing romance between Crawford and Gable. This was especially so on those days when he came home from the studio so exhausted he had to have a nap before dinner. Carole had her spies on the Metro lot, who assured her Clark was ever faithful, which made Carole suspect either Clark or Crawford or both knew who they were and paid them off. Carole had once confided to her close friend Fieldsie Lang, "It's tough for a gal to win in this town."

Soon she was alone in the trailer with Hazel. From a window they watched the men trudging off into the underbrush, the dogs circling and anxious for action. Hazel was delighted there was a phone in the trailer, and it gave her comfort. Phones always gave Hazel comfort. She was even more comforted when Clark assured her he had hooked it up to a jack installed for him outside by the phone company. The phone company didn't object, especially when it was pointed out to them a phone was necessary in case of an emergency, like a gunshot wound or an attack by an animal protecting both its turf and its skin. Carole pointed out there was also a phone antenna on the roof of the trailer, but it wasn't always dependable. Carole, deep in thought, was shaken out of her reverie when she heard Hazel say, "A penny for them."

"Mike Lynton and Lydia Austin deserve more than a penny. Is it true the Las Vegas mob are moving in on Mike's casino?"

"They're already in. They even did it fair and square as a tribute to Mike. They made a deal with his lawyer, who I'm sure pocketed an ugly sum for himself. It was a very smooth transition. They kept the staff intact, who agreed to stay intact, or else." Hazel ran a finger across her throat.

"Hazel? You rarely discuss the case. Don't you have any theories as to who carried Lydia off, who killed Mike?"

"Thanks for asking. Herb never does. I've nothing elaborate to tell you. I'm sure the way just about everybody else does that they knew something they were better off not knowing and had to be erased." *Erased.* Carole suppressed a shudder. Human lives snuffed out. How callous to refer to them as erased. She didn't say this to Hazel. Hazel wouldn't understand Carole's sensitivity.

Carole said, "Why do I keep seeing Takameshuga's ghost wandering around the periphery of the mystery, as though he knows something we don't know? And now that he's dead, probably won't ever know." She nibbled at a sliver of cheddar. "You know, I've been through this with Pappy and with Herb in a lot of phone calls, about which I must say, he's been the soul of patience."

"Honey, Herb thinks you've got a great analytical mind."

"He does?" squealed Carole. "How sweet of him! I happen to agree with him. I do analyze things carefully. I'm always analyzing the crap out of a script. Not that it ever does much good. Anyway, I chewed my way through this thesis a dozen times before but I can't shake it. Hazel, how do we know Takameshuga was on the ship?"

"It was on the ship's manifest. The one they have to file with the port authorities."

"Carl told me there was no manifest filed. The *Sarita Maru* snuck out of port as quietly as an actor slinking out of the Brown Derby when his latest picture bombs. And who released the list of the *Sarita Maru*'s casualties? I'll tell you who. The Japanese embassy as cabled to them by the pooh-bahs of Japan."

"Carole, you have me mesmerized. I'm fascinated. I haven't been this fascinated since Herb broke down and bought me a fox fur. *Could* Takameshuga be alive?"

Carole said firmly, "I wouldn't put it past him."

"Then he has to be in hiding someplace."

"You got it right, kiddo."

"Where is he?"

"I suggested Herb ask Mala Anouk but then it came to me she'd only shower him with blubber cookies. I have a suspicion her closets are filled with them. Mala's a pretty sharp babe, for all that display of Eskimo innocence."

"Who said Eskimos are innocent? In *Nanook of the North*, Nanook offers his wife to a visitor, explaining it's the polite thing to do in Eskimo circles."

Commented Carole, "So much for the unsophisticated North."

Hazel said, "Wouldn't it be rather amusing if we started a Takameshuga hunt?"

"No, I think it would be rather dangerous. Carl Arden is awfully evasive about our Oriental. He knows something we don't know and as far as he's concerned are never going to know. Pappy's sure Arden's a hell of a lot smarter than the sounds."

"So is Herb."

"Oh yes? That's nice. At last Pappy and Herb agree on something. I wish people would stop going around saying Pappy hasn't got too much going for him upstairs. Just because he's not a showoff like the rest of Hollywood's so-called intelligentsia. Christ. Even Marion Davies claims she's read *War and Peace*."

Hazel said, "Sure. But not in the original Russian."

Clark suspected there was a conspiracy afoot among the deer. They knew he was in the vicinity on the prowl, a Nimrod to be feared and avoided. The men followed Gable along a trail with which he was familiar; they were as silent as Clark had cautioned them to be. Jim Mallory almost choked stifling a sneeze, but managed to get it under control before his skin turned blue. Herb had a vision of the deer cleverly camouflaged and nudging each other as they watched the Gable caravan making its way through the woods, wet from the insistent drizzle. Jim asked Herb in a whisper, "Are we only supposed to shoot deer?"

Herb whispered back, "To Gable rabbits don't count."

The dogs were getting restless and darting in and out of the undergrowth. Oscar Levitt seemed to Jim Mallory to be on edge, as though he feared some sort of danger awaited them. Carl Arden looked brave and gallant, a true blue member of the FBI. Clark was disturbed by the dogs. They were too well trained to be acting so edgy and nervous. Something had them worked up into this frenzy; he had never seen them behave like this before. Oscar asked him if he had any idea what was bothering the dogs.

Clark suddenly had an idea. "The cave." Oscar said nothing. "We're near the cave. Maybe there's a dead animal in it and the dogs smell it. Let's go look."

He waved to the others to follow him and Oscar. The cave was hollowed out of a hillside, a natural formation. Clark and Oscar had sought refuge in it on previous occasions when storms were raging and expecting an animal to show up in a gunsight was a slim proposition. Animals were smart enough to seek shelter in a storm.

The dogs were now whining and barking ferociously. They had found something in the cave and were anxious to share it. Clark always had a flashlight strapped to his belt. He had it in his hand and snapped it on as they entered the cave. They had to lower their heads to keep from hitting them. There was a tunnel that led to the cave's interior and Clark led the way fearlessly. The noxious odor emanating from within was nauseating, but Clark persisted.

He was soon rewarded.

He and Oscar were the first to see the body holding center stage in the glare of the flashlight. Although it was badly decomposed, they could see it was the body of a woman. With red hair.

"Oh my God," said Oscar Levitt in a hoarse voice trembling with emotion, "oh my God! It's Lydia Austin! It's Lydia! Jesus Christ, she's been knifed!"

TEN

Half an hour later, the area was swarming with the police and the press. The hunting party was besieged by reporters and cameramen, Clark receiving a lion's share of the attention. MGM had dispatched several of their press corps to protect Gable but their efforts were fruitless. One press agent thoughtfully put a copy of *Gone With the Wind* in the trailer and when asked who was reading it, Carole told them, "One of the dogs." She hated the hullabaloo. Worse, she hated the reality that Lydia was dead. Since the phone in the trailer was the only one available, she listened to all the gruesome and sickening details as Herb described to his captain the discovery of the badly decomposed body.

Oscar was moaning, "The knife wounds! The awful knife wounds!" and Jim hoped he wouldn't start throwing up the way he did on Malibu Beach when Mike Lynton's body was brought ashore. Carl Arden couldn't take his eyes off Carole. Her face was ashen, a mask, and her mind was working overtime. For a moment, her eyes met Arden's and she knew he was questioning her. Her eyes moved to Herb Villon, the phone cradled between his shoulder and his chin, and she wished he'd concede the phone to Hazel though it seemed to Carole that Hazel had exhausted every contact she had before Herb impatiently and rudely snatched the phone from her freshly manicured fingers. Jim Mallory was the first to reach the trailer and after he ordered backup and an ambulance, Hazel grabbed the phone and called Lolly Parsons. Lolly was too drunk to talk to her but Dorothy Manners replaced her with alacrity. That was when Herb entered the trailer and pulled the phone out of Hazel's hands as she shrieked, "Tonight you sleep alone!"

The body was badly decomposed, Carole thought, that meant it was hidden away at least two weeks ago. She folded her hands and rested them on the table. She should be clenching her fists in anger and frustration, but that was too easy. She wanted Herb to get off the phone so she could tell him she suspected she'd discovered the identity of the killer. She was sure he had too, but both lacked proof. There had to be a way to make the killer crack. But most important, they had to figure out the connection of Takameshuga to the killings. She wasn't so sure Mala Anouk knew either. Mala knew something, but Carole decided the girl wouldn't understand the importance of what she knew. Maybe if she had a leather boot to gnaw on it might relax her into spilling what she knew. On the other hand, it might leave her with a mouthful of mud and Carole wouldn't wish that on anyone.

The rain was heavy, no longer a drizzle. The fauna of the area sensing there was no longer a danger from the humans, resumed stripping tree bark, though the dogs continued to worry them. Clark whistled for the dogs and they came tearing out of the woods, baying mercilessly with tails wagging. Clark clapped his hands and ordered them into the van, the floors of which were mud splattered and Carole didn't give a damn.

Herb was off the phone and Carole led him into the sleeping section of the van. She told him what she suspected and was glad to hear that Herb's opinion corroborated hers. There wasn't anything Carl Arden could do except wonder if Herb and Carole had come to a meeting of minds. Takameshuga was alive and well, but exactly where he wasn't sure. The FBI wanted the man for questioning.

Carole had asked Herb if he'd ordered a tail on Mala Anouk. Herb assured her he had, and the detectives assigned to keep an eye on her were certain to reach her before she heard on the radio that Lydia's body was found. Clark asked Hazel if she knew what was going on between Carole and Herb. "Whatever it is, I'll kill Herb if he doesn't tell me." Herb and Carole came back and Carole went to Clark who cradled her face in his hands. "You okay?" he asked her.

"Just dandy," she replied, and from her tone of voice Clark could tell she was on the warpath.

Oscar Levitt was seated near them. He had mixed himself a brandy and soda and drank it like a substitute for a blood transfusion. Herb was warning Hazel to stop bugging him, he'd tell her whatever he had to tell later, and went outside. The body was in the ambulance where an attendant was being lavish with an air freshener. They were to deliver the body to the coroner, who saw no reason to accompany them. From what Oscar heard on a phone extension listening to Jim Mallory, the coroner smugly said he could do the autopsy over the wire. Jim refrained from telling him most of his autopsy reports read as though they'd been phoned in, but laid off in deference to Herb and his chronic complaint that "autopsies ain't what they used to be." The Los Angeles coroners were celebrated for their slipshod work, a condition that would continue for many decades. Herb's favorite comment about coroners was that they couldn't even serve as chiropodists. He admitted that some of the staff was competent, but understood when they quit to take jobs as shoe salesmen.

Carole sadly surveyed the uneaten food. This was supposed to have been such a fun day. Poor Pappy. The rifle he was carrying was a new one, and he'd been looking forward to using it. Herb said there was no point in hanging around any longer and they prepared to go back to town. Jim Mallory helped Clark pack the trunk of the Cadillac. They said very little while they worked. Hazel helped Carole clear up in the trailer while the dogs, sensing something was up, went to the rear of the trailer and made themselves comfortable on the cots the Gables had installed when they acquired the vehicle.

Carole said with a wan expression on her face that she'd be happier driving back with Clark. Clark disconnected the phone and with only the aerial for reception, Hazel was having a hell of a time trying to sell an item to columnist Jimmy Fidler. Jim Mallory didn't envy the forensic boys their job of scouring the cave for clues. Not when it had contained a decomposing body for at least two weeks. Oscar Levitt wasn't feeling well and decided to go to the back of the trailer where he could lie down, much to the annoyance of LaVerne, whose cot he had staked out for himself but now was to be occupied by Oscar. Hazel wished the trailer was equipped with a typewriter but had to make do with a pad and pen.

Clark beeped the Cadillac horn several times to alert Jim Mallory they were departing. Jim beeped back and was positive he'd find his way home if he lost Clark in traffic. Herb sat in the front seat of the Cadillac with Clark and Carole. It was spacious enough for the three. Carl Arden was grateful to have the back seat to himself and took advantage of it by stretching out. He was glad he'd be more or less alone with his thoughts, which were occupied mostly with the possibility that Takameshuga was alive and well and sequestered somewhere in Los Angeles. What he didn't know was that Herb Villon had an idea where he might be hidden. He advised Carole, who said, "Why don't we go look now?"

Clark admired Carole's bravery. She had once told him one of her ambitions as a child was to be a lion tamer and stick her head in the lion's mouth the way Mae West did in *I'm No Angel*. Except Mae had audiences convulsing when she removed her head and said to the lion, "And where were you last night?"

In the Cadillac, Herb was all for stopping somewhere to let the precinct know they were going Takameshuga hunting and they should send some detectives as backup in case Takameshuga had company.

Clark pulled into a gas station. While an attendant replenished the tank, Herb phoned the precinct. Clark was out of the car examining the tires. Carl Arden suspected something was afoot. He questioned Carole. She turned around and faced him. "Herb and I think Takameshuga is alive and so do you. That's why you've been sticking around L.A." Arden said nothing. Carole deadpanned, "If silence is golden, you're Midas."

"I haven't contradicted you, have I?"

"The *Sarita Maru* was a blind. It was wired for an explosion at sea, a coverup for Takameshuga's escape. He's very big in Japan, isn't he? A general, some kind of high muck-a-muck, something like that."

"He's something like that." He didn't specify what.

"His wife is Mala Anouk's aunt."

"Mother."

"Mother! You mean he's Mala's father?"

"No. He's the mother's second husband. Her first was killed by an insane walrus.

Gored to death. She went to Tokyo to be with her sister, Mala's aunt. The aunt dutifully consoled her sister and introduced her to Takameshuga who soon was also consoling Mala's mother. Those Eskimos are pretty hot numbers for being from such a cold country."

Clark had resumed his position behind the steering wheel after paying for the gas. Herb was back seated next to Carole and had heard most of what Carl Arden had told Carole.

Carole said, "So Mala is the apple of her stepfather's eye."

Arden said, "I think it's safe to assume Mala is other kinds of fruit to him, especially a peach. They've been shacking up."

"Why that sly little minx!" Clark listened while pulling out of the gas station. Carole fumed, "Her and her goddamn blubber cookies!"

Clark said with an authority unusual for him, "How many times have I told you don't judge a book by its cover?"

"Too many times, and watch that son of a bitch passing you on the right." She asked Herb, "Is it too soon to go for broke?"

"Go for it, babe, go for it."

"Hee hee hee." Clark winced. "Takameshuga was here setting up an espionage system." Carl Arden's nod encouraged her to continue. "He masterminded the phony kidnapping scare along with those three jokers who were also supposed to be kidnapped, Oscar Nolan, Elmer Rabb, and Nathan Taft. They're German nationals, right?"

"Pola Negri, bless her heart, identified the three of them. Especially Nathan Taft. He, according to Pola, was very pushy."

Herb said, "Those three weren't on the *Sarita Maru* either."

"Goodness no," said Arden, "the ship was headed in the wrong direction. They left for Germany by way of Mexico and Northern Ireland. That part of the country is pro-German. Hitler's promised them the independence they're so hungry to get once he conquers the British."

"Never!" raged Carole. She asked Gable, "Do Larry and Viv suspect any of this?"

"Larry and Viv are too busy screwing. They came up for air every so often to study *Romeo and Juliet*. They're taking it to New York."

"How cute," said Carole. "They're both too old for the parts." She said to Arden, "You deliberately allowed Taft and his two buddies to get away."

"Not before we loaded them with a lot of misinformation."

"That makes me feel better," said Carole. "Takameshuga did some recruiting, right?"

"Right," said Arden.

"He was authorized to do any financing necessary."

"You're beautiful."

"You have to tell Pappy and Herb they're beautiful too. We worked this out together."

Clark said, "You deserve most of the credit, honey, don't minimize it."

"Well, I hardly expect to be awarded the Congressional Medal of Honor," said Carole modestly.

Herb said, "Oscar Levitt said he was having a part written into his movie for Mala. As Carole pointed out, after months of scrounging for backing, he's suddenly all financed. But he has a couple of problems, namely, Mike Lynton and Lydia Austin. Mike invested in the movie, one of the first to do so. The old buddy act. Oscar and Mike went back a long way. Lydia was working on Groucho to put up some backing too. Lydia knew what was going on with Takameshuga. She probably got it from Mala and then confronted Mike, her old lover, with the information. They decided there was something rotten not only in Denmark —"

"What have the Danes got to do with this?" asked Carole, slightly confused.

"Just a figure of speech," said Herb patiently.

Carole said, "The way I figured it, and Herb agrees" — Herb nodded his head — "Lydia and Mike decided there could be trouble with the Japanese involvement. Lydia confronted Oscar. Oscar panicked. He saw his movie in danger of going up in smoke."

Clark now spoke. "They probably met on his sloop. Oscar knifed Lydia. His performance in the cave was a beauty. 'It's Lydia, Lydia, she's been knifed.' A dead giveaway. No pun intended. With the body so badly decomposed, how did he know there were knife wounds and how the hell did he recognize Lydia?"

"Likewise his performance at the beach when Mike's body washed up," said Carole. "Obviously Mike got his on Oscar's sloop except Oscar didn't count on the tide delivering Mike's body to Miriam's doorstep, so to speak. He thought it would wash out to sea. What was that about the best laid plans?"

Carl Arden asked, "You think Levitt's wise that you're wise?"

Clark was looking through the rearview window and could see the van. "Jim's right behind us. He must realize we're taking a different route back."

Carole was all heated up, her adrenaline racing. "Why don't we nail Oscar now? What are we waiting for?"

"We're waiting for proof," said Herb.

"Oh," said Carole. "But supposing he tries to escape."

"He won't get far," said Herb.

"But how do we get the proof!"

Herb said confidently, "Oscar's a weak sister. He'll break down and then hire a hot-shit defense attorney. It won't do him much good."

"Oh," said Carole.

"What?" asked Clark.

"Supposing Takameshuga's not on Oscar's boat!"

Herb said, "My money's on him being on the boat. We've been keeping an eye on it. It's been loading supplies. Probably for a trip to Mexico where he would start his first lap back to Japan."

Carole said, "You know, if Mala clicks here Takameshuga might decide to settle down, send for Mala's mother, you know, mend his ways."

The silence in the car was deafening.

In the trailer, Jim Mallory was trying to figure out which way the Cadillac was heading. He had pulled in for gas as the Cadillac

304

pulled out of the station, but Jim wasn't worried about catching up with it. Now he was worried something was seriously up and wondered why Herb didn't have Clark pull over and tell him what was going on. He reminded himself Herb was to be trusted.

Not Hazel. She yelped, "Where the hell are we?" She tried looking out a window. The downpour was relentless. She hoped there wouldn't be mud slides. She didn't relish being trapped in one. She yelled, "Jim, where the hell are we going?"

"I'm following Herb."

"So where's he heading?"

"Search me."

They awakened Oscar. He arose from a troubled sleep that featured visions of Lydia Austin's body. He felt he was being watched. He was. Patty, Maxine, and LaVerne were sensitive to the whimpering he made while asleep. Patty thought he was cute but didn't attempt to lick his face. Also the odor of the brandy he'd been drinking put her off. Oscar looked out the window, at the rain coming down in sheets. He squinted. Christ, we're on the Pacific Coast Highway!

He leaped to his feet and entered the front of the van. "What are we doing on the Pacific Coast Highway?"

"Following Herb," said Jim innocently.

"Where are we going?"

"I don't know. But they're sure in a hurry. They're doing seventy. I can just about keep up."

Oscar had a sinking feeling in the pit of his stomach. Hazel asked him, "You feeling sick again?" Oscar didn't answer. He felt for the reassurance of the handgun he carried in an inside pocket of his leather jacket.

Hazel said, "We're passing Mike Lynton's joint. Damn Herb! What the hell's he up to?"

Oscar suspected what Herb was up to. He had slipped up. He was too quick to identify Lydia's body. He hadn't recognized it, the face was so badly deteriorated. He just knew it was her because he had brought her there. He intended to move it elsewhere but didn't get around to it because his only alternative was the Salton Sea near the cave, but there were communities there and he feared being apprehended. Now he feared Herb Villon was about to score a home run with bases loaded. And one of the bases held Ito Takameshuga.

"Jim. Pull over," said Oscar in a hoarse voice.

Jim, startled by the order, took his eyes off the road and caught a glimpse of Oscar's handgun.

Hazel gasped. Oscar was the killer Herb

was after. She had a scoop worth thousands. She reached for the telephone. "Don't touch the phone, Hazel!" Don't touch the phone? Was he inviting her to have a stroke?

Jim did the first thing that came to mind. He swerved the trailer and Oscar stumbled backward. Jim leaped from his seat and jumped atop Oscar, wrestling him for the gun. Hazel thought fast and got behind the steering wheel, bearing down on the horn.

But Clark had seen what was going on through his rearview mirror. He alerted Herb and Arden. Carole's hands covered her mouth. Clark had pulled over. Herb was out of the Cadillac and rushed toward the van, with Clark and Arden following on his heels. Carole wished they were working from a script. Then she'd have a gun. She had nothing. She felt naked.

In the van, Jim held Oscar with his hands behind his back. Hazel had the gun and Oscar pleaded, "Don't shoot! Don't shoot!" Herb entered the trailer, Clark and Arden still behind him.

"For crying out loud," yelled Jim in frustration, "what the hell's going on?"

Herb said, "Hazel, the gun's useless until you release the safety."

"Oh." Hazel handed him the gun and commandeered the phone. Carole entered the trailer, drenched to the skin. She asked anxiously, "Did he confess?"

Carl Arden accepted the gun from Herb as Clark and Carole hurried back to the Cadillac and Jim got behind the steering wheel of the van. He followed Clark to Oscar Levitt's sloop. The assistance Herb had called for earlier consisted of six detectives and they were milling about on the dock. Clark pulled over and Herb was out of the car yelling, "Are you guys nuts? Is the Jap on board?"

One of the detectives jerked a thumb toward the lounge belowdecks. There was only one crew member aboard and he looked bewildered. Herb, Carole, Clark, and Arden went below to the lounge.

"Mala!" cried Carole. The Eskimo, with a tear-stained face, was kneeling beside the body of Takameshuga. He lay face up in a pool of blood, his right hand still gripping the hilt of the dagger he had used to kill himself in the Japanese tradition.

Carole gasped, "Oh my God! He's committed Harry Carey!"

Carl Arden corrected her, "Hara-kiri."

"No matter how you pronounce it," said Carole, "he's dead."

Mala spoke softly, "He is with his ancestors."

Carole wondered if she'd given him some blubber cookies to take with him.

W. C. Fields and Groucho Marx weren't especially fond of each other, but on a whim, Groucho phoned Fields to join him at Romanoff's for a little memorial to Lydia Austin. Carlotta Monterey was at Groucho's side sipping a pousse-café. Groucho and Fields had ordered martinis and Romanoff grandiosely told them their drinks were on the house.

Softly Groucho sang, " 'Lydia, oh Lydia, oh have you met Lydia?' " and his voice broke. He choked back tears and Romanoff understandingly gently rubbed his back.

Groucho said good-naturedly, "Lydia did it better. Dear Lydia. How anxious she was for me to do a dramatic role. I thought of doing a new version of *Dracula.* Now that's a part I could really sink my teeth into."

Fields groaned. "What we should do, Groucho, is my new version of *Robin Hood.* I've had the vision for months. Groucho, you should play Robin Hood," a very magnanimous gesture on Fields' part, "and I'll play Friar Tuck, which you have to admit is perfect casting." He thought for a moment. "Now as for Maid Marian, I think Margaret Dumont is a bit large for the part."

"She's large enough to play it twice," said Groucho, searching for an excuse to make a hasty exit.

"And what do I play?" asked Carlotta petulantly.

"Why, my little frayed petticoat," said Fields, "you'll play third base."

In the plane flying to Atlanta for the world premiere of *Gone With the Wind*, Carole held tightly to Clark's arm. She was terrified of flying. Irene Selznick had plied her with sedatives, which didn't seem to have helped, and now she tried applied psychology. "Carole, tell us again how you captured Oscar Levitt and stood by while the Jap committed suicide."

Carole came alive. "You really want to hear it *again?*"

"Oh yes," said Mrs. Selznick while stifling a yawn, "maybe David will be interested in buying the film rights."

David O. Selznick glared at his wife. Carole screeched, "Pappy! Pappy! Did you hear that? David's going to buy the screen rights and we can play ourselves!" She began casting aloud. "George Brent would be divine as Herb. Joan Davis is perfect for Hazel. And of course Walter Pidgeon for Carl Arden. Now for Jim Mallory . . ."

"Jimmy Stewart," said Clark, realizing it made sense to humor Carole until the plane had landed.

"Oh perfect!" She released her grip on Clark. She leaned back in her seat, then said, as her eyes began to mist, "And for the girls, we'll find four unknowns. We'll hold a contest like David did to find Scarlett O'Hara. I still have the lease on the house our girls were living in. I wish Mala hadn't gone rushing off to Tokyo to join her mother. But she insisted her mother had said there were greater opportunities for an Eskimo girl in Japan."

Clark said, "Maybe she'll open a bakery and feature those goddamn blubber cookies."

Carole shrieked with laughter. The FASTEN SEAT BELT flashed on and Carole said, "Oh Pappy! I feel good all over! I'm happy!"

He kissed her cheek.

DATE DUE

GAYLORD

PRINTED IN U.S.A.